NOBODY'S PILGRIMS

NOBODY'S PILGRIMS

BY SERGIO TRONCOSO

an imprint of Lee & Low Books Inc.
New York

Cinco Puntos Press
an imprint of LEE & LOW BOOKS Inc.
95 Madison Avenue, New York, NY 10016
leeandlow.com

Edited by Jessica Powers
Typesetting by ElfElm Publishing
Book production by The Kids at Our House
The text is set in Crimson Text
Manufactured in the United States of America by Lake Book
First Edition
10 9 8 7 6 5 4 3 2 1

Library of Congress Cataloging-in-Publication Data

Names: Troncoso, Sergio, 1961- author.
Title: Nobody's Pilgrims / a novel by Sergio Troncoso.
Description: First edition. | New York, NY : Lee and Low, [2022] |
Summary: "Three runaway teenagers are chased in a road trip from the Texan frontera to
New England, by a drug cartel planning to unleash chaos unto the country."
—Provided by publisher.
Identifiers: LCCN 2021001765 | ISBN 9781947627413 (paperback)
ISBN 9781947627420 (ebook)
Subjects: GSAFD: Suspense fiction.
Classification: LCC PS3570.R5876 N63 2021 | DDC 813/.54—dc23
LC record available at https://lccn.loc.gov/2021001765

FOR LAURA DRACHMAN, AARON TRONCOSO, AND ISAAC TRONCOSO

CHAPTER ONE

Turi Martinez reads the mystery book that transports him to the forests of Connecticut and to the adventures of a boy on a raft on the Housatonic River. But Turi's neighborhood of Ysleta doesn't have forests and is surrounded only by the Chihuahuan desert on the United States-Mexico border. Leaves do not litter the ground like a multicolored carpet, as Turi imagines they do in Connecticut in October or November. Instead hot, coarse sand covers the ground and swirls in the air with every gust of wind. At the library of Ysleta High, Turi often loses himself in photographs of New England— church steeples, like sharp white cones piercing a blue sky; forests, dense and impenetrable; and layer after layer of misty green mountainsides in the faraway horizon.

Turi imagines building a cabin deep in a thicket of trees, next to a brook where he can fish. (He will have to acquire a taste for fish, which at present he doesn't have.) He will find a secret place where his aunt Seferina will never find him and his uncle Ramon will never bother to look. Turi imagines it will be like a real version of where Charlie Brown lives, with doghouses like Snoopy's and thick snow in the winter, green baseball diamonds and pumpkin patches, and a Thanksgiving dinner at a long, jam-packed table with red candles. Connecticut is the kind of place where a boy can cut his own Christmas tree in the mountains behind his backyard.

Turi imagines in this Connecticut that he will not be alone, yet not with someone like the woman with the big butt in the magazine that Turi taped on the blue wheelbarrow. He imagines someone beautiful and nice, someone still only a blur in his mind. Someone who won't mind someone like him.

Turi rereads the page where he stopped in *The Mystery of the Mighty Housatonic River* the night before. In the summer evening, the flashlight in his hand shakes as his eyes study the page. The feeling is slowly coming back to his sore hands after he carried chickens all day. His aunt allows him to use the flashlight as long as he pays for the batteries, so she got Turi a summer job at a poultry farm. Mrs. Garcia, the librarian, has loaned him the book, and five others, and instructed Turi not to bring them back until September. She has made him promise not to get into trouble and not to lose those books, since she checked them out herself from the Ysleta High School library. She once asked Turi about a bruise on his neck. He told her a story about his dog Princey jumping on him and his falling back and hitting a dead branch on their pecan tree. Mrs. Garcia was his favorite adult at YHS, and she smiled at him—a fake smile, Turi could tell—and noticed the nail mark at the end of his bruise. But Mrs. Garcia was nice enough not to ask more questions, and Turi did not look away from her face. Princey is not his dog, but the German shepherd Turi Martinez imagines he will one day have, maybe in Connecticut. There is no pecan tree in their backyard, just a mound of car parts, including an engine his uncle Ramon hoisted over their stone wall with a rope one midnight. The bruise—well, that doesn't matter anymore, because it eventually disappeared. Long ago in a dream, his dead mother Estela returned to him and kissed it away.

The boy in the mystery story, John, hates his family and escapes down the river. On this journey, he finds a canvas sack stuffed with money. The money belongs to bank robbers who bury the loot under a giant oak tree, but a black bear dug up the money sack and dumped half of it next to the river. John leaves the money where he finds it, but the robbers spot him as his canoe is rounding a bend on the Housatonic. They assume John has stolen the missing money. Secretly, they chase him and decide to kill him. Meanwhile, another pair of eyes in the flickering shadows follows the bank robbers and John.

"Turi, Turi! Where are you?" his sixteen-year-old cousin screeches like a bobcat through the cuartito's door.

His heart races to the present. He shoves the book under his pillow on his lap. His mattress is on the floor. The door swings open and slams against the wall.

"Did you take my joints? You miserable cabrón!" Vanessa yells, the naked light bulb framing a shadowy figure with long hair and wearing heels.

"Uh, no. Why would I want your stupid mota? Leave me alone and close the door. I don't do that shit." Turi grips the pillow just in case she aims a fist at his face.

"I-don't-do-that-shit," she repeats in a whine. "What a baby! You're a thief! I know you take things. Everyone knows."

"Maybe your mother took it. Or Raul. Please get out of my room."

"*Your* room? You don't have a room! You don't even belong here. We're doing Tía Estela a favor 'cause we're nice. Why don't you run away like a stray dog? It's bad enough we have to feed you and take care of you."

"I take care of myself. Leave me alone. I don't have your pot. *I'm* not the dog around here." Turi mutters these last words under his breath.

"What'd you say, adoptado? You insulting me? Say it loud, say it so I can hear it, like a *man*, so I can scratch your miserable little neck again."

"Search the room if you don't believe me."

With one hand feigning a punch, his cousin Vanessa lunges at the pillow in front of him. Turi clenches his fists and raises his arms in self-defense, but she only throws the pillow against the wall, revealing the book on his lap. She snatches it before he can grab it, and glances at the cover.

"Give it back to me. I haven't done anything to you."

"What a stupid waste!" she hisses, flipping the pages. "Don't you have any friends? Oh, I forgot, who would want to spend any time with a nerd like you?"

"Please give it back to me. Raul's Chevy always smells like mota. He probably took it. Told you, I don't smoke it."

"Maybe you should," Vanessa says, as she scans the room and twists slowly in front of him in her short denim shirt and ultratight black blouse, dangling the book on her fingertips. At Ysleta High School, Turi has regularly seen Vanessa behind the football stadium, smoking with seniors dressed like morticians. She once shouted at him—"Pendejo!"—from an entrance's shadow as he ran and sweated around the track in P.E.

"Sucio!" she yells at him as her eyes suddenly discover he's staring at her chest. She slaps his face with the book and throws it at him like a brick. A corner stabs him sharply under the sternum. Turi gasps. "Little pervert! If I find you took my joints, I'm gonna beat the shit out of you!" Vanessa stomps out of the room.

Turi pushes his door closed and jams an old pencil stub he found in the street into the doorframe, which connected the utility room he slept in to the main house through a small porch. He turns off the lights and listens carefully as he slips off his shoes. His socks are moist, his toes suddenly cold. No one is in the house on Corralitos except his cousin Vanessa. In a few minutes, she will be gone. Turi rubs the sore spot on his chest and inhales deeply, feeling a twinge of pain deep inside as if he's been impaled by an arrow. Closer to his bed, he yanks on a milk crate filled with the library books from Mrs. Garcia and a few school supplies he has bought himself or found over the past two years. Good pencils carelessly dropped on the linoleum floors of Ysleta High School. A plastic ruler cracked, but still intact. Three BIC pens full of ink. He uncovers a drain underneath the milk crate. Long ago this drain puzzled Turi. Perhaps this cuartito was intended as a bathroom and they changed their minds? Turi grabs a penny he keeps flush against one corner and turns two thick screws. As he pulls the drain cover off, a thin copper wire comes with it too, wrapped through one of the drain holes. At the end of the wire is a plastic bag from the Big 8 supermarket on Alameda Avenue. Turi glances at the light underneath his door. The light remains uninterrupted. No evil shadow lurks nearby to catch him by surprise. He listens and hears nothing. Quickly he unwraps the plastic bag, unrolls the smallest of three wads of money, and takes out the ten-dollar bill from his sock and wraps it tightly around the wad of money with a rubber band.

After everything is back in place, Turi takes off his clothes, loads the pile into the washing machine near his bed, and turns it on. Again, he listens for any noises on Corralitos. When he hears nothing, he runs naked to the shower down the hallway. He has to be done before anyone returns, before anyone—especially Ramon—remembers the teenage boy reading in the utility room in the back.

Before his cousins Raul and Vanessa return later that night, before Ramon's drunken shouts from the bedroom or the kitchen, before the screams, before the murmurs about him, Turi has cleaned up: he will not hand them an excuse to taunt him. He has eaten his dinner and hides in the cuartito at the back of the house, a room originally meant to store Ramon's tools, two shovels, the washing machine, a rake, and a rusty blue wheelbarrow next to the mattress on the floor.

Three years ago, his great-aunt Romita dropped him off at the house on Corralitos. He was a bewildered orphan. His aunt Seferina put him in the same room with Vanessa. Vanessa complained bitterly but quietly at first— Turi could often hear them when they didn't think he was nearby. He knew he was not wanted there. At Ysleta Middle School, the principal automatically put him in ESL classes with all the other students recently from Juárez. But Turi was so good at math and already an excellent reader in English that before the end of that first semester, he was moved to a regular eighth-grade class. By freshman year at Ysleta High, he was placed in Honors English. When Ramon returned from Santa Ana, California, like a sudden shift in a bone-chilling wind, Turi volunteered to move into the utility room. He sensed the danger. Those first few days, Turi watched Ramon saunter through the house like a mountain lion invading the El Paso Zoo. The man assumed he owned what he did not own. Ramon ignited a fever in Seferina's eyes, which became whispers and soft moans at night almost every night. Turi was embarrassed when he overheard those sounds, yet also fascinated. The same age as his cousin Vanessa, Turi had never been with a girl before.

From the moment the stink of Ramon's stale beer permeated the house, Turi separated himself as much as possible from anything Alvidrez. In dreams, his mother whispered many warnings to him. ("They are different from us, mi'jo. Do not become like them. They are lost souls.") He listened. But it chilled his heart whenever he was awake and could not easily remember the sound of her voice.

Turi was still his mother's son—she la Católica, la santita. Almost seventeen years old, Turi had an image of his mother forever etched in his mind, a memory from the last night he saw her alive when he was just a ten-year-old boy: her face turned toward him, only a trickle of blood on her forehead, after their Volkswagen flipped on the Pan-American Highway, her brown eyes wide open and still.

A few weeks earlier, right after finishing his sophomore year at Ysleta High School, he had pasted the inside of the wheelbarrow with old issues of the Mexican tabloid *Alarma*. He covered up the photo of the fat two-headed baby from Michoacán, Rigoberto Dos Cabezas, but displayed the silvery midget alien on a wall inside the blue wheelbarrow. He left visible only the surprised eyes of a Mexican actress wearing a red polka-dotted bathing suit, lying face down next to a young man in a cemetery. Was this how Aunt Seferina looked on her bed? Even thinking that thought made him feel guilty. What was *wrong* with him? He even imagined Mrs. Garcia in this coquettish pose one afternoon. Turi wondered if his mother, the ghost of his dreams, could also know he had been thinking those thoughts about Mrs. Garcia.

Inside the wheelbarrow, Turi arranged his underwear, four T-shirts, two pairs of jeans, and six pairs of socks. Seferina laughed whenever she saw the wheelbarrow, a mocking laugh of sorts that perhaps before Ramon's arrival would have also revealed admiration for Turi's invention and artwork. But even as his aunt had changed with her new man—was Ramon even his real uncle and was he even married to his aunt Seferina?—Turi also overheard stories of what had happened to Ramon in California. A vicious fight with a Black man who stole Ramon's tools at gunpoint and then beat him unconscious. Turi heard what he thought were Ramon's inebriated sobs and his aunt's whispers and entreaties to soothe him inside the house on Corralitos one midnight, self-pitying sobs interrupted only by angry shouts at the desert darkness engulfing all of them.

For Turi, the adobe house on Corralitos Street was never quiet anymore. At night the TV blared with novelas from Mexico that his aunt Seferina watched without watching until Ramon arrived with a fistful of cash—from where, or how, was always a mystery. "Bring me a beer, chula! Hurry up! Come here, don't go so fast. Come here, ay hermosa." That was what was left of happiness in the Alvidrez household.

"They might come in. They might see us. Espérate. Vanessa, Turi, they're here. Oh, my god, oh . . . oh . . . ay. Así, mi rey!"

When Turi would overhear these words, he wished all of them could leave for a better place together, but he knew that would never be possible. He understood what his ghost-mother had said to him in his dreams: the Alvidrez family belonged too much to this place, and too much to those parts that were foul and forsaken. Not everyone could escape or wanted to escape to find a different world. Turi was also from Ysleta. He had loved that place when his parents had been alive. But now he was also traveling to Connecticut in his mind and dreaming about his mother and wondering what she would say to him in the present, what she would do.

The screen door slams shut a few minutes later. Ramon and Seferina are out. Through a window, Turi sees their truck screech down Corralitos and disappear into the dust clouds on Southside Street. Tiptoeing to Vanessa's bedroom door, Turi overhears her talking to her friend Letty Jimenez about their Saturday night double-date with Letty's primos from Chihuahua, who are in town again.

Turi tries to close the warped door to the cuartito. A two-inch gap yawns between the bottom of the door and the unfinished cement floor of the room. Aunt Seferina slapped the top of his head hard when he once blocked the door with the wheelbarrow. She thought Turi was stealing from them (and he is, or as he sees it, simply taking back his money). She also accused him of stealing the earrings she couldn't find, her house keys, and a portable radio. But he has never taken anything but his own money.

Recently she upended his bed and books and neatly stacked clothes in a vain search for everything of value that was lost. Two nights ago, she found Turi's stash of crackers, pushed them carelessly to the floor, and crushed a corner of the box as she stomped out. "You ever block this door, I'll tell Ramon. Remember what happened to you the last time? Ramon's right: you think you're better than us? Is that it? Did my sister put that in your head? We'll see about that!"

Turi now keeps the door closed, but not blocked. He notices that if he keeps his room darker than the hallway, he can always see their shadows approaching his door. He also jams a stub of a pencil between the door and the frame to keep the warped door closed. The stub will pop out and roll on the floor unnoticed whenever Aunt Seferina shoves the door open to catch Turi unawares. If he is not imagining what it would be like to be with a girl, if he is not holding and squeezing himself under a blanket, Turi loves to read. A book in his hands, he notices, always deflates his aunt. (She has never caught him doing that other thing.) His mother Estela, Turi remembers, was also a reader. "Good reading is like dreaming and traveling through mountainsides with adventurous friends," or something like that is what his mother often said to him. Turi wishes he remembered her exact words. He wishes he had recorded her voice.

At night, Turi sneaks out through the garbage-can gate in the backyard, crouches down in the canal behind his house, and burns tumbleweeds, watching the moon's glow around him and the stars twinkling in the heavens. *I wonder what the stars look like in Connecticut. Through the darkness of the forest, the stars must look different. And during the summer, when it's not cold anymore, I can build a fort, I can hunt for snakes and frogs, I can climb trees, I can grow apples and peaches and strawberries, I can grow pumpkins. Gigantic pumpkins.* Nobody will find him in the canal, and he is free for a few moments. The call of another night also chills his bones.

The first time he snuck out of the house on Corralitos at night, he imagined La Llorona would get him, that weeping ghost-woman searching for her missing children that his mother had mentioned in her stories. Then he imagined La Llorona *was* his mother come back from the dead, in search of him. Could she be so far away and still look for him somehow? But now Turi just loves the silence and the stars and the glow of the fire. Many of his fears have disappeared. One night not long ago, a cop car cruised through the neighborhood and seemed to slow down near their house on Corralitos—perhaps they had seen the glow of the fire in the canal. He had to stomp it out quickly and climb over the trash cans to get back into their yard.

"Arturo! Are you back there! If you're back there, you'll be sleeping with the stray dogs tonight! Arturo!" Turi hears his aunt Seferina's high-pitched shrieks from the other side of the rock wall.

He remembers how different his mother's voice sounded from Seferina's, yet the teenager can recall only random phrases from his mother as if they were snippets of an old, almost-forgotten song. Is what he remembers his mother's voice, or just what he has made up in his head? Only after he immediately awakens from a dream, for a fleeting feather of a moment, is he certain about the sound of her voice. It never lasts long. But for those brief seconds, Turi knows he is with her again.

Turi is tired of Raul shoving his forehead and Aunt Seferina yelling through the thin walls of the cuartito for him to throw out the garbage. His aunt has never cared if he was late for school, but his mother did. His aunt has never cared whether he showered. But every night, Turi showers, because he imagines that's what his mother would have wanted him to do. His fondest imagination prompted by his mother's stories is when she washed him at night as a baby, in a washbasin big enough for only a watermelon.

Finally he opens the back gate.

"Get in the house, Turi, and sweep the front yard. I don't care if it's night and I don't care if you're tired from las gallinas!" Seferina yells, as Turi stumbles over the trashcans and closes the back gate behind him. The wail of an ambulance or police car on Yaya Lane echoes in the distance. The night has already hidden the Franklin Mountains to the west, yet in the darkness, Turi can still see the faint glow of lights in the horizon toward Ysleta High School on Alameda Avenue. The desert air is cool, velvety, and dry.

"I'm not going back. It's my summer, and I'm not going back. I can barely feel my hands. Look!"

Before he left for work this morning, Turi grabbed masking tape from a kitchen closet and wrapped his palms. Ten hours under the hot June sun, carrying chickens and stuffing them into cages. Somewhere in Socorro or

Clint, near the Río Grande River. He could only see the current of dark water like a giant snake in the desert during lunchtime. Older workers murmured to each other in Spanish, viejitos with skin so chocolatey brown, he thought he could hear it crinkle. The only other teenager at las gallinas was a boy the same age as Turi, with thick forearms and brown teeth, who spoke mostly Spanish and loved the Dallas Cowboys. Probably a pobre mojado.

"Oh, my goodness! A few pecks on your first day! And you want to quit? Are you my sister's son? Estela was a lot of things, but she was never a quitter."

"Don't talk about my mother."

"She was my sister before she was your mother. How do you think you're paying for your food this week? You're washing your jeans tonight. That chicken shit smells awful! We're sending you back to Tía Romita's next week. Back to Juárez. She won't make you work. She'll let you do whatever you want."

"*What?* Why—"

"Ramon and I decided. It's better for us. We don't have the money. We don't have the room. She'll take you this weekend and you can stay in Juárez."

"Until August? Until . . . until school starts? I'm American. I don't belong in Mexico!"

"Look, Arturo, plenty of Americans live in Mexico and we'll come visit you. Ramon's taking you on Saturday."

Turi glared at his aunt's eyes, and he knew she was lying. This would be forever. "I won't go. I won't. I don't care."

"It's better for all of us if you're with Romita in el otro lado."

"No," Turi says, feeling dizzy. "I hate you. My mother would hate you if she was here."

Under the floodlights of the backyard, Seferina only holds her hand out. Turi stares at her, for a moment imagining that hand will gently keep moving toward his chubby cheek to caress it. That's what his aunt's hand used to do, two years ago, before Turi became taller than her, before Ramon returned from California, before the house on Corralitos became like a prison for him. Turi remembers when his aunt *asked* him to help around the house in what he thought was an echo of his mother's voice. But with Ramon at Corralitos, her voice became different . . . *she* became different. "I'm sorry you feel that way. Well, where is it? How much did you make? Ándale! Don't give me those eyes!"

"Here it is. I'm not going. I hate you." He hands his aunt a crisp new twenty-dollar bill. The ten-dollar bill he hid in his sock after the truck dropped him off on Yaya Lane and Socorro Road is already underneath the drain in the shed.

She glares at him. She probably suspects he is keeping money from her. Even if she searches for it tonight while he sleeps, or tomorrow while he works, she will never find Turi's secret savings.

At night, once he is alone, once his head stops spinning with the awful news, Turi again imagines he hears his mother's voice in the wind. That's what calms him: "They are different from us, mi'jo. Don't worry. I will always be with you wherever you are."

CHAPTER TWO

Turi is up at five the next morning and at the corner of Yaya Lane and Southside Street a few minutes later. The desert sun of the border has not yet risen in the east.

When the same red farm truck that picked them up yesterday stops with a loud, screechy whine, this time Turi does not hesitate to jump in and does not fear the faces lurking in the shadows. This time he ignores them, waits for his eyes to adjust, and then furtively glances at who is in the truck as they drive to the poultry farm east of Ysleta, near Socorro or Clint, Turi isn't sure. Yesterday they were never told where they were, and Turi never asked. At least he'll be a few miles closer to Connecticut, he imagines, if he jumps out and runs away from Corralitos.

Turi is bigger than some of the old men in the truck, yet these viejitos are muscled and tough in a way he isn't yet. The other teenager Arnulfo Muñoz smiles at him with his brown teeth from the opposite side of the truck's bed, the only one who bothered to chitchat with Turi while they worked. Turi is lanky and uncommonly agile while Arnulfo is slightly shorter and somewhat squat like a boxer. Yesterday this flat-faced boy sought Turi out, and there he is again, waiting. Arnulfo is certainly a mojado, Turi thinks. This smiley semi-friend is what a brother would have been like if Turi had one, at least a brother from Juárez obsessed with the Dallas Cowboys. His mother would have handed Arnulfo a plate of enchiladas over the fence and said, "Pobrecito."

Turi imagines how Ramon and Seferina might try to abuse Arnulfo because he is from Mexico, or because Arnulfo's coolheaded stare might encourage them to think that he will work for anyone like a slave.

The eighteen-wheeler is already waiting for them outside the giant corrugated metal warehouse, with its load of hundreds of chickens in cages. Like a drawbridge, a ramp has dropped from the truck's open metal doors straight into the compound. Turi can already hear the squawking and screeching inside the truck. He can see the thick chicken dust pouring from its open doors, like a monster's yellowy breath, and wafting in the amber streetlight next to the truck. They are to unload and carry the chickens from the truck into the cages inside the warehouse. Workers will pop open a door, grab a chicken by its legs and then another one, and hand the pair to the next in line on the ramp. Turi and the other workers will carry these crazy beasts upside down, teeter down the truck's ramp, and not slip on the chicken shit or stub their sneakers on a broken board. They'll shove the chickens into the warehouse cages, two per cage. Thousands and thousands of these small cages are neatly aligned under cold fluorescent lights, with thick wooden planks in between each row of cages. Sawdust and pieces of feathers litter the floor. As soon as their bodies are through the cage door, the chickens will pop up and race around in search of an escape. But there is none.

Before he left Corralitos that morning, Turi wrapped his hands in duct tape. He also grabbed a pair of Ramon's gloves he found in a box in the cuartito. Yesterday he did not wear gloves. Now his busted blisters and welts feel pleasantly painful underneath the duct tape and canvas gloves. When the geezer Juanito hands Turi his first pair of chickens, the obrero smiles with crooked, golden teeth, the old face more maroon than brown like an oily paper sack with eyes. The chicken dust creates a permanent haze inside the eighteen-wheeler. The grit and bits of feathers sting his lungs.

"Turi, órale, you're back for another day," Arnulfo says right behind him.

"Well, yeah, I need the money." The chicken heads and bodies twist under his grip and stretch to peck Turi's thighs, but the teenager easily holds them away from his body. Yesterday Turi surrendered to the pain in the late afternoon, his shoulders and arms erupting with spasms, his head inflated with a weird dizziness. Yesterday the chickens mercilessly pecked his knees and shat on his sneakers with a vengeance. Turi remembers it as a death of sorts. This morning he feels stronger, angrier than the day before. Tightening his grip on the sinewy legs of his two chickens, he marches down the wooden planks of the warehouse to an open cage. A worker managing the cages steps away from him. Turi slams his chickens through the hole and shuts the cage door. Like panicked jack-in-the-boxes, the chickens pop up and circle the cages. Quickly, the worker fastens a clip to the door. That is the easiest job. Turi's turn to clip the doors after lunch will be the beginning of the end of his day. He will survive. More importantly, he has to think about what to do: he doesn't want to go back to Mexico—he *won't*—even if his great-aunt Romita is the only part of his family left that loves him.

"You think la migra knows about this place?" Arnulfo says, jogging up beside Turi. Arnulfo wears the same jersey he wore yesterday, dark blue with the number "33" in white on the front and "Dorsett" on the back.

"Probably. The river's just behind the warehouse."

Arnulfo hovers over him, with no sense of personal space, too friendly and too quiet at the same time. His two front teeth appear almost painted with brown blotches. Turi wonders if Arnulfo has ever boxed, with that squarish face and crew cut.

"You sticking with this all month?" Arnulfo says in English, in his heavy, northern Mexico accent.

"Don't know. I'm thinking," Turi says, staring straight ahead.

"Thinking by carrying chickens? That's funny."

"You from Juárez?"

"No tengo papeles. I'm out of here tomorrow. I'm trying to get to Nueva York. Wanna come with me?"

"I don't think so," Turi says, grabbing another pair of chickens. "It's good to get out of here. This is the kind of place the migra would raid. I'd raid it, if I could. I'd burn it to the ground."

"They'll get you too, carnal," Arnulfo says, huffing as he struggles to release his thumb from the grip of a chicken's claws. The thumb turns deep purple, the chicken tightening its grip on his flesh. Arnulfo's flat face never grimaces, as he wiggles his thumb free. Turi stares at Arnulfo's forearms again, thick with muscles from years of work.

A white-haired Anglo man glares at them as they enter the warehouse. Turi decides to wait to respond to Arnulfo. Yesterday this gringo with the Stetson, Mr. Dunbar, handed thirty dollars to each of them. Turi feels this man is trying to overhear and understand every word they say, in Spanish or English, even from the other side of the yard. Maybe the stoic Mr. Dunbar can even read their lips. Those blue eyes stare at every worker like laser searchlights examining brown granite. His mother would have never trusted that severe gringo.

"I'm not a mojado," Turi says, almost smiling at Arnulfo, who is shaking the blood back into his thumb. Arnulfo smiles back and winks at Turi, as if dismissing a mosquito bite.

"So why aren't you, like, in an office and shit? Why you doing this job?"

"I don't know. I'm thinking. Hey, 'Nulfo, so why don't you stay in Mexico? Is it really that bad? Just curious."

Arnulfo's face turns towards Turi and smirks quietly again. Not saying anything for a moment. Turi adds quickly, "I mean, I just wonder why you want to go to Nueva York. Why not Connecticut?"

Arnulfo grins, brown teeth stains and all. Yesterday Arnulfo had to tell Turi to stop harassing him about how Connecticut was better than New York.

"I want to work. Earn some money in dollars. Not a lot of opportunities in Mexico, not like here. My parents in Delicias are old and maybe I could send money back too. You and your Connecticut! Still on that, huh? Yesterday somebody else also told me that little state is not far from Nueva York. I'm not going to be caught by the migra by staying near the border. That would be stupid."

By lunchtime, their jeans are caked with chicken shit, welts dot Arnulfo's hands, and Turi's black sneakers are caked with a muddy, half-dried yellow goop. Mr. Dunbar stares at them from a cottonwood tree.

"Ese, Arnulfo. When they pick you up in the truck in the morning, where exactly are they picking you up?" Turi munches on his cheese sandwich smeared with jelly and a ripe banana, his favorite, quick-and-easy meal from Corralitos.

"On Americas and Socorro. Not far from the Zaragoza bridge. Tomorrow Juanito, the old guy with the James Bond teeth, he's giving me a ride to Kansas City. Where his son lives. After that, I'll figure it out."

"You trust that viejo?" Turi searches the farm to see if Juanito is nearby and doesn't see him under any of the trees next to the other workers dozing or finishing their lunch.

"El viejito offered me a ride. He asked me if I could help him drive and I said yes. He's also giving me fifty bolas. Should I stay in Ysleta and be snatched by la pinche migra? Don't think so, Turi. Don't think so."

Although he doesn't say anything to Arnulfo, Turi keeps thinking of Juanito as an old scorpion. His mother always gave animal names to neighborhood characters. The names would capture their essence in some strange way. Juanito would have definitely been un alacrán. The dark, sinewy muscles on his forearms, the ragged whiskers on his face, but also the old man's eyes: black, shiny, and cold.

By the end of the day, the sun descending behind the pyramidal Franklin Mountains to the west, Turi's body throbs with pain. His right bicep twitches with little spasms. Yet he has no trouble hauling himself into the truck. Yesterday he stumbled into the truck's bed like a sack of bruised potatoes as his legs collapsed underneath him. Today his body still half-obeys him and does not collapse under its own weight.

"Arnulfo, have a great trip to Kansas City. Don't fall asleep on the road, güey." Turi nudges Arnulfo, who smiles next to him as if to say, "No problem. I got this." The truck rumbles along farm roads covered with caliche and stops twice to let workers jump out in the middle of nowhere.

"You carrying chickens and thinking about Connecticut tomorrow? No way to spend a summer, no way. Especially if no one's after you. Look at my hands, ese. They're yellow. Can't feel this thumb. Goddamn gallinas. I'm gone at six in the morning. Can't wait."

Turi glances at Arnulfo's badly swollen thumb. Before Turi can open his mouth to tell him what he might do, Arnulfo Muñoz jumps up, waves at him from the bumper of the truck, and sprints toward a clump of trees near the river. "Cuídate!" is all Turi can yell at Arnulfo's back as number "33" sprints toward the trees.

The truck leaves him in front of the irrigation ditch on Southside, speeding off the millisecond his foot lifts off the bumper. Turi turns and slowly shuffles slowly down Corralitos. He's only thinking about washing his clothes for tomorrow, hosing down his sneakers and drying them, grabbing something to eat. It heartens him that no cars are in the driveway. Ramon, Seferina, Raul, and Vanessa, all gone for now. Saying "Alvidrez" has always felt like chewing on broken glass, yet Turi repeats "Alvidrez" like an expletive to keep his bladder from exploding before he reaches the bathroom.

Turi leaves his sneakers drying outside the back door near the cuartito, and climbs into bed and turns off his light. He has already assembled his lunch for tomorrow, and the brown bag is already in his room with a set of clean clothes in the milk crate. Nobody bothered him, nobody talked to him, and frankly that was a good night. Turi imagines Mrs. Garcia in her tight blue dress again, imagines she is ten years younger. He imagines he could talk to her and have something to say and she wouldn't treat him like a student. He imagines she is smiling at him . . . Turi's eyes flutter to a close in the darkness. He vaguely hears Ramon arrive somewhere inside the house on Corralitos, drunk and in mid-song.

"Di' you do this? Fuckin' little bastard!" Turi's door bursts open and crashes against the wall. The boy rubs his eyes and pushes himself off his mattress on the floor. Like a glass flung against a wall, the almost-dream is shattered.

"Wha—?" A powerful brown hand plants the door against the wall and shakes the drywall. Ramon's silhouette straightens and sways at the door's threshold.

Turi's eyes focus: he finds his uncle's red, rheumy eyes, the thick unkempt hair like dusty black straw on Ramon's head, the free hand pointed at Turi's face. Clinging to Ramon's body is a white sleeveless T-shirt with faded yellow stains at the armpits.

"The gloves, you little idiot! Los guantes!" Ramon slams a fist into the door. The door rattles against its hinges. His eyes lose their focus for a second.

"I used them for work today. My hands hurt. I needed them!" Turi squirms to a sitting position, his back against the wall.

"Di' I tell you could uze these gloves? You smell 'em? Look at 'em, cabrón! Smell 'em!" Ramon's arms are brown black, muscled, and tattooed. He shoves the gloves into Turi's face and drops them on his lap. Ramon steps back and sways in front of the bed in a drunken stupor.

Already dizzy from waking up so abruptly and the sudden putrid stench in his nose, Turi can barely make out the naked light bulb overhead, a weak and swaying moon.

"Di' I tell you could touch any'f my things? Di' I?" Ramon steps back again and stumbles against the door. His voice whines at the end of each sentence as he slurs every other word. Ramon's eyes wander wildly about the shed as if his head hears strange voices.

"I'm sorry, I'll clean them."

"They can't be cleaned! They're ru-ru-ruined!" Ramon picks up the gloves and flings them to the ground.

"I'm sorry. I'll buy you new ones."

"You bet y'r ass, you will!" Ramon stares at the room's walls as if he suddenly fails to recognize what room this is, what house this is, seeing and not seeing Turi, the boy cowering on the mattress on the floor. Turi finally notices Seferina nervously laughing behind the threshold into the house. She already seems half-drunk too.

"Ese, Ramon, chicken shit! Like you've been twisting off chicken heads all day!"

"Goddamn, li'l nerd, what's theez shit!" Ramon roars, kicking Turi's crate and launching his lunch, clothes, and books in all directions inside the little room. Ramon stumbles backward to the doorway, apparently not knowing what else to do. Slowly he turns to face Seferina, who wants to encourage him and hold him back at the same time, like a form of entertainment. Her hand is resting on Ramon's shoulder.

"I'll pay for the gloves . . . at least I'm working," Turi whispers, loud enough to surprise himself.

Seferina gasps.

"Wha' he say?"

"I think he said he's working. Unlike you, mi amor." A distracted grin spreads across Serafina's face, a hand rubbing one of Ramon's thick shoulders as if to sympathize and mock simultaneously with a touch. "Like he's the man of the house. He does give us twenty dollars every day, but that's not even enough for his food or this cuartito." She snorts at the naked bulb swinging above her head. Her hand soothes and caresses Ramon again, lightly dancing on his back.

Ramon lingers at the spectacle of his wife for a second, digesting her words and their meaning, and wheels around, legs far apart. "We're shipping you back to Mexico! Who-d-yah think you are? Ungrateful little . . . little—"

"I don't care what you do. I'm not going. I won't."

"You don't have a choice," Seferina adds, stepping in front of Ramon.

"You don't own me!"

"Wha' he say?"

"Ramon, querido, he says we don't own him."

"Who cares wha' ya think? Back to Juáritos, back to la nada, güey! Your sister, your sister . . ." Ramon vaguely stares at Seferina for a few seconds, losing his train of thought.

"I hate both of you!"

"Leave him alone, mi amor. Come on, let's go. Leave him to be miserable all by himself."

Turi starts sobbing and inhales in spasms on the mattress on the floor. Ramon stands still for a moment. Tears drench the boy's face as he clutches the blanket and pillow against his chest. A crazy, dizzying heat rushes to Turi's head. He wants to escape the suffocation he feels in this room, to fight back with triple the force. Turi hates the house on Corralitos. He hates what it has become under Ramon. He hates Seferina and all her stupid family. This room, the chickens, even the light bulb swaying like a pendulum above their heads—he wishes all of it would burn to dust.

"At least I'm not a drunk!" Turi screams hoarsely at both of them, not caring what happens to him, wanting to die more than he ever has in his life.

A swift kick connects with Turi's ribs and knocks him back against the wall. Red stars flash in front of his face. A rivulet of blood trickles from his mouth: Turi has bitten his tongue. He gasps and almost vomits on the bed as Seferina yanks the unsteady Ramon back. "Déjalo! Leave the little loser alone. Look at him, he's a little coward! Déjalo, Ramon!" She glares at Turi. "You're going back to Juárez, whether you like it or not!"

"Wha' you say?" Ramon challenges Turi again, one last time, staggering at the door's threshold, taking a step back and standing ready to view his handiwork. He is panting hard while Seferina still tugs at one arm.

Turi spits a little blood on the concrete floor and coughs. The boy is dazed. Inside his head, the room spins like an unhinged merry-go-round. The light behind Ramon inexplicably goes dark. A semifestive look in her glazed eyes, Seferina pushes her husband into the hallway and closes the door with another half-grin. In the velvety darkness, Turi's head recovers with invisible explosions, pressures, and echoes. His abdomen feels sore and tight, a dull pain there and not there, as if an invisible hand pressed and lifted against his stomach. He is okay, even if his mouth contains a small ball of blood and saliva. Turi thinks he hears distant murmurs, shouts, and even laughter in the recesses of Corralitos. A narcocorrido about the death of a Chihuahua musician blasts through the house with its polka beat. Turi lays on his bed, breathing in and out more easily now, swimming in this sound, and shuts his eyes. He is okay, yet no dreams come.

Past the time everyone else is in a bedroom asleep or on another joyride beyond Corralitos, Turi stirs in the darkest hours of that night. What wakes the teenager is a train's faraway whistle: the freight train rumbling east to west between Alameda Avenue and North Loop Drive a few minutes past three in the morning. He has always loved that whistle and imagined where it would go, the countryside it would cross. Turi wiggles his tongue inside his mouth, tasting a thin crust like copper underneath his tongue. He stretches his shoulders, arms, and legs. His ribs are sore, but not too bad. In the thick black of the night, he cannot see himself. He stands up gingerly and shuffles to the bathroom in the hallway as quietly as he can, his left knee buckling under him every other step. Each inhale reminds him of his ribs. He opens his mouth to see what he did to his tongue—spits out a bit of dried blood, rinses his mouth, washes his face, and gulps handfuls of water. Before he opens the bathroom door, Turi turns off the light and listens to the night. Nobody is in the hallway. Nobody is awake. Nobody walks the rooms of Corralitos. He walks into the hallway.

From their open bedroom door, Turi overhears Ramon's deep snoring and Seferina's heavy breathing. He quietly walks into their room. Turi can smell the Coors Golden Banquet in the air, even though their window is open. A sheet of moonlight falls over their bed. Next to the closet, Turi finds Seferina's purse and pinches out all the dollar bills he can find. On all fours, Turi searches for Ramon's pants under the bed, on the floor, and he finds them behind the door. Ramon's wallet also has a few bills, but Turi can't see the denominations. For all that trouble, the teenager might have only about twenty singles in his hand. Turi knows Seferina hides more money in the closet. But that rickety closet door has always squeaked loudly when it opens so he decides to leave their bedroom as quietly as he came in.

His flashlight in hand, the light dead from the naked bulb overhead, Turi picks up his books and his lunch, which is smashed into a messy pulp inside the brown paper bag. He dresses in silence, moaning softly when he twists his body to hike up his pants. On the mattress on the floor, he sits in his socks. The teenage boy flashes the light around the walls of the cuartito, tears blinding him. He sees the shine of his penny on the floor, picks it up, and unscrews the drain cover. Turi shoves the three rolls of cash into his jeans— throws his books, extra clothes, and the blanket into the milk crate. He grips the copper wire and pulls it taut between his fists. He imagines returning to the dark bedroom in the hallway, imagines wrapping it around Ramon's neck until it bites deeply into the dark skin, until the kicks stop forever. But even his mother would never have wanted revenge on any bad man. The boy opens his palm and drops the copper wire on the floor, tucks the crate under one arm, and slowly opens the back door. Outside Turi pushes his damp, clean sneakers on his feet. Under an amber haze from a streetlight, he walks away from the house on Corralitos. He wonders if his mother would have left Corralitos in the darkness, if she would have confronted her awful sister and fought back somehow. But his mother is not there to guide him anymore. In the silence, Turi steps into the murky shadows of Ysleta.

At the dusty corner of Americas Avenue and Socorro Road, Turi spreads himself onto the ground and falls into an uneasy half-sleep under the June stars. The smell of the cotton fields wafts over him. He imagines the Milky Way shining against the blue-black sky like a floating river of lights. Turi has always loved staring at the worlds beyond this earth. He can't wait to keep reading *The Mystery of the Mighty Housatonic River*. His ribs ache if he twists a certain way, and one side of his tongue is puffy inside his mouth. Like gigantic, heedless mechanical monsters, eighteen-wheelers roar by him on Americas and unleash rolling gusts of wind that disperse into the fields. He smells alfalfa and cattle somewhere faraway in the cool desert. After a while, as he drifts in and out of consciousness, his headache is gone and the pain in his midsection disappears as long as he keeps still. It is a beautiful summer night in the desert. His mother would have loved this night.

"What the hell are you doing here?" Turi hears a familiar voice say, as he feels a gentle kick at the bottom of one sneaker. He smiles even before opening his eyes.

"I want to go with you. Can I?"

"Don't know why not," Arnulfo Muñoz says, smiling at Turi almost as if he expected him to be there. A truck speeds past them on Americas, its headlights illuminating Turi's face like slow lightning. Arnulfo holds out his hand to haul Turi to his feet. Turi grimaces as he stands up. "What happened to you? You okay?"

"Fell down. Don't worry about it. I'm fine, ese. What time is it?"

"About, let me see, twenty minutes past—oh, here he is!" Arnulfo says.

A shiny navy blue Ford pickup, with a double cab and a large chromed toolbox in back, slides to a stop on the gravel. The old man Juanito stares at Turi, does not smile through his golden teeth. He waits a moment, then jerks his head for both of them to get in.

CHAPTER THREE

The truck heads north and east on Montana, toward the Guadalupe Mountains National Park and Carlsbad Caverns. It is almost an hour before anyone says anything. Johnny Cash and only Johnny Cash is playing on the stereo. Arnulfo smiles at the long black asphalt illuminated in front of them as if lost in the songs or the wonder of what Nueva York might be or just searching for the future somewhere in the horizon. Turi stares out the passenger window, wondering what the hell he has done and whether anyone on Corralitos, or anywhere else, will ever care. No one will find him unless he wants to be found. He imagines Mrs. Garcia at the beginning of school next September, angry and perhaps a bit worried about the books she has lent Turi and how her trust has been betrayed. Maybe she will even be worried about him. Maybe she will visit Corralitos to see what happened to her books and that boy with the bruise and why they have disappeared. Seferina, Vanessa, Raul, and especially Ramon? Turi hopes they rot under the hooves of the horned one. His great-aunt Romita in Juárez is the only one left from his real family, but he hasn't seen her in years. Finally he has escaped the border.

"So you going to KC too? Tienes chamba?" old man Juanito asks coldly, still staring straight ahead into the darkness of Route 62.

The desert is an abandonment of black around them, not a house or light or even a horizon. Only tumbleweeds flash near their headlights, with a vast expanse of nothingness beyond. Up close, Juanito looks grittier than at the chicken farm, his arm muscles shiny and lean under the dashboard lights. As the songs waft through the truck's cabin, Turi also notices Juanito's stupid grin and the occasional bob of the old man's head. All of that reminds Turi that Juanito seems as much of a Mexican grandfather as a Mexican scorpion. Turi is still glad Arnulfo is between them. Juanito's powerful musky sweat permeates the truck's cabin.

"Not yet. I'll look for work when I get there. I want to get to Connecticut, Señor," Turi says, trying to be polite. He is getting a free ride, and certainly doesn't want fifty dollars like Arnulfo, yet doesn't want to get dumped in the middle of nowhere. Turi stares at Juanito, who looks pensive and somber as the gravelly "Ain't No Grave" plays on the radio. The gold teeth hide and reveal themselves behind thick, dry lips.

"Shouldn't go anywhere without work, niño. You won't survive."

Turi says nothing but tries to smile. His mouth doesn't hurt anymore, but he can feel a certain thickness in his tongue. It doesn't matter because old man Juanito doesn't look at him and keeps his watery grey eyes on the rolling black asphalt in front of them. A tattoo of a snarling black dog or a wolf is on Juanito's forearm. "I'll do whatever I can," Turi says softly.

"Can you drive?"

"Sure," Turi says quickly. Yes, he drove before, many times from the empty parking lot of Ysleta High School when El Loco gave him a chance behind the wheel of his Chevy Camaro. El Loco lived two doors down from Turi on Corralitos and graduated from Ysleta High. El Loco's sister, also a high school sophomore, had a crush on Turi. He often accepted rides from El Loco back to their neighborhood in Barraca, with Antonia in tow, only for a chance at the black Chevy Camaro. For the past two months, El Loco allowed him to drive the Camaro on I-10 to Lee Trevino to drop him off at El Paso Fitness for two hours, but Turi always had to bring Antonia back to Corralitos and back to the gym to pick up El Loco. Turi even let Antonia kiss him at Blackie Chesher Park for one of those two hours, which he immediately regretted. It was like kissing a salty pretzel. But it was worth it to hear the sweet rumble of the Camaro's motor and to peel out of the park onto Zaragoza Road.

"How old are you?"

"Seventeen." Turi glances at Arnulfo, who still seems amazed at the night before them like a vacation. "And you?" The old man still doesn't seem half as tough as Ramon.

"Old enough to die at any moment." Juanito stares at the desert in front of them and sniggers with a half smile. More yellowy-black than gold, his teeth glimmer above the lights of the dashboard. "We're driving straight through. That's the deal. So if we take turns we should have no problems. We'll get there rapido."

Turi looks at Arnulfo again, who either doesn't hear or doesn't care. "How long is that? Straight to Kansas City?"

"Seventeen, eighteen hours, more or less. Depends how long we stop for lunch. We'll get something quick in a few hours, and keep going. 'Get Rhythm,' that's what we're doing."

"Your hijo expecting you? I mean, straight through. That's a lot of driving in one day," Turi says, shifting in his seat, and focusing on Juanito's forearms and what looks like a black, square cell phone in a shirt pocket. The old man only has whiffs of hair, and now that Turi thinks about it, Juanito's hair has been puffed into a sort of thin pompadour just like images of Johnny Cash that Turi has seen on the TV.

"Hijo?" Juanito asks, furrowing his eyebrows for a second. The old man turns to Turi, but then finds Arnulfo's distractedly amused face still staring at the white dotted lines that the blue truck is eating underneath them. "Oh, yeah. He's waiting for me," the old man says stonily at the highway in front of them. "We have an appointment and we can't miss it. We won't."

After an hour, the pickup slows on Route 62 behind a short line of cars in front of an immigration checkpoint. An idling Immigration and Customs Enforcement SUV with flashing red lights sits next to a small booth with a greenish fluorescent glow, a lone ICE officer inside. Behind him is a portable trailer office, the kind one sees in construction sites, and another SUV. Old man Juanito gently steers the truck at an angle, as if he's about to turn around. He nearly stands up in his seat to peer out the window and over the Honda Pilot in front of him. Then he straightens the truck back behind the Pilot. Juanito glances sidelong at Arnulfo, who is half-asleep, and at Turi, whose head rests against the passenger window. The officer has asked the driver of the Honda Pilot to step out of the vehicle, while two more agents immediately exit the trailer and start peering under the Honda's seats and gently knocking and feeling the open doors of the Honda. Oddly, the old man grins with his gold teeth, and fiddles with something embedded into the fold of the seat next to him. Turi sits up. After a few minutes, the Honda's driver jumps back in and drives forward.

"Good evening, officer," Juanito says. He glances at the ICE officer standing at the window with a flashlight in hand, but he is really just eyeing the camera in front of the pickup, high above both of them. Juanito elbows Arnulfo, who blurts "American" as soon as he fully opens his eyes. Turi repeats the magic phrase quickly as he tries to catch a glimpse of what Juanito has hidden in the fold of the seat. The old man asks for directions to

Lubbock, Juanito repeating "Lubbock" at the windshield and not even at the impassive officer, in a dark blue bullet-proof vest with a badge at the shoulder. The severe-looking Mexicano, with no trace of any Mexican accent, shoves a map in front of Juanito, and explains how to get to Lubbock. From the fold of the seat, Juanito retrieves what looks like a thick envelope made of map paper with squiggly red and blue lines. He carefully brings the envelope underneath the officer's map, and both envelope and map blend together. When the officer retrieves his Texas road map, the envelope underneath is also gone. Old man Juanito mutters, "Thank you," to the windshield again and drives carefully back onto Route 62.

After about five miles, Juanito slams on the brakes and skids the truck to a stop in the blue-black desert night. "Hey, cabrón, it's your turn to drive," Juanito says to Arnuflo. The old man then turns to Turi. "And you pay attention to him. If something happens to us, I'll kick both your asses! It should be easy driving to Kansas City from here. Stay on 62, and only 62, until Oklahoma City. Then north on 35 to Kansas City. Don't go over the speed limit, and let me know if you have any questions, problems, if anybody's following us."

Arnulfo shifts behind the wheel, rolling his shoulders and shaking his big head awake, and Turi rides shotgun. Juanito climbs into the backseat of the truck cab and lies down. As the truck pulls onto Route 62, Turi glares at Arnulfo, but does not say a word.

CHAPTER FOUR

The clueless Arnulfo drives steadily past Carlsbad. Before Hobbs, Juanito is snoring in the backseat. Turi glances back: sure enough the old man's eyes are closed, and a silvery line of saliva dangles from his lips.

"Oye, güey," Turi whispers, one ear still cocked to hear the snoring.

Arnulfo takes his eyes off the road for a second and smirks at Turi.

"You see what happened at the checkpoint, what Juanito did?"

"What? What are you talking about? The checkpoint?"

"Keep your voice down!" Turi hisses harshly, waits for a second, and catches Juanito's rhythmic snoring with his ears again. He stares through the dark murk of the backseat. The old man is still lost in sleep.

"Juanito gave the migra guy some feria, güey."

"Money? Why would he . . . ? Serious? What are you talking about?"

"Told you to keep your voice down. You were half-asleep. We're probably carrying contraband and shit. Don't you pay attention?"

"You're making it up. I don't believe you. Serious?"

"Yes, of course I'm serious."

Arnulfo glances suspiciously at Turi for too many seconds. Turi jabs at the road with his finger. "Pay attention!" he whispers. In the back, Juanito is still snoring. Turi lifts his index finger to his lips.

"Juanito, the old man? You're joking. He's going to see his son in Kansas City. What are you talking about?"

"Look, 'Nulfo. This guy's running contraband, drugs. Think about it. Why drive straight through? When I mentioned his son earlier, he looked at me as if I was out of my mind. He's lying. I saw him hand an envelope to the migra guy."

"You saw him?"

"Yes, I saw him. He's using you, me, as drivers, güey. Drug mules."

"I don't believe you." Arnulfo stares at Turi: the smug smile is gone, the lips are flat, and under that massive forehead, Arnulfo's tiny eyes glare at Turi as if he has just pushed him a bit too far. The teen tries to get a glimpse of Juanito through the rearview mirror by twisting his neck, but the old man is too far down, lying on the backseat.

Turi worries Arnulfo will stop driving, won't believe him, will blurt out something stupid, will eliminate the only advantage they have: the old man Juanito assumes they are still oblivious dupes in this scheme. Again Turi points a finger at the road. Arnulfo drives steadily into the night toward the Texas panhandle, but Arnulfo is frowning at the windshield and occasionally at Turi. Arnulfo grips the truck's steering wheel a bit tighter, knuckles white. He stares at the road, his eyes two tiny slits in an immobile death stare.

We're in danger, Turi thinks. *We need to get out of this mess.*

Who knows what Juanito will do after they arrive in Kansas City, or even before. They are more than expendable: nobody will even search for them if Juanito pumps bullets into their skulls somewhere in the middle of this wasteland. Turi could spell it out for Arnulfo, could tell him what probably awaits them at the end of this ride. But maybe Arnulfo already knows, maybe that's why he's angry.

This is exactly why Arnulfo was brought along. Because he's undocumented, because he can be easily used, because he'll do what he's told, because no one will give a damn if he disappears. Turi was the little surprise that ruined those plans.

Behind them, Juanito still snores.

"Let's keep driving, okay," Turi whispers. "Let's think of a plan. When we switch drivers. That's when we'll do it. Just keep driving."

"What if you're wrong? What if you didn't see what you think you saw? What if the envelope didn't have money in it?"

"You kidding? Why would I make it up? You think Juanito was handing him a wedding invitation? Let's think of a plan."

"To do what?"

He's not sure what. That's part of the problem. "Let me think. Just please, Arnulfo, keep driving."

After almost two hours, they are on the northern outskirts of Lubbock, and Turi has whispered to Arnulfo that as soon as they are past the city lights, and into another stretch of darkness on the road, they will stop at a rest stop. They will stop the car, and when Juanito wakes up, they will tell him they need to go to the restroom. They will tell him they want to switch drivers. When the old man is in the can, Turi will get the hell out of there and leave Juanito behind. Arnulfo twists his head and gives Turi a sidelong look like a brother sizing up another brother, half impressed, half in doubt.

"Please, just do exactly what I say. See that rest stop coming up? Let's hope no one's there. As soon as we stop, give me the keys."

The truck slows as it exits the highway. Turi points to the spot where he wants Arnulfo to park. Not too close to the cinder block restrooms, but not too far either. Nobody else is in the inlet of asphalt next to Route 62.

The stars punch pinpricks of light into the Stygian sky. The moon is three-quarters full. Rancid smells from the green trashcan barrel waft through the air-conditioning vents as soon as the truck stops next to it.

"Wha—? Why the hell we stopping?" Juanito growls groggily from the back as he pushes himself up.

"I need to pee, we're switching drivers," Turi declares, staring at Arnulfo whose hands still grip the steering wheel with white knuckles, not moving. Turi jabs his thumb toward the window and yanks the keys from the ignition before Juanito sits straight up and rubs his eyes. Arnulfo glares at Turi.

"Where the hell are we?"

"We just passed Lubbock. I gotta go!" Turi blurts as he flings open the door.

Arnulfo opens his door and also steps outside. Turi sighs, relieved. *Somebody has to take control*, he thinks. He's not going to end up dead in the middle of nowhere.

The teenage boys enter the milky darkness of the cinder block bathroom, dimly lit only by moonlight. Turi imagines a desert bobcat lunging at their throats from a dark corner or from underneath a stall wall. The stink of dried urine and shit gags him before he steps outside to glance at the truck. Arnulfo is still inside the cinder block tomb of the bathroom. Turi sees the cab's light flicker on inside the truck. He can see the vague, moonlit figure of Juanito creakily step out and slam the passenger door shut, stretch his hands to the blue-black sky, and undo his pants as he pees about two feet from the truck.

"Arnulfo! Where the hell are you?"

"I'm right here." From behind him, a steady, deep, disembodied voice. "What if you're wrong, Turi? What if you didn't see what you think you saw? I'm not sure I wanna—"

"Listen to me. He's peeing next to the truck, goddammit. I'm not wrong, 'Nulfo. I saw him give money to the migra. Please, just do this: get into the passenger seat. Just get the hell in, 'cause if you're not there, I'm leaving you. Not trying to be mean, 'Nulfo. But we're both going to end up dead if we don't ditch this old man."

"Okay. But if you're wrong, if you're wrong, we're about to ruin everything. No Kansas City. No New York. No Connecticut. Nada. You saw him hand over money? You sure?"

"Yes. I *saw* him."

"This is so screwed up. I don't understand—"

"You think we should *ask* him? You mean, so he can put a bullet in our heads right now?"

"No, that would be stupid."

"Exactly. 'Nulfo, I *saw* him. He bribed the ICE officer, goddammit. The officer was expecting the bribe. They've probably done this many times before. Why won't you believe me?"

"But what are—"

"Just get in the damn truck. Lock the door on your side. That's all you have to do." In the bluish glimmer of moonlight, Turi starts walking slowly toward the truck. He doesn't look back. If Arnulfo isn't behind him, if Arnulfo can't think on his feet, if he panics at the wrong time, if he doesn't believe him, so be it. Turi will escape this fiasco one way or another. He is bigger than the old man. The only problem will be if Juanito carries a gun in his pants. The chances are that he doesn't. The chances are that if the old man does have a gun, he has left it in the truck as he slept.

As Turi marches toward the truck, he suddenly hears quick footsteps slapping the pavement behind him, and glimpses the shadow of Arnulfo sprint past him like a ghostly running back. He jumps into the truck. As Arnulfo locks the passenger's side door, both doors lock automatically. Turi is still ten feet from the truck.

"What the hell is that idiot doing?" Juanito hisses in front of one of the truck's darkened headlights.

Through the windshield, Turi throws a sharp glance at Arnulfo crouching behind the dashboard as he walks briskly around Juanito. Does Arnulfo not notice that both truck doors are locked? Did he lock them on purpose? Arnulfo's lips are a straight, indecipherable line below tiny black eyes following Turi's every step.

"Heard a growl in the bathroom. Noises. An animal, maybe," Turi says, thinking quickly, almost to the driver's side. He can smell and feel Juanito's stale, sticky breath in the cold air like a sheet of rust hanging in the moonlight. Turi fingers the truck key in his pocket: if he takes the key out, Juanito may grab it.

"Pinche güey. Probably a javelina or a skunk! No es nada. We need to get out of here and get going! We don't have time for any games."

Turi raps on the driver's side window and points at the lock. For a flash of a second, Arnulfo's smirk returns. Turi gives Arnulfo a look. Turi imagines an invisible hand reaching through the glass and strangling Arnulfo. As soon as Turi hears the lock pop open, he turns around, Juanito less than two feet away, and shoves the old man with all his might and weight into the little ditch next to the curb.

"Hey! You son of a bitch!"

Turi slams the truck's door, hits the lock with his elbow, jams the key into the ignition, and revs the motor. He can see Juanito struggle to get up and climb out the ditch: Turi shoved the old man's chest hard, and he heard a pop or a whoosh as he pivoted toward the truck. Maybe he knocked out the old man's air. Just as the reverse gear engages, Juanito's hand is at Turi's window, pounding against the glass. Out of the corner of one eye, Turi glimpses the irate dark figure. He floors the accelerator and yanks the wheel away from the curb. *Does Juanito have something gripped in his hand? A rock?* Turi winces and waits for the explosion of glass, but sees only Juanito's shoulder as Turi clips it with the wing-like driver's side mirror. The truck roars backward, sending the old man careening and spinning like a whirling dervish into the desert darkness.

Turi yanks the gear into drive, and the truck lurches onto the highway. He stomps down on the accelerator and finds only flashes of moonlight in the rearview mirror where Juanito once stood. Like a blue marlin released into the ocean's depths, the truck swerves on the highway between the two empty lanes, leaving a cloud of dust in the desert's midnight murk. The head-lights turn on and slice into the night.

"Shit! Shit! Sorry about the door! I didn't—"

"Freakin' A, Arnulfo. Why the hell you lock both doors?" Turi glances at Arnulfo involuntarily shivering in his seat and holding himself with both arms. Turi is also suddenly cold. "Wonder what happened to the old bastard."

"Now they're going to come looking for us."

CHAPTER FIVE

John Dunbar hangs his prized Evilla de Oro warily on the rusty nail at the back of the dilapidated shed. Before he pulls a pair of pliers from his jeans, he wipes a speck of blood from his black Lucchese boots and flicks the cotton-wood leaf into the desert wind. The nicknames his workers have given to him? El güero and The Stetson. The morning sun palpitates, a fiery shield in the sky. For miles, the landscape is empty and quiet. The Río Grande is just over a ridge line in the horizon. With the pair of pliers, he grips the emblem from the gold badge and works the eagle free, leaving a clean-cut edge in the metal sharp enough to slash and gut a fish. This weekend, he will add the eagle to his tools and odds and ends in his fishing shack near Ruidoso, deep inside the Lincoln National Forest. What is left of the badge will be obliterated in the grinder, along with a few other items, as soon as Dunbar returns to the poultry farm. As a gold Christ-on-the-Cross dangles from a fine, oval-link chain on his neck, he kisses the tiny figurine rever-ently. "Cuida mis niños, Dios Todopoderoso," he says in perfect Spanish, which has often startled his Mexican workers. Few have ever expected or gotten used to the intimate song of their mother tongue coming from such sky-blue eyes.

His reddish skin glistens with sweat over freckles and stubs of blond hair. Dunbar turns on the black cell phone in his pocket: it has been off as he has worked through the night. As the phone acquires a signal, he grabs the Stetson hat on the rusted nail and listens to a message with a sudden frown. He calls the unknown number back immediately.

"What the hell happened, Juan? Where are you?"

"Señor, I'm at a convenience store. Outside of Lubbock. North of it. I had to walk all night until someone picked me up on the highway and dropped me off here. I'm bleeding, señor. My head has a chichón the size of an orange. My god. I'm surprised I'm not dead. I tried walking back all the way to—"

"Where's the damn truck?"

"They took it! They almost ran me over, hijos de putas! My cell phone, my—"

"They? What do you mean 'they'? Who else was in the truck? Not just that illegal? What the hell did you do, Juan?"

"A friend of his joined us. I thought he could help us drive and get to KC faster. Two boys. I couldn't just say no and keep the illegal. It was both of them or nothing. It's the kid that worked for us a few days ago. He was at the farm too, the young mojado's only friend. Another teenager but, maybe, an Americano. Son of a bitch—"

"Shut up, Juan. Right now. The packages? That special delivery?"

"In the truck, Señor. I'm sorry. I made a mistake. I know that. I should never have brought that other kid too. I just wanted to go as fast as possible. Señor, please forgive me. Thank god, I had my wallet still. I'm on a burner phone I bought—"

"I'll send Chucho and Eduardo to pick you up right now. Call them in about an hour—they'll already be on the road to Lubbock—and tell them exactly where you are. They'll be there in a few hours. Stay put and wait for them. And let me tell you, Juan, our friends in Guerrero will not be too happy about this, so you have one focus, one job only: find that goddamn truck. I'll tell Chucho and Eduardo the circumstances."

For seconds, silence hangs in the air between the two cell phones like the pause before an assassin pulls the trigger on his target.

"Señor, please. Please, Señor. I'll find the truck. We'll find the truck. The packages, nobody will find them in—" A heavy click suddenly terminates the call.

Dunbar spits on the dirt and marches into the shed. On a wooden table long enough for a man to lie flat, wet spots of water dot the wood as three men spray every inch inside the shed with a mixture of bleach and water and wipe clean other surfaces on the walls and floors. As soon as the blond man walks in, the chatter in the room ceases, a blanket of silence over them. It is as if the tiny Christ-on-the-Cross on the chain is staring directly at them, alive, with eyes ignited by blue fire. The cleaning becomes suddenly more vigorous. Dunbar inspects the room, his eyes quickly scanning every edge and corner. In one shadowy recess, he spots something not quite flat, a small gob. After a few quick steps, his black boots are in front of it: the bloody remnants of a finger, fingerprints still on a piece of skin, a bluish fingernail dangling.

"Let me tell you, you numbnuts, if I find anything else, anything else in this room, all three of you will join our friend at the poultry farm. Pick this shit up, and get the rest of the rag bag, and anything else, anything, to Dagoberto at the grinder." Before he finishes the sentence, one of the old Mexicanos cleaning has already grabbed the gob and flung it into a thick plastic bag sagging in the middle of the floor. Dunbar pinches the mangled Border Patrol badge from his pocket, what is left of it, and flicks it into the bag too. Then he again touches his fingertips to his lips and lets them envelop his golden talisman.

By evening, Dunbar has gotten Turi's name from Juanito and has also dispatched Chucho and Eduardo to Lubbock and questioned the truck drivers at the poultry farm. Dunbar has driven to Yaya Lane and Socorro Road and asked a few questions to kids playing baseball in an empty lot of the Barraca neighborhood of Ysleta. In front of a house on Corralitos, he is waiting. Tony and Ruben sit in the back of the SUV like silent gorillas at attention to their boss in the driver's seat. Dunbar's deep blue eyes do not apparently blink from their focus on the crooked porch and half-broken chain-link fence of the house.

"Just remember," Dunbar says quietly to the windshield in front of him, "we need their cooperation. But we need to get a message across. After tonight, you two will be checking on them, to see if they've made any progress locating those boys and that truck."

A teenage girl arrives at the house on Corralitos first. Then a woman, the mother, with a man grabbing her ass as they stumble through the doorway. The lights turn on, and the faint sounds of laughter can be heard through the one-inch crack of the window in the black SUV. After a few seconds, Dunbar steps out of the truck, and his two men march behind him.

The meet and greet begins friendly enough on Corralitos: el güero knocks on the door, the woman answers, and all three are invited inside after exchanging pleasantries. Through the nearly closed front door, one can hear pleasantries faintly exchanged, Ramon's voice beckoning them to take a seat on the sofas, murmurs and explanations, and one sudden near shout, "What has this little cabrón done! He stole your truck in Lubbock?" Another voice, Seferina's, chimes in, "Lubbock? Vanessa, check the back, and see if anything else is gone! Vanessa, check everything! See what's missing!" More murmurs and explanations come through the half-opened door: "No, we haven't heard from him. We don't know anybody in Lubbock. He doesn't have a cell phone. Call the cops. Where the hell would he be going? How should we know that?"

The front door closes shut almost in slow motion. But Ramon's shout still rings like a mission bell into the empty darkness of Corralitos: "Get the hell out of my house! Who the—" A sharp thud behind the door. Scurrying and screaming. Seferina's and Vanessa's intermingled screams, like dueling fire truck sirens, distinct yet both piercing, and then sobs, deep guttural sobs from only one. "Dios mio! You're killing him! You're killing him!" Another deep thud and moan. At the same time, in the same moment, even higher pitched screams, a grotesque symphony, from Vanessa, the screams of someone lost in a living nightmare. The screams reverberate in the cool desert night. Even a cat runs away to hide underneath a pile of rotting wood next door.

"Help me! Please, my god, help me!" Ramon's voice now different, begging, still deep, still a man's voice, but begging: "No, please, we haven't done anything. Vanessa, don't fight them! Vanessa! We don't know where he is! We're not even his parents, my god, my—" Curses and cries from a grown man.

Surprisingly, Seferina's voice is the most resilient, the most defiant, until it isn't. Until only the unique timbre of her sobs can pinpoint that she, too, is breaking. An intermittent silence, soft sobs, then shrieks, and again silence. For three hours, the black SUV stays in front of the house on Corralitos, like the hand of a god that ushers in a reckoning.

After a while, only an occasional sob or groan escapes from the house.

The neighbors have already turned off their lights and forbidden their children to step into the streets. Their dogs strangely do not bark any alarm. The quiet is so sudden, it appears as if the neighborhood is spontaneously praying. More murmurs and entreaties sound through the crack underneath the front door. "We'll help you find him. Just leave us alone. Please, dear god. We'll help you find him. That little son of a bitch will pay! Look what you've done to us! Look! Just leave us alone. We know. We won't tell anyone! Just leave! For god's sake, just leave. We know. Don't you think we don't know that? Where is my daughter? My god! No, please, don't!" A half scream rises and falls in a fraction of a second, followed by coughing, soft whimpering. One final exclamation, "We don't want your money! Vanessa! We'll help you find him for nothing. But, just . . . Please, leave . . ."

Murmurs and instructions. The three men march out in the same order as they marched in. The SUV's motor roars to a start and leaves only a small dust devil dancing on Corralitos. After a while, one bedroom light flickers on like a weak yellow candle. Guttural moans and only one shriek in half-hearted anger interrupt the desert night, the edge of the edge of the world. "They're coming back. You know they're coming back. We have to find him. That goddamn pendejo! I'll kill him if I find him first, dear god. I don't care what they want. What has he gotten himself into?"

Dunbar checks his stocks on his personal cell phone. He has done well today, especially the security portfolio he has constructed this year after reading an article in *Barron's*. John Broaddus Dunbar is still inside his SUV, which is inside his huge garage, after dropping off the men in Socorro at midnight.

His ranch is beyond Clint, miles from the poultry farm, which he owns too. At the black electronic gates, higher than two men and stronger than a dozen, everything is quiet. The guard is alert but not visible from the caliche farm road. Others are at the corners inside the complex, alert and also invisible, just as he has trained them. Dunbar owns dozens of acres around him too, yet he believes he owns too much land. Too much of his father still in him, too much of the past, too much of the border mentality that disdains New York and London and what those places can deliver to someone with a little brains and perspective. The two-feet-thick adobe walls of the garage and around the entire complex always seal out the noises from the desert. Sitting in his SUV is where he exhales and gathers himself before entering his home and greeting his children. Alone is always where he finds the most peace. Dunbar closes his eyes in an attempt to find a holy solace. Suddenly his body aches and begs for the bed: it has been almost forty-eight hours since he last slept.

Before he walks into the house, Dunbar puts in an after-hours buy order for more stock in a large pharma, a safe bet but also the only one developing what will soon be desperately needed. He already owns the Swedish counter-part, the other half of the equation, and while he waits, he collects tens of thousands of dollars in dividends. The stock order will be filled tomorrow at the opening bell. Eventually, he will also have to inform his boss in Guerrero of the "slight problem" with the transport of their special shipment to Kansas City. He is sure he can never convince his boss to be patient, so he wants to avoid this call as long as possible. Don Ilan, el Luchador, will be more than angry, yet Don Ilan also needs Dunbar to move the regular cargo to where it needs to go. That cargo is flowing north like blood gushing through the heart of a marathoner. Dunbar does not want el jefe Don Ilan and his friends more involved on this side of the border. That line on a map has always given Dunbar a measure of independence from the secretive Don Ilan, but it has also never kept out assassins or prevented secret wars between producers and distributors. The losses could be great if that special shipment is not soon found. The losses may be catastrophic and cause the beginnings of a bloodbath that has happened only once every other generation. But that dark chaos is still only one of many possibilities.

"Daddy!" A little girl, eight years old, shrieks on the other side of the SUV's window in the garage. "Come out, Daddy!"

Dunbar opens the vehicle's door gently and lifts her high in the air, above the roof of the SUV, and carefully swings her around, avoiding the thick metal posts that hold up the floor above them. "Sweetheart, I love you," he says, scanning his daughter's cheery face. He can tell she can't wait to reveal something. Her blue eyes, just like his, glimmer with excitement. "How did you do on your multiplication test today?"

"Ninety-six, Daddy! Ninety-six!"

"That's my smart girl. I am so proud of you."

She wraps her small arms around him as he carries her into the house and kisses him on the cheek and whispers something about her older brother, popcorn, and the sofa, but he doesn't quite hear every word. He thinks of everything he could lose if his men don't find that blue truck.

CHAPTER SIX

Ramon and Seferina drive across the Zaragoza International Bridge, through Waterfill, and to the Avenue Ejército Nacional on their way to the Central Camionera. Romita lives on Calle Rodolfo Fierro, which isn't far from the central bus station in Juárez. Ramon and Seferina won't get lost as long as they head to the boonies around the Central Camionera. They have avoided Juárez since the drug violence skyrocketed in recent years, but that is the past. They have no choice at the moment anyway, and they also have no more ideas. At Rodolfo Fierro, they stop at a half-finished adobe shack, one room without a roof, and another with just a corrugated sheet of metal sloped to one side. On a faded blue door riddled with cracks in the wood, the number "13" is crookedly hand-painted in white, less than two feet from the dusty street. Looming maquila warehouses surround the few narrow residential streets, the people an afterthought to the business at hand.

"Pásenle, pásenle," a fat old woman says, opening the creaky door, which dangles above the curb a good foot from the floor. They have to step over the concrete threshold from the street to walk inside the shack. "Seferina, mi Dios Santo, how long has it been?"

"Tía Romita. How are you? You remember Ramon?"

"Your esposo? Ramon? What happened to your face, hijo? Jesús, María, y José!"

"I'm fine. A car accident. Señora, we can't stay long. I'm okay." Ramon stares at Seferina. His features hardly resemble a human face: his eyes are a deep magenta; one cheek is unbelievably swollen as if a lemon has been embedded under the skin; a chunk of his hair is missing, and his swollen lips glisten with a mixture of dried blood and pus, as if they were injected by a Botox sadist. Ramon limps over the curb and slumps into a rickety wooden chair next to a fire.

"For dinner. Please stay for dinner. I have some fresh frijoles on the stove, with chorizo, mis hijos."

"Tía, we really can't stay long. We came to say hello. To bring you some news."

"Come, let me look at you. You too? My god, what happened to you?" Doña Romita holds Seferina's face by the orange light of the fire and studies it carefully. Two black eyes, the left a deeper purple than the right. Seferina seems mostly intact, except for those eyes. Ramon twists in the chair, grimacing every few seconds, and breathing heavily in short gasps.

"We came, Tía, because of Arturo."

"Oh, god, please no, he didn't die in this car accident? Please dear god, take me first. Take me first! My poor niño! The only one I have left from Estela's family!"

"No, Tía, Turi's fine. As far as we know. But he's run away."

"What? He ran away? Where? With who?" Doña Romita speaks in a singsong cadence, trudging to the kerosene stove next to the fire, swaying unsteadily as she walks. The old woman collapses on a wooden bench that once was used to stack corn. That is the only chair that holds her. The other chair is for her cat, Gatingo, who jumps off to inspect the guests, a surprisingly large and well-fed animal. The walls inside Romita's shack are bare adobe, yellow straw jutting out from the dried mud, spiders and niños de la tierra roaming the crevices and corners and holes underneath the corrugated metal sheet. All the little creatures avoid the chonky hunter. Outside, the occasional passing car roars but a few feet from the front door.

"We don't know with who. But we need to find him, Tía. That's why we're here."

"You think he'll be coming here? Back to Juárez? I don't think he even knows how to get here. He was just a little boy when he left." Gatingo slips in and out of Romita's hairy legs as if to convey, "You are my human. I will protect you."

"No, Tía. Not here," Seferina says, glancing at Ramon who seems in perpetual pain. He is ready to leave. He is ready to go home. Ramon has told her what a waste of time this will be. He is glaring at her now through his redder-than-red devil eyes.

"How old is Turi? He ran away? Just like that? Quizás tiene una novia."

"No, Turi has never had a girlfriend. He's not yet seventeen, Tía."

"I first got married when I was fifteen, Sefe. Don't be surprised, niña."

"Anyway, if you hear from him, if he comes this way, you need to tell us. It's important. Very important. I don't know who else he has, or where he would go. But you never know."

"I haven't seen him in at least two years. But I'll get word to you. Somehow."

"Tía, here. Take this, but don't spend it all. Your neighbor, what's her name again, Doña Letty, or Lela—"

"You mean Adela? This is too much."

"She still has a phone?"

"The only one on this block."

"If you hear from Turi, if he contacts you, anything, give us a call. Pay Doña Adela a ten-dollar bill for the call to El Paso. It's more than her entire monthly phone bill, I'm sure. Just pay her, and call us immediately. The rest is for you, Tía. You need it to take care of yourself."

"Dios mio. Really? God will repay you, mi'ja. One thousand times. He's probably having fun somewhere. Starting a new life. Wasn't Turi happy in Ysleta? What's this about, niña?"

"Tía, Turi stole something valuable. From school. And we're responsible if we don't find him, if we don't get it back soon."

"Turi? But he always loved school. He's a reader just like Estela was. Just like her mother, my sister Dolores. Always perdida in stories, lost to the world, searching for another place faraway. Dreaming, from Satevó to Juárez to América. From one generation to another to another, esa es la herencia. How could he steal anything?"

"He got involved with some gente mala. Malísima. Gangsters, cholos, narcos. We need to find him. Tía, please, just do it. Or we'll end up paying for his misdeeds. They are threatening to take our house, Tía. Please."

"Your house? My god! What kind of disgraceful government is that? That's worse than Juárez! He's just a niño and didn't know what he was doing. I'll give you everything I have, everything."

"Señora, that's not going to work."

"You tell them I'll work for them. I'll cook for the school. Anything. They can't do this to you. He's just a niño. Forgive him, mi Dios, for he knows not what he does."

"Tía, you have to promise. Give us a call. Promise you'll do that."

"Muy bien. I promise. But . . . stay for dinner. Frijoles con chorizo."

"Tía, we can't. Ramon's not well, as you can see. And we have to go look for Turi. Well, at least Ramon does. That's what we're thinking. As soon as he's able. It's important we find Turi. We can't fight the government for what Turi did. Before I forget, we also brought you two dozen tamales from La Tapatia in Ysleta."

"God will repay you, my dear. Dios Nuestro Señor will save us all. Pray, do you pray, mi niña?"

Ramon snorts and wipes the bloody snot from his nose on the leg of the chair. Gatingo crouches in front of him, as if the animal is about to launch itself at his throat. The cat's eyes glow uncannily in the firelight.

"Yes, Tía Romita. I pray. I'll pray to find Turi. Call us, if you hear from him. Letter. Phone call. Anything at all. This is important." Seferina beckons Ramon to stand up, one eye on the cat. She hands Doña Romita the bag of tamales.

"Tonight, after dinner, I'll pray for Turi's soul. I'll pray a special devotion to San Antonio y San Judas Tadeo. Saints of the lost and the desperate." Doña Romita speaks in her garbled voice to their backs, as they leave. She makes the sign of the cross in their wake. Gatingo jumps on his chair again and stretches his claws into the night's air. "Cuídense, mis niños."

"I need to lie down. My head's exploding." Ramon winces and spreads his broken body on the couch. "What a waste of time! I told you it would be a waste of time with Romita."

"Ese pendejito doesn't have anyone else. He's not coming back here, not after what you did to him. Turi might contact her. We need to have something to tell them when they come back. We need to show them we're trying to find ese güey."

"Well, I'm gonna rest for a few hours and then I'm driving to Lubbock. El güero said he was north of Lubbock. Son of a bitch. I'll kill all of them if they come back. I'll get a gun at Academy, goddamn it. Bring me a beer, mi reina."

"Well, that might not be a bad idea. A gun. But look, Ramon, mi rey, not for them. At least not now. They're looking for him. They know we don't know where he is. And they also know we might find him, we might be the only link to finding him. Think about it. They won't find him and their goddamn truck if they kill us." Seferina hands Ramon a beer, another one in her other hand. "But if they can't find him, we might need to defend ourselves."

"We're not calling the police."

"If we call the police, we're dead. I know."

"Sons of bitches. I don't know who I hate more, ese pendejo Turi or those cabrones."

"It doesn't matter at the moment. Can you drive to Lubbock in your condition?"

"What choice do I have?"

"And? Do what?"

"I don't know. Say, 'I drove there. Looked around. Couldn't find him.' My head feels like a jackhammer's on top of it."

"Ramon, look, I have a plan. You go to Lubbock, north of Lubbock. That's what they said. This is exactly what you'll do: gas stations, McDonald's, any place you think Turi would stop in. Think like a sixteen-, seventeen-year-old with a truck. Try several highways going north, going in different directions. We'll look at a map. You can call me when you're there. Say you're looking for a runaway. Your nephew. That's the truth. Somebody's bound to see him. Anything we can report to el güero when he comes back. And we'll also be ready if el güero is pissed off if we find nothing. We'll be ready. I'll go to Academy while you're in Lubbock. Don't worry, we'll be ready."

"Sixteen? Turi's sixteen?"

"Well, yeah. His birthday's tomorrow. Sixteen for one more day. Little bastard. Hope he's rotting in hell, wherever he is. Hope he's rotting in hell and left their truck where they can find it."

"I would've killed them if they had raped you or Vanessa. I would have. You know that, right? Vanessa, well, she seems okay. Bring your stuff over here and make me feel better before I go."

"Y Vanessa?"

"What about her? I think I saw her in her room earlier."

"Yeah, she's fine. She's a tough girl. She can—"

"Mom, Dad, they're here to pick me up! See ya!" Vanessa yells in a blur, not even looking at them as she sprints through the living room and runs out the front door. Just at that moment, Seferina and Ramon realize a car has been idling in front of Corralitos. Immediately a door slams shut and the car screeches down the street and disappears.

CHAPTER SEVEN

"Eduardo," Chucho says, his eyes not on the road and not on the slim volume on his lap. If he reads too much on the road, he may throw up, and that's the last thing he wants to do in front of Eduardo. Chucho stares at the Adonis in a black T-shirt behind the steering wheel, wondering what he is thinking, whether he is thinking.

No response.

"Eduardo. Are you listening?" Chucho finally stares at the Texas highway in front of him, somewhat exasperated, and wonders why *he* thinks what he thinks. Life will always be easier, if he doesn't have . . . if he doesn't want . . .

"Yes," Eduardo says finally to the windshield in front of him.

"We are almost there. Twenty, thirty minutes. Abernathy. That idiot Juanito should be at that exit north of Lubbock, at a 7-Eleven. That's where the old man said he would be, that's what he told The Stetson."

Eduardo smirks.

"You like that name, don't you?"

For a second, Eduardo truly smiles. When that hulking giant smiles, Chucho wants to fly out the window, to soar into the desert, toward that delicious smile he imagines should be in the sky. But is anything behind it? *Am I just creating what I want there, instead of what's actually there?*

Eduardo is silent again. Chucho continues: "Do you like poetry, Eduardo?"

"Poetry?"

"Yes, poetry. Can I read you a poem before we get to pinche Juanito?"

"Poetry?"

"Yes, a poem I like. Here goes." Chucho looks at Eduardo, who stares at the road, their SUV cruising at 75 mph, his arm muscles occasionally rippling gently underneath and over his black T-shirt, the brown skin perfectly bronze under the Texas sun. Chucho keeps staring at Eduardo, wondering if the man gives a damn, but at once Eduardo turns to him, with that massive neck and chiseled face, and asks with his eyes, "So where's the poem?" Or at least that's what Chucho thinks.

When Chucho reads the line about allowing the animal inside your body to covet what it wants, he can see the Herculean Eduardo shudder just the slightest bit at the shoulders, and when Chucho mentions the geese flapping hard in the sky to get home, he thinks he sees Eduardo's brown eyes glisten. But are they truly glistening, or is that just another fantasy in Chucho's mind?

"Who wrote it? You?"

"No, a poet named Mary Oliver. 'Wild Geese,' it's called."

"So a 'wild goose' is inside me?"

"Something wild. At least that's what I think she means. An animal. Something beyond good and evil. The world wants us to be what we are. Beyond any judgment."

"She mean we can do anything?"

"Maybe more like, 'We can *be* anything.'"

Eduardo smiles for the longest moment of their trip. Every second seems the most exquisite tonic for Chucho.

"Right here, stop here," Chucho orders Eduardo. Eduardo has been driving their black Escalade since leaving El Paso County. He is an ex-Marine from Socorro. He turns the wheel toward the Valero Corner Store just south of Wichita Falls, Texas, his muscles twisting thickly from under his T-shirt. Chucho runs his fingers through his bleached blond flattop and looks as military-minded as Eduardo, but with a difference: instead of a tight T-shirt, he wears a button-down light-blue dress shirt with a gold rope chain dangling loosely under the collar. A tiny diamond stud is in his left ear.

"But we never went all the way here. Not to Wichita Falls," old man Juanito in the backseat says softly. Chucho turns his head ever so slightly and sees Juanito staring at the back of their heads with a blank look. In front of them, the flat green pastures give way to a small downtown in the distance. A black "Denim and Diamonds" sign welcomes motorists on the highway.

"We have to assume they kept going north, maybe to Oklahoma City, but probably not to Kansas City. Not unless they're idiots. You were going to KC, and they know you were going to KC, so that's not where they're going. They know we'd come after them." Chucho's eyes linger on Eduardo for a few seconds, but Eduardo does not notice. *Why do we have to carry around this no-good pinche Juanito with us?*

"They're just two stupid teenagers that don't know any better. Who knows what the hell they would do."

"Listen, el jefe wants that truck. At the moment nothing else matters. Your ass is on the line. I don't think you want to go back to el jefe without the truck." Chucho yanks the truck door open. "Stay here, while Juanito and me go ask this guy if he's seen the truck and those pendejos."

"Little bastards. They surprised me. Maybe I can buy some Motrin. You see this chichón on my head?"

Chucho ignores him. "Look, ask the clerk. You're looking for your grandkids that ran away. Describe the truck, the two kids. Can you do that?"

Chucho and Juanito walk into the fluorescent brightness of the convenience store, which gives it the glowy appearance of being underwater. After a brief and unsuccessful conversation with the pimply-faced clerk, Juanito buys Motrin for the bump on his head. Chucho pays for drinks, sandwiches, snacks. He also remembers the CornNuts, the silent Eduardo's favorite.

Back in the truck, Chucho glances at the map on his iPad and gives directions to where he wants Eduardo to drive. Eduardo pulls the SUV onto the highway again and revs the motor. Chucho knows Eduardo likes to be told what to do, likes it when someone else is in control. Even as physically powerful as Eduardo is. Everyone is silent for a few minutes.

"How long are we staying out here?" Juanito asks.

Chucho hears the old man gulping down the pills in the backseat. He turns his head slightly, and some of Juanito's Snapple trickles down his cheek, which he wipes off with his forearm. The old muscles twitch underneath his tattoo of a snarling black wolf. *No vale madre. What a loser.*

Chucho ignores the old man again and focuses on the road. "As long as it takes. We're driving and stopping everywhere these punks might have stopped. To Wichita Falls, Oklahoma City, Tulsa, Wichita-en-la-nada-Kansas, and KC if we have to. El jefe needs to find that truck." He rips open a tuna sandwich. Now he imagines Eduardo as a brown-skin version of Michelangelo's David behind the wheel. Not a glance at the food, not a word from his mouth, nothing other than an uncanny focus on the highway and what their next stop will be. Chucho pinches open the bag of CornNuts and stands it in an empty cup holder. As if suddenly smelling the salty corn nuggets, Eduardo grabs the bag, tips it into his mouth without taking his eyes off the road, then glances for a second at Chucho in mid crunch. He smirks again.

"What if we can't find it? What if no one knows where they went?" Juanito says too loudly behind them.

Chucho turns around this time, glares at the old man. Juanito is holding his hand to his forehead as if he has a fever. "You don't want to go there. Don't think you want to tell that to el jefe. Think about how to find this goddamn truck."

"What if we . . . well . . . report it stolen? What if we do that?"

"Did that knock on the head make you stupid? You know why The Stetson wouldn't do that under normal circumstances." Chucho notices the way Eduardo's lips tighten into another smile as he drives. Eduardo really loves that nickname for Dunbar. "You know why he wouldn't want the cops or la migra to stop or impound any of his vehicles. And these are not even normal circumstances. This is worse. This involves Guerrero, güey. This is el jefe del jefe. Don-fucking-Ilan. And your sorry ass isn't worth spit in comparison."

"So why the hell did he ask me to do this if it was so important? Why, dear god?"

"Goddamn, Juanito, I've thought about this for hours on the drive up here, and I'm guessing el jefe thought moving this for Guerrero on the down-low would be best. Just like a regular drop. Too much firepower, too many people, and you attract attention, especially from our enemies. Make it appear like a routine delivery. No big deal. Ese, we're always being watched. Whether we like it or not. I probably would've done the same thing. The best way to avoid trouble is not to attract it. You were also steady, cabrón. Without a problem for years. But now we do have a problem. A serious one for el jefe. You just fucked him over with his boss."

"Dios mio. You talk to him? What did Dunbar say?"

"Find the blue truck, that's what The Stetson said." Another snarly smirk from Eduardo the statue, but maybe that one's aimed at Juanito and the shit-hole he is in. "Maybe, maybe . . . if we can't find the truck, if we can't find those kids, he might roll the dice and report it stolen. Maybe he might bet on the stupidity of the cops somewhere in the middle of nowhere. But I doubt it. I don't want to go there . . . yet."

"He just told me, 'Take this truck to Kansas City. As fast as possible. Take cualquier pendejo to help you, if necessary. It's an important delivery, but I want everything normal. I'll tell you later where you're going.' Never saw anything. But I could tell something was in the passenger door. Seemed heavier when I closed it. I know trucks, I could tell. What was Dunbar moving for Don Ilan in this shipment to Kansas City?"

Chucho stares at Eduardo's massive shoulders, rocklike. A He-Man.

They drive north on I-44 toward downtown Wichita Falls, Texas. He does not answer Juanito, who is still poised on the backseat, his stinky breath on their necks, waiting. Chucho turns around slowly, staring hard at Juanito with a look that seems to presage a spit to the face. The old man suddenly slumps away from them and against the backseat and rests his head on the back window of the truck. He looks like a brown insect trapped against glass.

"El Grupo Guerrero, Don Ilan, el Luchador . . . They're the ones who decapitated that entire police force in Chilpancingo. Put them into barrels of acid along the highway. Entambeados. I've seen the newspaper photos," Juanito continues softly behind them after getting no answer.

Chucho still ignores him. The old man seems dizzy and green, trying hard not to throw up in the backseat. *That's what you get for fucking up, viejo.*

"Hechos pozole. Made into soup in barrels. Except for the heads: they left them on top of the barrels for everybody to see. One of them with a Mil Máscaras mask. The Mexican version of 'Construction Ahead,' cabrón. Like the orange barrels over there!" Chucho points to the median of I-44, next to an overpass, with a half snort. Again, there it is—Eduardo's nearly imperceptible, but this time rather lovely, smirk. "Except I think their barrels were bigger, rusty, white and blue."

"Ay, Dios de mi vida."

CHAPTER EIGHT

It has been almost two days since Turi and Arnulfo escaped El Paso, and one day since they abandoned Juanito at the rest stop north of Lubbock. Turi stays on Highway 62 to Ralls, then veers east on 82/114 to Wichita Falls. He knows the old man Juanito demanded they stay on 62, so Turi wants off that road as soon as he can. If they are carrying contraband, Juanito's friends will be looking for the blue truck, and they will start looking where Juanito was left behind.

They eat breakfast at a Denny's in Wichita Falls. Turi and Arnulfo buy a map at a Mobile gas station and drive north to Oklahoma City. They spotted only one state trooper on the highway: the ramrod-straight, crew-cut Anglo was ticketing a motorist by the side of the highway. Turi kept the blue truck in the slow lane at the speed limit.

On I-44 in Chandler, halfway to Tulsa, Turi exits at another rest stop in the middle of more flatlands. Both of them sleep for hours, drained. Turi keeps the pickup's keys in his pocket.

"You think, hey, you think they'll find us? Hey, Turi, you awake? You think they'll find—"

"What? Ugh, I twisted my back in my sleep! Oh, god. Think it's time to get going again. East on I-44, and we'll see where that goes. What'd you say?"

"They're going to kill us," Arnulfo says, rubbing his eyes and glancing at the highway across the near horizon. The rest stop is grim. Only the occasional eighteen-wheeler roars on the road a few feet away. "I dreamed—I dreamed . . . I think they're going to find us. If what you say is true, if Juanito paid the officer—"

"Nulfo, I *saw* him. With my own eyes."

"They're going to find us."

"They might, but I don't think so. Not if I can help it." Turi focuses on the reddish shadows of the few trees next to the asphalt. It is early evening, and the sun just setting in the horizon of endless fields to the west. The blue pickup is warm and smells of sweat. Their gas tank is still nearly full after their stop in Wichita Falls. Turi still has at least two-and-a-half rolls of money in his jeans, and maybe Arnulfo also has some cash.

"Maybe we should get rid of the truck here," Arnulfo says. "Right away. I don't want to get mixed up with any—"

"Here? And just walk a hundred miles to the middle of nowhere?"

"Well, you're right. I know you're right, but—but . . . I just want to find work. I don't want any trouble. Just work." Arnulfo stares at the busy highway in front of them.

"I figure we have at least a couple of days. Maybe a bit more."

"Before what? Before they find us?"

"No, before our luck runs out. Before—before someone stops us and asks us about 'our truck.' I don't know."

Arnulfo stares quietly at the windshield. Turi tries to catch Arnulfo's eyes, because obviously something is on his mind. Finally he says, "I usually know what to do. But right now, I—I—"

"Nulfo, you can trust me. I don't want to steal this truck. I don't want to steal anything. I just want to get to Connecticut and get you to New York or anywhere closer. I won't get us in any trouble. I'm trying to get us out of it. Juanito, the old man, I don't know what he would have done to us if we hadn't left him behind. We did the right thing. I know we did. I just want to celebrate . . . another birthday." *How much can I really trust Arnulfo? Do I really know him and what he'll do if we get into trouble again?* Turi thinks.

"Your birthday? Today? How old? I don't even know how old you are."

"Seventeen. Today I'm seventeen."

"No chingues! Seventeen? Come on! Me too!"

"Yeah, we're almost adults."

"I don't feel like an adult. Not really. Not even almost."

"Yeah, well. We got rid of that old bastard. We have the truck. We can fill it up. We can keep going. That's what matters." Turi lifts himself up to air his seat.

"You don't think they're going to find us and kill us? Just wanted to get to Kansas City. Find work. I don't know, find a place, and now . . . *this.* I'm not going back to Mexico. I'm never going back to Mexico."

"And I'm not going back to Ysleta. Look, Arnulfo, they haven't found us and if they don't find the truck, they won't find us. We leave the illegal stuff to whoever finds the truck. Not our problem. I'm going to Connecticut. You can go wherever the hell you want. You're free."

"What's in Connecticut?"

"What's in Kansas City?"

Suddenly and simultaneously, the two boys scrunch down into the front seat and turn their heads. Another car pulls into the rest stop and parks on the other side, about thirty feet away. Turi glues his eyes onto the gray sedan, his fingers slowly inserting the key into the ignition, and then straightens up when he notices the driver is a lone woman with a baby in the backseat. She is on her cell phone as soon as the car jerks to a stop. Arnulfo has bent his stocky body forward into the well of the cab as if he is studying his sneakers.

Turi taps one of Arnulfo's shoulders, breaks the thick silence. "Just remember, they don't want us. They want the truck. We're nothing to them." He keeps an eye on the woman in the sedan.

"That's exactly what I'm worried about."

"As long as a cop doesn't stop us and ask for our driver's licenses. As long as we don't do something stupid to call attention to ourselves. We'll be fine."

"Let's get out of here." Arnulfo's leg is pumping on the floor mat, as if willing Turi's leg to do the same and step on the gas.

After six hours on I-44, Turi keeps hearing an occasional buzzing sound behind him, or he thinks he does. The hum of the blue truck on the highway will suddenly be interrupted by a strange, almost imperceptible buzz like a bee trapped in a glass jar. Arnulfo is in and out of sleep next to the passenger window.

"Hey, 'Nulfo. Wake up. I need your help."

"What? Everything okay?"

"Yes, hey, look in the backseat to see what's making that buzzing noise. I don't want to stop and it's annoying."

"I don't hear anything," Arnulfo says as he unbuckles his seat belt and peers over the backseat. Turi hopes a cop won't see him and stop them. That's the last thing they need right now. "The backseat's empty. I don't—"

"You hear that! There it is! What the hell is that?"

"Let me . . . just . . . climb over. I think I know where it's coming from . . ." Arnulfo drops onto the backseat. *At least he's not unbuckled and visible in the front seat anymore,* Turi thinks. Arnulfo's head disappears in the rearview mirror just behind Turi's seat.

"Well?"

"Turi, it's a cell phone, in the door compartment. With messages. I think—I think it's Juanito's cell phone . . ."

"Holy shit! What the hell do they say?" Turi is still focused on the highway, but he's frantically glancing back and forth at the rearview mirror.

"I don't want to—I don't want to . . . read . . ." Arnulfo stares at the phone. He looks stunned, his face ghostly white. His head disappears behind Turi's seat again, and when he reappears in the rearview mirror, he is no longer staring at the phone but at Turi, with frightened brown eyes. "There's also a gun."

"Oh my god!" Turi glimpses a sign to a national park slightly south of them, after St. James, Missouri. He immediately exits the interstate. The road is in the wrong direction, not east, but he has an idea. "We need to get off the road right now, right here. Just leave those things where you found them and I'll look at them once we stop. 'Nulfo, you okay?" His friend has scooted away from the side where the cell phone and the gun were found in the door compartment directly behind Turi.

Arnulfo buckles his belt and stays behind the empty front passenger seat, as if avoiding a box with a diamondback rattlesnake next to him. "It says they're going to kill us."

❧

On this late morning, Turi is exhausted from driving. They have been driving, on again, off again, without a decent night's sleep. On Highway 8 at Steelville, a drive-by town where the tallest structure is a rusty, silvery water tower, he stops and tells Arnulfo to come outside to the driver's side of the truck. Before they step into the store, in between the open truck doors, Turi checks the cell phone in the door compartment behind him—the black gun next to the phone he avoids touching as if it's alive—and sure enough, the cell phone reads "Sin Servicio." He shows Arnulfo standing next to him. "No cell service. This is exactly where we want to be. Let's get something to eat." Arnulfo looks puzzled as Turi leaves the phone in the door compartment and steps into the supply store. Arnulfo follows him.

Turi purchases bread, peanut butter, jelly, a six-pack of plastic water bottles, which he intends to refill along the way, five bags of pemmican, and toilet paper. Arnulfo keeps bumping him from behind, not saying a word, not even looking up at the store and what it might have to offer. Two men donning canvas hats and vests stroll through the claustrophobic store, also picking up provisions. From afar, their chest pockets appear to have feathery, hairy bugs on them, but up close, Turi can see they are red, yellow, and green fishing lures. One man nods at Turi, and he nods back and forces a smile. They ignore Arnulfo. The men are fair-skinned—like Mr. Dunbar at the poultry farm. The girl at the cash register is also blond. Turi notices how dark both he and Arnulfo are in comparison, as dark as the weather-beaten wooden crates against the wall. Even if they don't mean to attract attention, they will attract attention: the quicker they drive into a trailhead on Highway 8, hide the truck in the trees and hide themselves, the better for them. Turi notices the blond girl is about the same age as he and Arnulfo, and her biceps are as big as theirs. She suggests a trailhead into the Mark Twain National Forest and gives him exact directions to the Berryman Trailhead from Highway 8. She stares at their blue pickup through the window. But it isn't a hostile stare. Her eyes remind Turi of the eyes of an eagle he once saw on a computer at the Ysleta High School library: clear, direct, and ready. "Have fun, guys," she says as they walk out the store.

Arnulfo seems satisfied with Turi's choices for provisions and hands him a twenty-dollar bill back in the truck, covering over half the expenses. Turi doesn't say a word. Arnulfo is suddenly calmer after they have left I-44, after the isolation of Steelville surrounds them like a warm fog. Other than a German shepherd barking in the dusty parking lot, Turi notices nothing is happening in Steelville, not a soul is on the street, and only a few old cars seem abandoned, like apparitions from another time. The outpost is miles from the main highway of I-44. One store offers "Fountain Service" above a red Coca-Cola sign. Next to it is a coffee shop with a yellow sign of a turbaned fortune-teller proclaiming "You Need a Cup of Coffee"—both are empty—and an antique shop is closed next door. Only the hardware store and the convenience store with canoe rentals have any customers. Turi shifts the truck's gear into reverse. He spots the blond girl offering a quick, friendly wave through the store's grimy window. *That cute girl's been staring at us the whole time.* Turi grins nervously back. For no reason, he flashes her a peace sign. Arnulfo turns to Turi with a what-the-hell-is-that look.

"Why do you care if Juanito's cell phone has service?" Arnulfo finally asks as soon as they pull away from the gravel parking lot of the supply store. "Did you read what he sent to us? Or whoever sent those messages to Juanito's phone? They're angry. He and his friends know we have his cell phone and gun."

"I'll read them as soon as we hide this truck. We'll bury the gun in the forest somewhere. Nobody will ever find it. We'll bury the cell phone, destroy it. I read somewhere, in a magazine in Mrs. Garcia's library, that phone companies can track you by their cell service."

"So they know where we are? Oh my god." Arnulfo shivers as if a draft of cold mountain air has drifted suddenly through the truck's window.

"Not if the phone has no service. That's why this is exactly where we can stop and get rid of those things. They won't track us, even if they were tracking us before. I'm not sure they were, but . . ." A shiver also suddenly climbs Turi's spine as he loses his train of thought.

In a few minutes, they maneuver off Highway 8 into the trailhead, turn briefly north onto a dirt road, and find signs to the Berryman Trailhead. Cars are not allowed past a certain point, so they park the blue pickup under the shadows of thick pine trees in an empty parking area, as far from the dirt road as possible, which is also hidden from Highway 8. No one will find them there. They read the rules of the park at the trailhead. It is free for campers and hikers as long as one does not leave any trash, or take any rocks or plants from the forest, or damage the Mark Twain National Forest in any way: "Leave No Trace Behind." Rangers are in the area and will periodically visit the trailheads to assist anybody who needs help or has questions. But other than those pamphlets, the forest seems devoid of humans. As they walk around and near the truck, they hear only birds chirping in the distance, the wind meandering through the pine needles and leaves, and this dense silence around them. Turi and Arnulfo decide to hike for a mile or so to bury the gun and the phone somewhere deep in the forest where no one will find them. Turi drops the gun in a paper bag, but he carries the phone in his hand and has not yet read the messages. When Arnulfo looks at him strangely, Turi shows him that the phone still reads "Sin Servicio."

"I'll read the messages right before we bury it," Turi finally responds as he leads the way. They will return to the truck to eat and sleep in the cab. With every step into the forest, Turi leaves behind a bone-numbing exhaustion.

"This is beautiful," Arnulfo says. "¡Qué chulada!"

"Mark Twain National Forest. We were so lucky to find it at the right time on the highway." Turi jumps over a rock at a slight incline. He moves steadily and powerfully like a bear. He is also in awe of this palpitating green around them and how eerily it makes them its center.

"You've been here before? Or read about it?"

"No, no. I know the book, the writer."

"Someone wrote a book about this forest?" Arnulfo can catch up easily with his quick, short stride, but he keeps looking up at the trees and sunlight filtering through the leaves. He looks almost happy in contrast to that deathly stare Turi saw in the rearview mirror when Arnulfo first glanced at the text messages on Juanito's phone.

"No, 'Mark Twain' was a writer. A long time ago. Over a hundred years ago. Estaba bien loco. He loved adventures," Turi says, leading the way up the trailhead. "He wrote one of my favorite books. Señora Garcia gave it to me. Well, she didn't give it to me, but she let me have it for the summer, so I could reread it. *Huckleberry Finn*. It's one of the books I have in the back of the truck." Turi grips the cell phone tighter in his hand.

"Quién es esta Señora Garcia, güey?"

"She's my teacher." For a moment, Mrs. Garcia in her tight blue dress flashes in Turi's mind. Wishing he had a photo of her, he wonders what she is doing this summer in El Paso. He also wonders why he didn't chat more with that blond girl in the store earlier this morning: it never occurred to Turi that *she* would look at him. In the forest, every step seems to reinvigorate his body. He feels the blood coursing through and around his aches and bruises. He imagines flinging the cell phone against a tree and smashing it. But not yet.

"And este 'Jaques-eri Inn'?"

"'*Huckleberry Finn*.' With an H. And Mark Twain wasn't his real name. The writer."

"He lied about his name? Why'd he do that?"

"Well, I don't know. I guess he wanted to be another person when he wrote books. When he told stories. His real name was Samuel Clemens. And he always dressed in white."

"Like a panadero?" Arnulfo stumbles on the stub of a bush, but rights himself after one step.

"Yeah. White hat. White suit. Like a *fancy* baker. He had this big white mustache too, like those old fashioned bigotes the circus strong men have. Wild white hair too, like he needed a haircut two months ago." Turi finally drops the cell phone into the paper bag, and although the paper bag is in his left hand, the cell phone seems miles away. He stretches and wiggles the fingers of his right hand, which had gripped the cell phone. As he hikes, his hand feels like a part of him again. The paper bag even seems like a lunch.

"He should have been in a book, el loco. His books must have been good, 'cause he got a big forest named after him. You ever see more trees in one place in your life?" Arnulfo is still looking up as he walks, captivated by the green ceiling.

"You ever read him in Spanish in Mexico, 'Nulfo? Twain's books are good."

Following a trail tamped down with dead leaves, they keep hiking into the forest. Turi feels a silence that breathes surrounding them. He walks ahead of Arnulfo and turns around after a few steps to see if his friend is still behind him. He, the teenager from Juárez—who a few days ago was carrying chickens with Turi on the border—seems as out of place as a rhinoceros among this verdant splendor.

"No, never read him at our school in Delicias."

"No problem. It's a great story. So there's this kid, Huckleberry Finn. His best friend is Tom Sawyer, and Huck, that's his nickname, he lives in Missouri, where we are now. But it's over a hundred years ago, when this country had slavery. They live next to this gigantic river called the Mississippi, and Huck's running away from home . . ."

As they march and stumble north to and past the Berryman Trailhead, Turi recounts the story, sometimes backtracking when he forgets a crucial fact or event, explaining the perils of Huck and Jim, the enslaved man running away, the odd situations, the adventures along the Mississippi River, the floating house and dead body. Without breaking his stride, Turi reenacts certain scenes he thinks funny, or he tries to mimic the accents, what he imagines might be Huck's and Jim's voices. Once Arnulfo gets a sense of the story and its characters, he adds to it, poses a what-if to a certain scene, or invents another exchange between Huck, Jim, the duke, and the king. Turi and Arnulfo riff off Twain's characters in their version of *Huckleberry Finn*. They spin untold stories and other possibilities with these personas, entertaining themselves as they march through the trees. Once in a while, Turi also notices how eerily mute everything is around them, beyond their voices and laughter. For many minutes, Turi forgets he carries the paper bag in his hand until he sees it there, almost surprised by what he holds in his hand, until the sudden weight of it causes him to remember.

Turi and Arnulfo jump over a small stream and climb over and through a rock formation, following a good trail bedded with pine needles, leaves, and small branches. No one else is there. They hear no other sounds except their voices or the cracks of branches underfoot or the thumps of their footsteps. For forty minutes they forget about the blue truck, and forget who might be looking for it, and forget about the paper bag.

"I'm tired. Why don't we turn around here?" Turi asks, staring at his hand with the paper bag for a moment before he turns to look at Arnulfo's face.

"What about that?"

"Let me just read the messages and we can dig a hole here." Turi takes out the phone, Arnulfo sits down next to him, as if knowing it will take a while to absorb the words. A bed of pine needles surrounds them.

"I only read the first one. You don't have to read all of them, Turi. If you don't want to. One was enough for me . . ."

Six unread text messages are on the cell phone. Still it reads "Sin Servicio" in the middle of the forest. All the messages come from the same number. The first one is awful enough: "You two motherfuckers are dead! Hijos de la chingada! I will kill you for what you did to me! You are dead. You understand who I am? You understand what I will do to you? The best thing you can do, if you have any brains, is to leave the truck and tell us where it is. Just leave it, lock it, and text me an address. If you want to live. That's the only way you will live. We will never stop looking for you and that truck. Little pendejos. If you don't do that, you better pray we don't find you. But we will. Your choice." The other messages, shorter, are only more threats, which get more specific and graphic as whoever sent the text messages never received a response from Juanito's phone. Arnulfo stares at Turi in awe as he not only reads beyond the first message but reads all of them, and then rereads them, as if committing them to memory.

Suddenly Turi stands and picks up a large rock. He smashes it against the cell phone, pounding it repeatedly until it's in pieces. The two boys dig a hole with sticks, then kick the cell phone's pulverized pieces inside. Turi drops the paper bag with the gun into the hole. They cover everything with dirt, leaves, and sticks, and place a large rock on top. They look around. The forest is silent. For a moment, Turi forgets what is in the hole as he sees everything around them and how perfectly it camouflages what they have done, what they have brought into the forest. No one will ever find the cell phone and the gun buried in the middle of the Mark Twain National Forest.

"Let's go back. I'm hungry and it's lunchtime." Turi walks back to their original path and starts following it with Arnulfo beside him.

Only when they are far away from their turnaround in the forest does Turi mention *Huckleberry Finn* again. They talk about the story again, but in a different way, as if they are trying to talk about the story rather than losing themselves in it. They even bring up brief memories of their previous conversations on their way to the turnaround, as if trying to recapture something in those conversations that is now lost forever. Arnulfo asks many questions to clarify a scene or to understand why a character does what he or she does. But he seems like he's trying too hard. The lingering excitement of the story, in real time, slowly peters out as they come closer to where they began, as they recognize rock formations revealing how close they are to the parking lot and the blue truck. Most of the last few minutes, they walk in silence, in an air that seems to envelop them with a mysterious purpose, the sun at high noon, bright in the cloudless sky. The temperature has never climbed above the mid-seventies, yet Turi and Arnulfo sweat from their hike.

At the still-empty parking lot, the blue pickup in one corner under a penumbra of trees is a relief to both of them. They are beyond tired; they slept only a couple of hours each the night before. But Turi also feels a sense of dread in the silence. *What will happen to us?* he thinks. *Is Arnulfo right? Will they find us? We can't stay in the forest forever.*

CHAPTER NINE

After lunch in the parking lot surrounded by the forest, Arnulfo says, "What if the narcos are still tracking the truck? What if they put something in the truck? To track it? A guy from Juárez told me once about this thing they can put into any car, LoJack, and a lot of Americanos were putting them into their cars and trucks because they were often stolen in Mexico. What if they put the same thing in this truck?"

"In the forest, there's probably no signal, just like the cell phone. So that's another good reason to hide here right now. But wouldn't they have to report the truck stolen to the police?"

"I don't know. I don't know how LoJack works. I don't know if the narcos have their own way of tracking it without the police."

"I mean, it must also work by electricity. Think about it. So if anything's in the truck, it must be tied to the battery somehow. Maybe we can disconnect it if we find it." Turi wipes his mouth and jumps off the truck bed. "Here's another thing: what about the drugs? What do you think they're hiding in the truck?"

Turi opens the blue truck's doors on the driver's side and starts moving the seats. He sticks his head underneath for a better view, shoves the front seat forward, and peers at the floor of the backseat.

"What are you doing?"

"Looking for the drugs."

"Looking for—"

"Where do you think they hid them?" Turi is now trying to yank up the backseat, to see if it pops open somehow, but he is only able to release a middle compartment with a cup holder. Nothing. He taps the floor, taps the seats, listening, not knowing exactly what he is listening for.

Arnulfo goes to the other side of the truck, half-heartedly opens the passenger's side, and pretends to look under the seats. But mostly he is staring at Turi as if he is trying to understand why a cat focuses on any sudden movement with such attention. "Wh—wh—why, why are you looking—"

"Aren't you curious, 'Nulfo?" Turi is already dragging himself underneath the truck, a cloud of dust wafting up to where he was next to the driver's door a few seconds ago. "I can't see anything anyway, but I don't know much about trucks. Do you? 'Nulfo!"

Arnulfo sticks his head down for a better view. Turi is flat on his back underneath the blue pickup. He drags himself a few inches on the ground toward the motor in the front and then a few inches toward the rear wheels. "What?"

"What if it's money? What if it's not drugs, but money?"

"Money? Why would they—"

"I don't know. I don't see anything down here. Not anything that seems weird, out of place. You know anything about motors? I don't think this truck has a LoJack."

"Why?"

"Well, Juanito's text messages. Whoever sent them. They didn't seem to know where the truck was, they wanted us to leave the truck behind. They wanted us to tell them where it is."

"What if you're wrong, Turi? What if they're tracking us by satellite as soon as we leave the forest? They'll torture us. I've read about what they've done to traitors in Juárez, whoever betrays the drug cartels. Killing us will be the last and easy part. They'll torture us first, Turi."

"Arnulfo, please. Calm down. I really don't think this truck has a LoJack. Do you know anything about motors?"

Turi is already dragging himself out, pine needles dangling from the back of his head, his arms and forearms covered with more dust and debris. He brushes off his pants, shakes his head, quick slaps from one arm onto the other. "We're wasting our time," Arnulfo says after a moment. "Let's look for the LoJack."

"Let's pop the hood. That's where the battery is. That's where it would be connected."

"The what? The hood?"

Turi yanks open the door on the driver's side, peers at the markings on the buttons underneath the dashboard, and finally presses one. The hood jumps open.

Turi lifts it open and studies the motor. Arnulfo walks to one side, staring guardedly at the carefully twisted metal, wires, cylinders, belts, plastic tubes, and battery, a machine that fits perfectly in its space. "I don't see anything, do you?" As his eyes try to find better angles to see deeper into the motor's workings, Turi jiggles and pulls at a few of the thick tubes and wires.

"If we find something . . . are we, like, disconnecting it?"

"It depends."

"It depends?"

"Depends what it is. The drugs, if we find the drugs, we could get rid of them."

"I don't think we want—"

"Shit! Oh, my god, shit, shit, shit!" Turi yells as fluid—what looks like oil—pours from the bottom of the engine.

"What have you done! Turi, hijo de la chingada!"

"I'm trying to stop it!"

After a few minutes, the flow falling under the motor stops. Turi's hands are black and slick with oil. He wipes them on his jeans. When Arnulfo starts the truck, an even bigger splash of oil drops to the ground. The truck's oil gauge flashes an ominous red dot.

Arnulfo refuses to talk to him for an hour. Turi finally volunteers to walk back the three miles or so to the store in Steelville to get help. But it is more than three miles, and probably closer to five miles, to get to the Steelville store: Turi walks for almost two hours under the relentless afternoon sun.

Turi explains what happened to Molly, the blond girl at the store. She seems happy but puzzled to see him returning, his pants smeared with oil and no blue truck in sight. She calls the owner of the store, who knows about car engines. While they wait for him to show up, Turi finds out more about Molly Crump.

She is also seventeen, almost eighteen, and was born in Steelville, which she calls "a dump." She lives with her brother, his girlfriend, and their baby. Turi doesn't ask about her parents. What seems mesmerizing to him, however, is how beautiful she is, yet she doesn't seem to know it or care. Her white T-shirt is grimy from moving crates at the store, and her blond hair is unruly with strands matted down at her temples. Her hands are scratched, and her nails are dirty from work. But for Turi, Molly would have been one of the most intriguing girls at Ysleta High School: not of the fancy set, not those pretending to act muy muy, but a natural blond amid ninety percent poor and working-class Mexican students from the border.

People might have assumed Molly was from the better side of the railroad tracks—because of her blond hair and her "Mizzouruh gal" English—yet Molly is a trabajadora, a working-class white.

For the first time, Turi knows how little he understands of the world beyond the border. He hopes Molly doesn't notice him catching glimpses of her chest and the perfect shape of her body in her jeans and even the muscles that ripple from her arms. He would have found her intimidating at YHS, but here in the store in Missouri, her blue eyes seem to welcome his every word. When Turi tells her, "Yes, I'm Mexican, from El Paso, Texas," those blue eyes only seem to dance with real intrigue. "You boys should stay here until the morning. By the time your truck's fixed, it will be nighttime."

Molly winks at Turi in a friendly way, which startles him.

The owner, an old white-haired man named Mike, doesn't say more than five words to Turi when he finally arrives at the store with a bag of oilcans. He motions Turi to join him outside. Molly begins to close the store but Mike shakes his head.

Turi lingers next to her, finally says goodbye, thanks her for her help and for staying with him, and stares just a second too long at her high cheekbones and lopsided smile and what looks like a smudge of dust near her lips. He would have loved to get to know this Molly a lot better. She waves at both of them as they exit and get into Mike's truck.

Mike doesn't say much more to Turi as they drive to the Berryman Trailhead on Highway 8. Mike probably sees him as a pain-in-the-ass kid who doesn't know shit about trucks. He's only doing it because Molly asked him to.

Mike finds the loose valve that released the oil and mutters something about, "Shouldn't have popped that easily—maybe it was just ready to go. Better here than the middle of nowhere."

Turi pretends to understand what Mike is doing, but Arnulfo is mute and still. Mike stares at both of them and shakes his head. "One hundred and fifty bucks. For the oil and my time. Just a loose valve. I would take it for a tune-up sooner rather than later."

"One hundred and fifty dollars? Turi, really? Isn't that too much?" Arnulfo asks as he looks at Turi.

Mike stares impassively at both of them.

"Arnulfo, it's okay. We have it. Thank you, sir." Turi hands Mike the cash and he drives away in the early evening. Turi can feel Arnulfo's glare even before he turns around to see it.

"He took advantage of us, Turi. That's what that old man did. And we let him."

"Nulfo, what are we supposed to do? Argue with him? Fight with him? We didn't have a choice. I'm sorry, but we didn't have a choice."

"He charged us too much 'cause we look Mexican."

Turi raises his hands to the sky as he walks away.

As the evening darkens, the boys eat and talk in the blue pickup's open bed. Turi remembers something he read at the trailhead about animals being attracted to any food left outside. The trailhead disappears in the evening shadows. They stay another hour in the truck's bed, talking about what they can do when they arrive on the East Coast. High above the ground and surrounded by the truck's thick blue walls of plastic and steel, they still feel safe. But as the evening metamorphoses into night, and the birds cease their songs, a deeper silence shrouds them. Arnulfo's leg pumps rhythmically against the ridges inside the truck's bed as he sits over the metal hump of one of the back tires. He says finally, "Do we even have enough money to make it to the East Coast anymore?"

Turi stares at the darkness above and around them like a gigantic black dome. Only the rays of a half-moon reach the disappearing ground. He ignores Arnulfo's question and says, "Why don't we go inside, 'Nulfo? You take the back, where there's more room, and I'll be in the front seat. Let's bring our backpacks inside too."

They decide that maybe tomorrow morning they can find a stream to wash their dirtiest clothes before they get back on the road again.

As soon as the pickup's doors slam shut, both of them exhale and say nothing to each other. The night surrounds the pickup like a sheet of black plastic. Darkness presses against every window as if they are at the bottom of an endless sea. *What on earth have I done?* Turi wonders.

Soon enough Turi can hear Arnulfo's snoring in the back. *We are safe for now,* Turi thinks, *and the truck works again.*

No one will find them in the Mark Twain National Forest.

He takes out his flashlight from his backpack and reads chapter after chapter of *The Mystery of the Mighty Housatonic River*. Strange questions float in and out of his head like black and yellow butterflies. *Do* they have enough money for gas and food? Where are the drugs or money hidden in the blue truck? Could the truck have a LoJack they couldn't find? What exactly is hidden in the truck? Could the contraband be embedded in the seats underneath them? How much money does Arnulfo have and will he keep sharing it to reach Connecticut or New York? Will Juanito's friends report the blue truck stolen? What can they do if a police officer stops them, or if the old man Mike reports them as suspicious teenagers? That's another reason Turi just wanted to pay Mike quickly: to avoid trouble. What if they argued about the bill, refused to pay him, and he reported them to the police? A forest ranger could still kick them out of the park tomorrow or report their truck to the authorities. They do look like they don't quite belong in this forest in the middle of Missouri.

As the cool night air wafts into the blue pickup, Turi can see no bruises on his face in the mirror, but he suddenly feels extraordinarily tired after their long day and his long walk. His ribs are sore. His body aches. Corralitos seems like eons ago. Soon enough Morpheus wings him to another world.

Rap, rap, rap. Rap, rap, rap. Somewhere deep inside a black sea, a noise. Turi's eyes are blurry. Slivers of light flash in his eyes through the trees, the sun's rays. *Rap, rap, rap.* He has not been dreaming. He pushes himself up and finds the pickup's window on the driver's side. It's Molly. What is she doing here?

Turi rolls down the window. She's alone. Behind her is an old maroon Impala. She dangles a large paper bag next to her head, smiling and waving. Her eyes are lively, and her smile is gentle, but she appears mischievous. "Brought you boys some submarine sandwiches. Just wanted to say, 'hi'."

Molly stands almost at attention, slightly leaning in to hear Turi's soft voice, her face on the verge of a smile. Turi is amazed he's talking to her.

"Yes, thank you. I'll wait for Arnulfo to—hey, 'Nulfo! There he is. Come out here and meet la Molly."

"Ooh, I like that. 'La Molly.' Sounds like a singer's name. Like Beyoncé. La Molly MC. I took Spanish a few years in middle school and freshman year in high school. Had to drop out to help my brother."

"Arnulfo, this is Molly Crump from Steelville. The girl from the store who helped us yesterday, 'member?"

Still trying to absorb this morning surprise, Arnulfo shakes Molly's hand, stares at Turi, rubs his eyes again, and straightens his shirt.

"She brought us sandwiches."

Arnulfo glances at Turi again, but says nothing, his eyes and mouth in a polite smile. Arnulfo looks up and down at Molly, the blue streak in her hair, her dirty white T-shirt, and finally her sky-blue eyes.

"Just wanted to say 'hi' and see where you guys are headed. Mike came by the store after he helped you with your truck last night. I was cleaning up. Can't believe he charged you one hundred and fifty dollars! Didn't say anything to him, he's my boss . . . but one hundred and fifty dollars! Not that many kids around here my age, you know," Molly says. She glances at Turi as if to say, "Is he okay with me? I'm not trying to cause any problems."

"I told you he charged us too much money, Turi!" Arnulfo blurts out. He doesn't seem angry, just happy to be vindicated.

"Let's sit down. It's fine. Do you want some water, Molly? That's all we have." Turi yanks open the latch of the truck's gate. "Thank you for the sandwiches, but you didn't have to do that . . . maybe you can tell us about a good trail around here."

"Well, the sandwiches won't make up for what Mike charged you, but I wanted to do something. Oh, do I know trails. Every one of 'em. There's a cave, you know, not far from here. This is a very nice truck by the way."

"'Nulfo, sit down. Relax. Everything's okay. You're making me nervous. Don't act like you're from el rancho."

"Ranch-hoe? Like ranch, somethin' like that?"

"Well, when you say someone's acting like they're from 'el rancho,' it's like saying he's from the countryside, a bit too shy, not knowing sophisticated ways."

"Well, Arnie-ulfo—did I pronounce that right?—I'm from el ranch-hoe too, so please, no worries. The ranch-hoe of Steelville." She jumps onto the back gate of the truck and sits cross-legged near the edge in one swift, athletic move. "I'm just a country gal from Mizzouruh."

"Nice to meet you, Molly. I like 'Arnie.' My best friend from Juárez used to call me that. You can call me 'Arnie,' también."

"Arnie it is, then. That's not in Texas, this War-ez, right?"

"No, it's in Mexico. Just across the Río Grande from El Paso, Texas. Right on the border." Turi notices that Arnulfo stares at Molly's eyes for one moment too long. Arnulfo clambers up the bumper and into the truck's bed and sits precariously on the edge of the truck's panel, his feet on the tire hump, near them, but not too close.

Turi jumps onto the metal gate next to Molly. She twists her trim body to face both of them. Turi imagines that Mrs. Garcia—if she were blond, if she were a teenager, and if she lived in Missouri—maybe she would look like this Molly.

"Love to see that cave. A real cave? Like one you could stand in?" Turi gathers himself while Molly half smiles as their eyes come together again. She is one of the most beautiful girls he's ever seen. It is almost hard to look at her, as if he's staring into the sun, yet what brings him back to her is that she's unpretentious, she's staring right back at him with a smile. "Is it far from here?"

"Oh no, less than an hour. Off the Berryman Trail. Found it last year when I explored a section off the main trail. It's big. All of us could fit in it. I imagine it's used by black bears in the winter."

"There are bears here?" Arnulfo pumps his leg against the floor of the pickup's bed, nervous.

"They run away from you, if you make enough noise. Unless, of course, they don't. Unless it's an abnormal bear."

"An abnormal bear? You mean, like the bear's crazy?" Arnulfo twists awkwardly on the edge of the truck's panel.

"Well, some bears get used to humans. Stop bein' afraid of them. Stupid people leave food outside their tents or even throw it away on the trails. If we have a drought like we did a few years ago, there's not enough food to go 'round." Molly glances at Arnulfo, then back to follow the contours of Turi's face for a few seconds. He blushes. Arnulfo's leg stops pumping on the truck's bed.

"Hey Molly, here's a question. I mean . . . would you show us the cave? It'd be cool to see it. What do you think, 'Nulfo?"

Arnulfo pretends to smile, but says nothing.

"Yeah, I'd love to. It's my day off. Mike might hang around a few hours, but he's usually gone fishin' too or workin' on his house."

"We want to wash our clothes, right, Turi? In a stream or something. That's our plan before we hit the road again this morning."

"Wash your clothes in a stream? I mean, if you went for a fun swim, maybe I would join you. But you'd have to take a shower immediately after. And if you wash your clothes in a stream, you guys would stink all the way to Connecticut and New York. Don't do that. Use the washin' machine and shower at the store after we hike to the cave. That's the least I can do for you guys. I use it all the time and no one's there today. Not Mike. I've got the keys." Molly's hands are on her hips.

"Wow, Molly. You are the nicest girl in Missouri. Thank you. Molly la Milagrosa."

"'Grosa,' yikes. That doesn't mean, like, 'gross,' does it?"

"No, no. 'Mila-grosa.' From like 'miracle.' 'Miracle Molly.'"

"Ooh. Thanks. I should get a T-shirt with that. That'd be so cool."

As they hike the Berryman Trail to the cave, Turi and Arnulfo learn more about Molly Crump. She has never left the Midwest. She lives with her older brother Jim, and she gets along with him okay, though he has a girlfriend Molly despises. That feeling, according to Molly, is kind of mutual. Corina wants Jim's attention, wants Jim to do this, wants him to do that, and expects Jim to take care of her and their new baby. Every penny has to be spent on Corina and the baby, and there aren't many pennies to go around. Jim works a series of odd jobs in the lumber industry, construction, and trucking, so it is mostly Molly avoiding Corina, and Corina fighting with Molly and reporting her version of events to Jim. He tries to keep the peace from afar.

A few years ago, Jim and Molly's parents died in a house fire. Molly survived by climbing through a window in the middle of the night. Jim was on a date with Corina.

Turi tells Molly about losing his parents in a car accident in Mexico. Arnulfo is quiet, asking questions as he follows behind them. When Molly tells a joke about Corina, Arnulfo laughs in an exaggerated way, with his mouth open and his body nervously shaking with mirth. When he stumbles forward on a rock, he gently grabs Molly's shoulders before falling down, grins at her red faced, and claps Turi on the back. Molly smiles and asks 'Arnie' if he is okay. It takes Arnulfo a few minutes to recover himself.

Maybe Arnulfo has not been around too many girls in his life. Neither has Turi, but he did spend a lot of time with Mrs. Garcia.

Turi notices that Molly is in great shape. Her jeans fit as if they were tailor-made for her. Turi and Arnulfo sweat and puff hard for air as she easily climbs over rocks on all fours, jumps over dead tree trunks, and pulls herself over a rocky outcrop in front of the cave. On ledge after ledge, Molly smiles and waits patiently for them to catch up, not bothering to brush away the blond strands on her face.

At the entrance, the secret cave smells musky. Molly says a skunk has probably been a recent visitor. A perfect place to hide from one's enemies, Molly continues, for a Native American or for a mother bear and her cubs looking for the right home for the winter. They climb down and return to the Berryman Trail. When they reach the blue pickup again, Turi pulls out three of Molly's sandwiches—there are six enormous submarines wrapped tightly in white butcher paper and masking tape.

"Saw you holding your side when you were climbing. You okay?" Molly chomps on one end of a submarine.

Turi imagines the bruise underneath his shirt is suddenly visible, even glowing, and rubs his side instinctually. He had almost forgotten about it until their long hike. "Oh, that's nothing. A fight. Back in El Paso. An asshole. It's a long story. Maybe I'll tell you about it one of these days."

Turi has never met a girl like Molly, one who is so impressive in his eyes, yet wants to be friends with him.

"You told me you fell down. Liar."

"Sorry about that, 'Nulfo. I was embarrassed. Got kicked by a bully." Turi looks at his feet for a moment and then turns his face to Molly. Her bright blue eyes are waiting for him, still warm and gentle.

Molly keeps working on her sandwich for a while, munching, glancing at the air in front of her, as if in a trance. "Well, we've got plenty of those in Mizzouruh, believe you me. You boys are super nice."

The boys follow Molly's maroon Impala back to the center of Steelville. Arnulfo is again unusually quiet. Turi imagines he might be uneasy about using a stranger's shower or Molly catching a glimpse of him naked, or even Turi. Maybe 'Nulfo is worried someone will spot the blue truck, which is working perfectly again. But Steelville is again a ghost town, and the Impala and Ford pickup are the only vehicles in front of the convenience store on Main Street. Molly opens the store and leaves the "Closed" sign dangling on the door. She shows them where the closet shower is in the back. Arnulfo goes first while Turi washes their clothes in the washing machine in another storage room. Molly nods silently at him. Turi expertly manages the machine's controls and the amount of detergent. The room reminds him of his shed on Corralitos, and for a few seconds, he scans the floor for a secret drain.

"Turi, hey, now that Arnie's in the shower, I wanna ask you a question. It may sound kind of crazy, but it isn't. Been thinkin' about this idea. Let me just explain for a second. Corina and Jim had another awful fight last night. Three in the morning. They thought I was asleep, but I wasn't. They were arguing in the living room. The baby has to sleep in their room. I've got the only extra bedroom. The baby doesn't let them sleep. They're miserable with each other. Corina hates me. They've been fighting like this for months, but this fight was the worst. I'm afraid they're going to break up or Corina will move back with her parents and take their baby with her. And it will all be my fault.

"Now I've hung around with you guys, hiked with you. I know I'm not just daydreaming. Think this might work. Both of you are really nice boys. Arnie's kind of quiet. But you're definitely good guys."

Molly reaches for a crumpled paper bag underneath the register, in a storage shelf deep behind books and papers. She shoves her hand in the bag and shows Turi a fistful of ten- and twenty-dollar bills. Hundreds of dollars.

She continues: "This is all mine. Ain't stolen it from anybody. I've been savin' it here. Away from Corina. Away from my brother. Turi, can I go with you guys to the East Coast? I'll pay my way. Just wanna ride out of here. That's all. Just a ride and nothing else. But we can't tell my brother. I'll leave him a note on the windshield."

Turi stares at Molly and tries to think of something to say, but he can't. He is dumbfounded. Arnulfo steps out of the restroom, his hair still sleek and wet. "You know, the cold's on left, and the hot's on the right. Took me a while to figure it out. ¡Híjola!"

CHAPTER TEN

They wave goodbye to Molly in the parking lot. Turi turns the blue truck toward the Berryman Trailhead instead of returning to the highway.

"What are you doing?" Arnulfo says.

"We're going to wait for Molly. She's going to meet us at the supply store in two hours. She wants to come with us."

Arnulfo slams his hand down on the dashboard. "What the hell is wrong with you, Turi? She can't come with us! Are you crazy?"

Arnulfo jumps out of the truck as soon as Turi pulls to a stop where they were the night before. Dust swirls in the air.

"Nulfo, she has money. She's smart. It will be better for us."

"What are you talking about? Qué chingada, Turi! We're picking her up in two hours? Who the hell made you the boss? We can't do this!"

"Look, I should've asked you first. I know. My mistake. 'Nulfo, calm down. Please think about it. I'm asking you now. We're talking about it now."

"Is that what you told her? Is that . . . We're not picking her up! Tell her that!"

"Look, 'Nulfo. Just for a second, let's calm down. We won't look like two Mexican teenagers anymore with Molly, okay. Not like what they're looking for anymore. Here's another thing, she has money, okay. Hundreds of dollars. She's saved it. She showed me. She can help us. She can also drive."

"If the narcos get her, if the narcos get us . . ."

"No one's going to get us. We'll tell her, or we won't tell her. We'll have to figure that out."

"So you're lying to her? Is that it?"

"Well, we both are. Maybe we'll tell her later, I don't know."

"Turi, these narcos will kill us all. It's bad enough for us. And now you're getting her mixed up in this. Do you know what they do to women in Juárez? They rape them, they enslave them, they dismember them. What if she finds out the trouble we're in, what if she turns us in? That's what the narcos will do to us too!"

"I think we stand a better chance with Molly. I think she can help us."

"Do you like her, is that it? You and that buenota? Is that why? Is that what she wants too?" Arnulfo said, his fists still clenched, but the brown was returning to his face.

"She wants a ride. That's it. Don't be a pendejo, 'Nulfo. I should've talked to you first, I know. But I didn't have time . . . I thought it would be a good idea . . . it happened so fast. Yes, I like her, but that's not the point."

"Fuck you, Turi. Fuck you. Is that what you want to do to her? Is that it? Stop shaking your head, güey! What if she gets us in even more trouble? What if she turns us in after she finds out?"

"She won't. I know she won't. She'll help us. We can get to New York or Connecticut or wherever and we can go our three separate ways, if we want." For the first few seconds of their argument, Turi imagined he might have to fight Arnulfo. Now he suddenly seems only an angry stranger.

"Maybe I like her too, güey." Arnulfo took a step closer to Turi, with a menacing, challenging smirk.

"Go for it," Turi says, turning his face away from Arnulfo. "You're such a goddamn charmer."

"And you are? I think we're making a mistake. You're thinking with your verga, güey."

"That's what you think. I'm thinking what will work, that's all. And why not? We need the money. She'll help us drive. Molly's smart and she works hard. That's why I like her. What's wrong with that?"

"I'm sure her ass has nothing to do with it."

"You know, 'Nulfo. *Stop* it. Let's stop talking before, before . . ."

"Before what?"

"You know, 'Nulfo. Let's just stop talking before we begin to really hate each other. Don't be a culo. We're giving Molly a ride. Period."

"This will be a disaster, I know it."

"We can't drive all night either. She'll get suspicious. She'll know we're in trouble. But we'll drive as much as we can every day. The three of us."

"You see? Already we're screwed. This will be a disaster, I can feel it in my bones."

As they pull up in their shiny blue F-350 to the store in Steelville, Turi can see Molly taping a note to the windshield of her Impala. The note is in a baggie.

Arnulfo is stoic in the front seat. The store is closed. Why isn't Molly telling her brother what she's doing?

Turi begins to load Molly's gear. Arnulfo stands next to the passenger door and half-heartedly grabs a duffle that Turi hands to him with a look.

Turi puts bags of groceries and a pillow in the backseat behind the driver's side.

"Thank you! I am so grateful to both of you," Molly repeats for the third time, leaning toward them, as if she wants to hug them but isn't sure.

They are loaded and ready to go. Molly is practically jumping in place. Turi looks at Arnulfo: Molly's enthusiasm has melted his resistance some.

"We're happy you're coming with us, Molly. Better to split the costs three ways, right, 'Nulfo? The driving. And we can always use the company." Turi wants to get on the road before Arnulfo changes his mind or blurts out something stupid or nasty.

Questions circle and sting the inside of his mind like wasps: Should they tell Molly how they took the truck? Will Juanito and his friends ever catch up to them? Most importantly, what will happen to Molly, to them, if . . . if they are caught? Maybe they can tell Molly about Juanito and what happened at the immigration checkpoint once they are on the road. She can decide if she still wants the ride to the East Coast. But Molly will never turn them in, Turi is certain of that. She will help them, if she decides to help Turi and Arnulfo. Or she might just walk away. But she will never do anything to hurt them. Turi also knows he is the one who has put her in danger. For the past two hours, he has been wondering if he is doing the right thing. *I like this Molly. What is wrong with me? If something happens to her, if they catch us, it will be my fault . . . all my fault.*

"Mind if I take a few pictures before we go? I can't believe I'm finally leaving old Steelville!" Molly wipes a few strands of the blue streak in her blond hair away from her face.

She beckons Turi and Arnulfo to her side, and with her long arms takes a cell phone selfie of the three of them in front of the truck. Another one in front of the supply store. A third one—with a timer as the phone is propped on the truck's hood—the three standing next to each other, Steelville's water tower in the background. In the last photo, after she counts down before the camera clicks, Molly unexpectedly wraps her arms around Turi and Arnulfo: Turi is frozen in a nervous laugh, while Arnulfo has a leery, awkward smirk.

CHAPTER ELEVEN

"Jefe, me permites un momento?" A man in a black polo shirt addresses Don Ilan politely. The boss wears a light green, pinstriped dress shirt and sits in his sprawling office. But what has always unnerved every visitor is the wrestling mask that covers his head: this time it's the silvery mask from El Santo. The floor-to-ceiling glass doors open to a deck overlooking the Pacific Ocean.

"Come in, come in. What do you hear from Dunbar's man in El Paso? The package for el Tapado should've arrived two days ago." Don Ilan passes his hand over his shiny head, as if stroking the hair that should be there. No one has ever seen Don Ilan's face. His hands are massive.

"It still has not arrived in Kansas City. I asked our friend on the border for more details."

"And? What has that pinche Dunbar done with the package? Where the hell is it?"

"That's just it, jefe. I think they lost it. I heard they gave it to one of their regulars to drive to the drop and two kids stole this viejito's truck and they're looking for the kids now." The man in the black polo shirt gulps as he delivers the news to Don Ilan.

"That son-of-a-bitch gringo! Kids? No tienen el producto . . . nada? El Tapado's our best customer! Not a man we want to disappoint! That pendejo

Dunbar knows that too!" One of Don Ilan's hands closes into a tight, rock-like fist.

"The kids don't know what's in the truck. Our distributor Dunbar has sent people after them. The viejito's with them. As long as the truck keeps moving, nothing happens to the package for two weeks. After that, who knows. It could deteriorate, release. I'd rather not be in any city in Gringolandia."

"So it's lost, but in a truck? Eventually they'll find the truck. El Tapado has been expecting this important package. Let me talk to him again. I can get him to wait, but only so long."

Don Ilan stares into a nearly deserted bay near Barra de Tecoanapa, south of Acapulco, Guerrero. Three women in bikinis are being photographed near the calm cerulean water. They appear to have jumped out of the pages of a Victoria's Secret summer catalog, with a twist. All have painted their faces in whimsical manners, as animals or skeletons, in a tribute to el Luchador, their nickname for Don Ilan. In unison, they wave at Don Ilan as they laugh and wiggle their hips into a pose. South of them, a bright white yacht is anchored a few hundred feet from the shore. Three small motorboats sit on the beach next to two armed men. A third man loads packages onto the boat next to an all-terrain mini truck. Around the villa next to the palm trees, grim expressionless men scan the cliffs instead of staring at the sweethearts primping for the photographers. Each man grips a machine gun like a soldier, and they grunt a few, terse words into a black headset occasionally. Above the deck of Don Ilan's office are red clay, roof tiles, and a parapet with more men with guns. Beyond the roof, the dark blades of a helicopter peek out from the front of the villa.

No man has ever dared to mask or paint himself in honor of el Luchador for fear of a deadly misunderstanding. They know he wants to see their faces, but he doesn't want anyone to see his.

"Dunbar doesn't yet know we know?"

"That's right, jefe. I expect that soon he'll tell us, but only if he can't easily find it or if he needs our help. Our man in Clint is keeping me informed. Every day."

"Dunbar's calling me later today and I'm sure it's to give me the bad news I already know. Send el Hijo de Huerta to El Paso right away. Don't wait any longer. Tell him it's a special favor for me." Don Ilan's squarish jaw with its flat nose underneath the mask evokes the maw of a spectre. Many think their masked boss reminds them of an evil Tenochtitlan idol in a disguised human form.

"But jefe, he's relaxing after Chilpancingo, he's—"

El jefe's green eyes turn toward the man in the black polo shirt who stops talking as if their green shimmer cut his vocal cords. Stoic, the man gulps again. "I'm sorry, jefe. I'll call el Hijo right away. I'll tell him exactly what you said. I'll inform him of the circumstances of our distribution problem."

"Good." Don Ilan returns his cat eyes to the girls on the beach again. "Tell him I don't want him to do anything to Dunbar or anyone else in El Paso—yet. I want him to find the truck. I want to know what's happening in El Paso. I don't want the gringo Dunbar to know el Hijo is there on my behalf. As soon as Dunbar knows el Hijo is there, he'll know I sent him, he'll know I don't trust him to get this problem solved quickly. Then the gringo will go to his friends in Juárez to come back at me. That son-of-bitch has never known his place! He thinks the American border protects him, gives him an advantage. Once he knows I might replace him, then it gets more complicated.

"Tell el Hijo to take whoever he needs for this work, or he can go it alone. He'll probably enjoy being in the States for a while after Chilpancingo anyway, as long as the Americanos don't run into him. This requires a little finesse from el Hijo, but he is capable of it."

"Yes, sir."

"You see the payasa in the black bikini?" Don Ilan strolls further onto the deck and points only with his green eyes. The open sleeves of his dress shirt undulate with the breeze from the cliffs. The man in the black polo follows his boss, but at a distance.

"Yes, sir."

"After I fuck her all night tonight, every which way, every pleasure . . . After I have her for hour upon hour . . . no one will ever have her again. She's been flapping her mouth too much."

"Yes, sir."

"Pride. It's what gets you in trouble. Don't ever forget that. The petty human being and pride. You start thinking you are more than you are, without earning that pride. More than dust. More than a little heat on an afternoon at a beach. Until it's too late. Until your time is gone in a moment. The best ones realize that while they are here. How precious life is. How little life is. The mask that life is. They start a journey through many deserts that will take thousands of days. They will create a real work of art before their afternoon is gone. Others just pretend to take that journey. They wear masks when their faces have no masks. For those pendejos, their work will never be much, but it will be something. Great ecstasy can be a small work of art too. So I will help her achieve the only thing she can achieve in this life."

"Yes, sir."

"And you know why she can only achieve that? Because she knows only a superficial way to be, posing for photos, posing when she talks too much, posing to seem bigger than she is. Muy falsa. That's why." Don Ilan scans the shore he owns, the endless water to the horizon, and even the depths beyond. His head glints in the sunlight. He casually walks back to his desk and sits down again.

"Yes, sir."

"Not all are Wild Beasts. Not all live between the danger of death and precious life. But that's what Wild Beasts do. And God has ordained that men, and even women, can be Wild Beasts. Living in between real life and death. The pretenders, like our friend down there, they assume a pride they have not *earned* in their lives. The pretenders have a limited capability, a certain minimal greatness they can achieve. They have made their choices. They have not faced the emptiness in their souls. They have not struggled to fill that hole in their chest. They take 'can' and turn it into 'is'—without the work. Their stupid, petty pride soils our world, with half-men, half-women, pretenders, followers, the nice and well-mannered, the seekers who don't want to pay the price. The naked faces with the most grotesque masks. The cheaters and the strivers who don't see that the only struggle that matters is the one within them. This struggle that calls you to a Battle, to a Quest."

The man in the black polo warily scans Don Ilan's desk and notices the spiral notebook where his boss has scribbled many paragraphs in pencil, with "QUEST" and "WILD BEASTS" and "PRETENDERS" in capital letters. Carefully printed lists are underneath each heading. He wonders if he is on any of those lists. "Si, Señor."

"We are images of God. Some soil that image with their pretending. Don't be one of those, my friend. Others make the real choices to live life openly as a journey of danger, unpredictability, and consequence . . . and they pay for that journey with their blood. Wild Beasts, my friend. The world is nothing without them. The greatest accomplishments are achieved because of them." Don Ilan gradually reclines in his black leather chair, puts his feet up on the desk, and twirls an ornate dagger in his hand. The empty leather sheath lies next to his papers.

"Thank you, sir."

On the east side of El Paso, beyond Clint, a black cell phone rings late at night. Dunbar slumps into his gray sofa. He recognizes the number. It is Don Ilan again. He already spoke to him earlier today. The Stetson lies on the coffee table, waiting for him.

"Don Ilan, I told you earlier what I know. We don't have the truck yet. I've got two of my men and the driver still looking. We're also waiting for one boy to contact home. We still have time."

"John," the voice says loudly, in what seems a harsh tone, but what is just an excellent satellite connection with the phone volume set at maximum. The voice is a heavy baritone with a Mexican-Spanish accent in English. "What you didn't tell me earlier is this: how much time do we have exactly? The arrangements?"

"Easily fifteen days. Maybe as much as three weeks. The blood samples are in six different containers in the passenger door, wrapped in three different packages each. They won't break—unless the idiots have an accident. All six containers are cooled from the movement of the truck and are kept at the right temperature. The cooling lasts at least forty-eight hours, maybe seventy-two, without a recharge. As long as they keep the truck moving, the cooling unit gets recharged. The containers, as I said, are very well insulated."

"We aren't going to wait much longer before we act. It's good that you're not lying to me."

"Don Ilan, I would never lie to you."

"There you go, my friend. Your second lie to me today. But it's unimportant. I'll overlook it. Tell me what happens if these six containers aren't cooled properly. Let's say they don't break, they don't have an accident. But the truck is abandoned, gets overheated. What happens?"

"As long as the containers are intact, nothing. No danger to the public. Nothing to release it into the air, to animals or humans. After a while, our special product for our customer goes bad. The blood samples become inert. Even if they are later found and exposed to the air."

"I've heard from el Tapado already. Our dear friend. He is waiting too, in Kansas City. Our *best* customer, as you know. But today he's already demanding replacement blood samples. He has his own timetable. A Midwest plan to start, I think, followed by plans for the East and West Coasts. Va a desmadrar América. You understand how difficult it was to get this product for him—from the czar's men in Pushchino—how expensive it was and how much he's already paid us. I don't even know if they have replacements. If you don't find this truck, and soon, you will be working for me free of charge for years."

"Don Ilan—"

"Listen, my friend. That's actually a good outcome for you. And you know it. I don't want things to end badly between us. And they easily could. Just like that. Give me an update in three days. After that, well, I won't be happy at all. I won't keep trying to hold back el Tapado, who does not like to be disappointed. God help you if he is not as patient as I am. Think of a Wild Beast of God, my friend."

Dunbar hears a click, and the cell phone goes dead. *Goddamn masked son of a bitch*, he thinks. *They'll be here looking for the truck too, I'm sure. Wait three days and that's when I'll be dead. Maybe . . . maybe he means it, that I can work this out, if we don't find the truck, and maybe he's already sent someone to replace me . . . But it will cost him too much. The bloodshed, new men up and down the organization on the distribution side, the disruption to his pipeline. El Tapado is just one of his best customers, but it's like the lottery with el Tapado, only one great order every five years for his international plots. And yes, this may be his biggest plot against America. But I'm the one who makes money for Don Ilan every year, every month. It's not worth it to him to start a war. Not now. Not on this side. Maybe he does mean it. Maybe he just wants me to relax before he tries to put a hollow point in my head, or worse. Yes, his style is to be much worse. Like mine. That's why we've always gotten along. His style is always to send a message no one dares forget. Just like mine.*

Dunbar picks up his hat with one hand and his second cell phone with the other. The Stetson is comfortably on his head. He glances at his financial news alerts and notices the Swedish counterpart to his biggest US pharma holding is moving higher, not by much, but still higher in European trading. These two companies possess control of the possible vaccine for Marburg-B, although in reality it is the Swedish company that is testing this vaccine. The American company has only funded most of the research and acquired distribution rights to develop it in the United States, if a catastrophe unfolds.

Dunbar remembers reading the symptoms in a journal, perhaps six months ago: first confusion, prostration, high fevers, diarrhea, nausea; then bloody stools, mucosal and visceral hemorrhaging; finally convulsions, coma, and death. In the Congo, eighty-three percent of infected muertos como perros, as Don Ilan would say. A devastation if it hits cities and places not ready with a vaccine, which of course will be everywhere.

Once Dunbar heard about el Tapado's plan to incite mayhem and unrest in the United States, and Don Ilan's offer to locate and purchase this key product for el Tapado, Dunbar strategized about how he could take advantage of the future chaos. El Tapado is devious, Dunbar has to give him that. Maybe millions will die like dogs. But as reports come in, if this crazy plan ever unfolds, everyone will rush first to understand this pandemic, but by then it will consume the dry plains like wildfire, and the cities too: Los Angeles, New York, Chicago, Kansas City, the first city. After an understanding of this new Black Death, government, businesses, individual investors, everybody will be throwing money at the only two companies that possess a vaccine—the prototype to a vaccine—and Dunbar already owns shares. His trust in Switzerland owns even more shares. A singular concentration of his investments, started six months ago.

As the devastation rolls across the country, the vaccine in mass production, he will of course hide with his family and men in Clint or Socorro, or even somewhere more remote. No one will be allowed in from the outside, and Dunbar will have his own private Wall to keep out "infected aliens," which will be just about everybody. He will be *there*, en la nada, fortified, as soon as he knows their customer—the notorious el Tapado—has been successful, as soon as Dunbar reads about that first outbreak of Marburg-B, as soon as Patient One has been identified in the press. Isolation is key. Isolation and wealth. Shoot-to-kill orders for all outsiders. And the vaccine. Dunbar is already working on getting a few samples of the prototype vaccine, at a steep price, for his family. Dunbar will be rid of ever needing Don Ilan again and can escape this business. Dunbar will have too much, and he will eliminate many enemies. After a plague of biblical proportions, this country will be cleansed, weak. He will have everything he wants. Even if he abandons Clint to escape to his hideaway in Costa Rica.

CHAPTER TWELVE

"So whose truck is it? It's gorgeous!" Molly says.

Turi glances at Arnulfo, who stares an I-told-you-so at the windshield and keeps driving in steely silence. Finally Turi says, "It's Arnulfo's."

"Oh, really. So you can buy an American truck and put Texas plates on it, even if you're Mexican? Didn't know you could do that." She glances at the map on Turi's lap and at the GPS console on the dashboard.

"Yes, of course. We *both* bought it. I saved enough money with Arnulfo and we bought this truck in El Paso. To go east."

"Oh . . . I see. So you guys are, like, friends, huh. Question: are you really runaways or something?"

"Nooo—we're not runaways," Turi says quickly, flustered, staring at Molly. She is smiling at them. She doesn't seem perturbed, but more amused by their company. Covered with nearly invisible blond hairs, her arm occasionally rubs against his. Turi thinks it is strangely warm, as if she has an oversized heater inside her body.

"I don't really care if you are. I'm runnin' away too. Arnie, c'mon, you can tell me, are you guys runaways? From the ranch-hoe?"

"No . . . we're . . . not."

"Ar-nul-fo, just tell me, is this beautiful truck yours and Turi's?"

"Yes. Yes." Arnulfo twists his thick shoulders behind the wheel. He points an air-conditioning vent right into his face and frowns.

"Is this really your truck? Your parents' truck? Something like that?"

"No, this is our truck," Turi says. "We're fine, Molly. We just want to get to Connecticut . . . but we're fine, really. I'm not from the rancho, by the way, but Arnulfo is."

"I'm sure we're fine. Look, don't worry. I'm grateful you guys are givin' me a ride. As long as the cops aren't lookin' for us in our cool, blue, stolen pickup. I just don't want to end up in jail. Hah, hah. You know my dad was from New Mexico?"

"No, I didn't know that. That's next to El Paso," Turi says quickly. Arnulfo looks angry or worried or annoyed, his forehead flushed, his small eyes aimed only at the road. "Have you ever read Mark Twain?" Near an off-ramp, a highway sign pointing back to the Mark Twain National Forest catches Turi's eyes.

"Oh, Turi. One of my absolute favorite writers. *Huckleberry Finn.* Had to read him, since half the county was named after him. But then I reread him, just for the heck of it. Read Tom Sawyer too. You're smilin', you like Twain too?"

"I got *Huckleberry Finn* in the back of the truck. With my other books."

"No way! Oh, I *knew* there was somethin' about you guys."

"You tell her you stole them from the library?" Arnulfo says, finally relaxing in his seat, his fingers lightly holding onto the steering wheel. The cloud above his head seems to have dissipated. For the first time since they started driving with Molly, a half smile crosses Arnulfo's face.

"I didn't *steal* any books from the library! I borrowed them from Mrs. Garcia—my teacher—who told me I could have a whole bunch of books all summer."

"But you're not goin' back to El Paso, are you?"

"No, I'm not. I'll mail her back the books, once I have a place, once I'm settled in Connecticut."

"Well, at least we have some cool stolen books in the back, even if this isn't a stolen truck. I was hopin' this ride was going to be exciting. Hah, hah. An adventure." Molly's voice is throaty and enticing, almost like a radio announcer's voice telling a story.

The landscape of pine trees and dirt roads slips by them, like a photograph whose subjects are always, but not quite, coalescing. The truck's air-conditioning hums perfectly in the June heat. Only a few cars pass them in the opposite direction across the double-yellow lines of Route 8 and then Route 21. In less than two hours, they are south of St. Louis on Interstate 255 and already seeing signs to Interstate 70, which will eventually take them to Terre Haute, Indiana and beyond. On the interstate, the landscape has shifted to blurry images of trees zooming by and a flat expanse interrupted by slanted on- and off-ramps. When they cross the rust-colored arches of the Jefferson Barracks Bridge, all of them whoop at being on top of the mighty Mississippi River—and at finally crossing east of it.

Turi looks at Molly out of the corner of his eyes. The two of them have a lot in common. He really likes her, likes her teasing and her way of being so natural—easy in a way he has never been, confident. Is it right not to tell her about the truck and old man Juanito and the possible contraband they are carrying? His stomach twists itself into a knot. If they stay safe, if they are safe, this knot should release itself into nothingness. But that's only going to happen when they get rid of this truck.

It seems like Arnulfo is finally relaxing.

Arnulfo tires and Molly takes a turn driving for several hours on Interstate 70. Then Turi is at the wheel as they approach Salt Fork State Park in Ohio. It's almost midnight. They've been driving eight hours straight. They stop only for gas and to go to the bathroom. They should find a safe place for the night. Turi wonders if maybe they should keep driving all night. Maybe Arnulfo is thinking the same thing. But what will he tell Molly if she asks them why they are in such a crazy hurry? That narcos are trying to find their stolen truck?

The dirt road into the 24-hour campground is pitch black. A few RVs are parked next to electrical outlets that protrude from the ground of pine needles like disembodied arms. But most of the parking stations are empty. Turi parks the blue truck at a cul-de-sac that signals the end of the road, clicks on the internal cab light in front. Who's going to sleep where?

"Okay, I'll sleep in the back," Turi volunteers before anyone has a chance to say anything. "'Nulfo, you can take the backseat if you want where there's more room, and Molly can have the front seat. That okay?" With a slight smile, Arnulfo looks like he doesn't care.

"Well, that's fair. First, I'm the new one here," Molly says, her eyes on Arnulfo, who is taken aback for a moment, but smiles broadly after a second. Outside a sheet of blackness presses against every window in the truck. "But I'm also okay to sleep outside, done it dozens of times in a tent at Twain, and this is a nice, comfortable truck bed. Even better. I'll get my sleeping bag out."

"Molly, let's flip for it, okay? I like seeing the stars anyway."

"Really, that's my favorite part too. As long as we don't have food around, or outside, we won't attract any animals."

"Heads it's me, tails it's you outside." Turi digs a quarter from his pocket and flips it, almost hitting the cab ceiling. It lands with George Washington face up, his hair in a queue. Before anyone can say anything else, Turi steps out into the darkness. With the cab light momentarily on, Turi climbs into the truck bed, and the truck bounces. In a moment, he steps off the truck again and brings Molly's sleeping bag and a blanket for Arnulfo, who is already in the backseat. But he waves it away. "See you in the morning. Let me know if you need anything else from back there."

"Tomorrow it's my turn, okay."

"Deal." Turi closes the door. The truck bounces and rocks gently as he settles himself and moves their backpacks and gear in the truck bed behind them to create a space for himself.

After a few minutes as he stares at the dark sky above him, Turi hears the truck door open carefully and someone step outside. The door clicks shut softly.

"Hey, Turi. You mind if I hang out with you for a bit back here. Not sleepy. And Arnulfo's falling asleep."

"Can't sleep either. It's nice out here under the stars. Not too hot, not too cold. I like the smells of the forest. The piney scent. The wood. Everything's so quiet."

The truck bounces as Molly climbs into the truck bed.

"What's keeping you up?" Molly asks. She sits at one end of the truck bed. Turi pulls himself up to lean against the cab. He can see her silhouette. When the breeze sways the branches in the trees, the slivers of moonlight reveal her face.

"I dunno. Nothing in particular. Just want to get somewhere. Find a place to live. I'm thinking about when I'll get the books back to my teacher,

Mrs. Garcia." *Did we miss the LoJack in the truck? Could there be another device that is tracking us? Are we really safe hidden in these trees?*

"You like her, don't you?"

"Uh, Mrs. Garcia? She was always very nice to me. My family, my aunt and her family, the ones who adopted me, they weren't. That's why I left."

"What's she like, this Mrs. Garcia?"

"Well, she's very smart. Young for a teacher. My youngest teacher. Not too old. I'm guessing in her late twenties. But I don't know." Turi's darker thoughts have dissipated from his head.

"Is she pretty?"

"Come on! She is, but that's not why I like her. That's not the only reason I like her."

"Hah," Molly says gently into the cool mountain air. In the undulating moonlight, Turi cannot clearly see Molly. He imagines she is smiling just as he is. "Okay, first, what does she look like, and second, why do you like her? Why do you *really* like her?"

"Brown hair, almost black, short but with a little curl at the end. She told me once she loves to dance to keep in shape. Modern dance, whatever that is."

Molly snickers into the night.

"She's married, by the way," Turi continues. He is glad they are obscured by dark shadows, so Molly can't see how red his cheeks are. Yet this mask of darkness also emboldens him in a way, to keep revealing what has only been inside his head for so long. "Why I like her—*really*—is because she listens to me. She likes that I read. She pays attention. She's different from the other teachers. She's different from most of the other people I know in Ysleta."

"Is-leh-tah. Am I saying it right? What a cool name. What does it mean? That your neighborhood?"

"Yes and yes. I think it comes from 'isla.' Spanish for 'island,' but why they called it that in the middle of the desert, who knows. An old Spanish mission's been there for hundreds of years."

"What color are her eyes? This Mrs. Garcia," Molly says in a mockingly seductive near whisper.

"Her eyes? Brown, I think. She has these *big brown eyes!*" Turi says in an exaggerated husky voice, playing along.

"Oh, you dog! Knew you had a crush on her! Just knew it."

"So *what?* She's nice to me. I needed someone to be nice to me. Everyone else was awful."

"Hey, who hasn't had a crush on a hot young teacher! I have."

"Okay, your turn. You found out Mrs. Garcia is keeping me up. What's keeping you up?"

"I'm more *wholesome* than you," Molly says. In the moonlight's shadows, Turi thinks he sees Molly grinning from cheek to cheek. He snorts. "My brother. That I didn't tell my brother." Suddenly the forest around them is quiet again, with more shadows like dark ghosts wafting across the blue truck.

"That you were coming with us? I thought that was a little gutsy of you, but it's none of my business."

"He'll be mad. Jim, he would've tried to stop me, I know. That's why I didn't tell him."

"Just tell him tomorrow morning. That way he won't worry. He won't find you, unless you want him to find you."

"My brother, he loves me. He's the only family I've got left. But—but he's different. Your Mrs. Garcia is different in a nice way. Well, my brother's different in another way. Sometimes not so nice, even if he means well. He doesn't have a choice with me. I was gonna leave sooner or later anyway and he'll be happier without me there. He has a girlfriend who is kinda his wife already. *Corina.* And a baby."

"You don't like this Corina?"

"That obvious, huh?" Molly waits for a few seconds before she continues. "I could call him tomorrow, just to tell him I'm fine and where I am. I was plannin' to wait maybe one more day."

"And you are fine. You're with us!"

"I know. That's one reason I feel lucky tonight."

"Just tell him and he won't worry. That will be that."

"Good idea. I think I'll leave my phone plugged into the socket down there. I'm going to sleep."

"Have a good night, Molly. I liked talking to you."

"Same here. *Big brown eyes!*" At once Molly jumps out of the truck, and the truck bounces again.

"Shut up." Turi chuckles, not sure whether she heard him or not. He can hear her footsteps crunch on the gravel around him as she plugs her phone into one of the RV park's electrical outlets next to the truck. He imagines she is grinning at him, though it is too dark to see.

The truck door closes with a soft but forceful click. Turi wiggles into his sleeping bag, tries to fall asleep. The night air eventually takes him to a dream with stars all around him, as if he is flying through the Milky Way and escaping into the night and entering a strange new world. But the snap of a falling branch interrupts his dream. The memory of Molly has faded into the other strange murmurs of the forest. Dark shadows fly above him and send shivers through his body and keep him at the precipice of sleep.

CHAPTER THIRTEEN

"You met these guys three days ago and now you're hitchin' a ride with them? What the hell?"

"Jim, c'mon, they're very nice, even polite. Remember 'polite people'? Once in a while we get those unicorns in Steelville, except usually they're old fishin' guys in, like, a Marilyn Monroe world. Look in your sock drawer."

Jim Crump pulls open his sock drawer with a creaky honk. Corina found the note on the Impala at the Steelville Supply Store and drove away without even looking for Molly, without wondering why Molly would not be at the store to give her the car keys in person. Jim was busy driving to St. James for a job interview that afternoon, and so it wasn't until late that first night when he realized something was wrong: Molly was gone without a word. He imagined Molly had somehow found some friends to hang with, even a boyfriend, or maybe she had gone on another overnight camping trip, yet Molly would have said something to him, even in passing. Not to ask permission, but to let her older brother know where she would be. In silence, Jim rips open the white envelope with Molly's letter and reads it slowly.

"How do you know these guys aren't going to leave you in a ditch somewhere? Rape you? You don't know who the hell they are. Get your ass back here, Molly! You crazy?"

"Jim, calm down. These guys are nice. Read it later when you calm down. You know I couldn't wait to get the hell out of Steelville. Turi and Arnulfo are from Texas, drivin' east. Boys my age. Dad's best friends from New Mexico were Mexican. These boys are just like them. And I can handle myself. *I'm stronger than these boys.* But they're nice, I tell you. I'll call you again when I can. Just didn't want you to worry. *Turi* told me to call you, *that's* the kinda kid he is. If I can't get a job, or if I can't get settled somewhere, I'll come back. How else am I gonna get anywhere, see anything? Kansas City's great, but it's still Kansas City."

"Molly, listen to me. Technically, and I'm just talkin' technically speaking here, you know, you're still a minor. A goddamn runaway minor now, for god's sake! Mom and Dad would never let you go. *Never.* You kiddin'?"

"Well, Mom and Dad aren't here anymore. And I know Mom wouldn't want me to stay in Steelville. She would've wanted me to get the hell out. I could go back, make Corina miserable—make *myself* miserable—for six months, then I can go wherever I want as an eighteen-year-old adult. No one can stop me then. Be legal sooner than you think."

Jim is silent for one too many seconds on the cell phone line. He is reading Molly's letter, three sheets of paper which crinkle as he reads every line, their history, how she wishes he'll be happy with Corina and their baby, how Molly knows the silent burdens he has carried since their parents died. The drawer creak-honks to a close again.

"Thank you for what you wrote, Molly. Know you're an adult already. Know that. Realized that a long time ago. You don't take shit from the old farts at the store and I don't imagine you'll take any shit from those guys giving you a ride."

"Jim, you know, they're *boys.* Teenagers my age. If they lived near Steelville, I would have asked at least one of them to go to the movies. Turi was born in Texas. The other guy, the quiet one, Arnie, I think he's Mexican. I mean Turi's Mexican, but born here. Arnie's Mexican Mexican, I think. Look, I'm sending you a couple of photos right now. See?"

"I tell you, if somethin' happens to you, I'll hunt those guys down. You tell them that. I don't care where they're from or where they go. Molly, where the hell are you?"

"Jim, listen to me. I'm fine. We're in Salt Fork State Park in Ohio. Please don't worry. *I want to do this.* I'll let you know where we are every couple of days, okay?"

"Cannot believe you. You're beyond stubborn." Jim breathes hard into the phone and for once feels powerless. He also knows Molly knows he won't start chasing her half-across the country. What would be the point? So she can leave, angry, six months from now? Jim spits a wad of tobacco into a trash can. He wishes he were outside, beyond these four walls, beyond these problems that never seem to leave him.

"Jim, please, relax. Everything'll be fine. Everything'll be *great*, I know it! I'll let you know how things are and where we are, okay? I'll call you when we get to Connecticut, for sure, or wherever we're going. Got money saved up. Got my clothes. Packed my campin' gear. I know how to work. I'll find another store, but somewhere better than old Steelville. I'll land on my feet, you'll see. I can handle these guys. But I don't need to handle anything. They're really nice, I tell you."

"They look like two dorky Mexican kids. You're out of your mind."

"Look, Corina will be happy. You'll be happy 'cause Corina will be happy. You get an extra room for little Mason. And most of all, I'll be happy. It's better this way, believe me. I'll be fine. Nothing bad's gonna happen. I can handle it."

They are silent for a moment.

"I don't know why you hate this town so much."

"We gonna go through this again? I mean, seriously?"

"You can hike 'til you drop, you can stay with us as long as you want. I'll talk to Corina."

"And do what? Work at the tackle shop my whole life? Fight every week with Corina? See no one? Get to joke with old guys who live to fish 'til I'm old and broken too? I mean, every kid I knew has already moved or found jobs in St. Louis or Kansas City or just disappeared. The closest kid I knew in high school, for that one year, was twenty miles away! A white trash jerk. I'll come back and visit. I'll come back and visit *you*."

"Well, there's no talkin' you out of it. I see that. You're as stubborn as Mom. Just don't like those guys givin' you a ride out of here."

"Okay, we're about to hit the road again. I'm fine, believe me. They're doin' me a favor and they're happy to have me. I'll call you in a day or so, okay?"

"That's a nice goddamn pickup they have."

"Jim, okay, I'm going. I'll call you."

"Take care of yourself, Molly." Jim clicks the phone dead just a split second on the quick side.

Kevin O'Callahan from Redtec assigns him to Manuel Aguirre, one of his crew chiefs, to work on the demo for the two bathrooms Redtec is renovating in the St. James Winery, the first job in two years that pays Jim almost twice the minimum wage. A damn good job, as long as Jim can keep it. The drive from Steelville is also only thirty minutes to the winery, about as good as good could get. Manuel spends the morning laying out plastic sheeting in and around the employee bathrooms, sheeting that drops all the way from the winery ceiling and is held by metal pressure posts which Manuel has shown Jim how to apply without damaging the floors or ceilings.

Jim imagines they will just start ripping shit out to get ready for the new bathrooms. Watching Manuel carefully lay out the brown butcher paper from the bathroom worksite to the exit door to prevent their dust and debris from soiling the office carpet as they work—watching him affix the thick paper to the floor, exactly and meticulously—is frustrating. But, Jim keeps working. He is looking at Manuel on all fours, like a dog, his ass half out of his jeans, a sight which bothers him. When Manuel turns around and points at a wobbly metal post and says, "Pay attention to la madera up there, the wood, before it falls on your head!" Jim imagines throwing him a middle finger. As he trudges up the ladder to tighten the metal post, Jim thinks, *Goddamn him telling me what to do*, but then at the top of the ladder he remembers what O'Callahan said when he hired Jim: "You listen to what Manny wants and how he wants it. If you want to keep this job, you make sure Manny's happy. He knows how we do things at Redtec. He knows exactly what we stand for and how to keep the customers happy. Manny's been with me for eight years. You have a problem, you talk to him. You have a problem with Manny, don't bother coming back to work."

At home, Jim is exhausted from their prep work. They have begun to pry free the old drywall and 1950's tile in the winery bathrooms, the debris of which Manuel gently placed (not threw) in a huge plastic trash can with casters, so as not to make noise for the winery employees on the other side of the plastic sheets, so as to roll it out over the boards they have placed over the brown butcher paper and not damage the carpet. Manuel, always in control. Manuel, always so genial but firm. Manuel, confident about what is next and how to do it. All while Jim holds back every muscle, waiting for his instructions, secretly angry at being bossed around with an accent. And afterward, the endless sweeping and tidying up and picking up every scrap and laying down fresh butcher paper for the next day—all of it left Jim drained. Is it from work or from the pent-up tension in his mind? Mexican boys took Molly, and his sister joined them happily. Now his immediate boss is one of them too.

"What a goddamn world we live in," Jim utters half-heartedly. He stares at the computer screen in their bedroom. Corina is working on dinner, and the baby is mercifully taking a nap in Molly's old room. Maybe life will get better. Jim also sees Manuel's work ethic and the fact that Manuel doesn't give him any bullshit and waves goodbye with only a "See you tomorrow, Jimmy," despite the fact that Jim is not exactly friendly for eight hours. Maybe Jim is being too hard on Manuel. But damn him if he ever gives Jim any bullshit, if that Manuel ever does anything unfair to Jim, if he ever so much as gets any kind of pissy attitude toward him—Jim will respond. And hard.

As Jim waits for his computer to boot up *Fairbairn News*, he thinks about his father and his stories about New Mexico, how the old man always wanted to go back with Jim's mom, but never did. Jim admired his father and even kind of loved him. After both parents died in the fire, Jim even hated both of them for dying and leaving him to take care of everything, to suddenly go from being a boy at home to being a man in charge of one. Only Molly was left. Only Jim was left. Only the frayed stories of their family were left. His father, Gary, was a delimber operator in New Mexico, moved to Missouri with a timber company, and that's where he met his wife Sarah, Molly and Jim's mother. Fair-haired and fair-skinned, Gary had a hulking look—that linebacker body—he bequeathed to his son. Jim remembers his schoolmates abusing him about his unruly blond hair and older kids picking fights with him because he was their size. In grade school, some African American kid named Ronald punched him out of the blue on the playground and spat in his face and yelled, "Cracker," which Jim misheard as "Slacker," until a friend explained it to him. In high school, he remembers the Halloween Dance when Jessica told him she needed "a little time and space to think things over." Had it been because the week before Jim had enthusiastically told her he wanted to go to community college, as if this would somehow impress her? And he did want to go, but what he glimpsed in return was Jessica's crestfallen face. Poor white disappointment at being stuck in the middle of nowhere, that's what he saw reflected back in his face. It took him a year to get over that emotional punch to the gut.

In rural Missouri, Jim felt somewhat cursed most of his life, trapped in limited circumstances, even though he also loved the simplicity and freedom of the American countryside. When his parents died, the curse became as real as a Missouri spotted skunk. But what was the point of feeling mushy about his past? Why feel sorry for himself? How was that ever going to help him? Jim has only had time to work and keep all of them afloat. That was what mattered then, and that is only what matters now.

Fairbairn News features a story about a professor at an Ivy League school canceling a midterm because of the trauma of the US Senate's confirmation of a right-wing Supreme Court judge. A photo of a crying baby is at the top. Another section focuses on a story of an illegal Mexican immigrant raping and killing a young girl in a Kansas City, Missouri suburb. The immigrant was deported three times, a druggie, only to return across a defenseless border. Jim hasn't read a newspaper in two years, after the regional weekly that he often used to start fires in their fireplace went out of business. A photo of a young white guy next to a haystack, donning a trucker's hat emblazoned with "Proud American," adorns an ad for more political paraphernalia from *Fairbairn News*. The male model can easily pass for his brother (if Jim had one). He watches a few short videos of political commentary and allows his body to recoup itself as he smells Corina's lasagna in the oven and overhears not a peep from the baby. This is always the best time of the day for him, the evening, when he is done with work, when he can relax, when he can reconnect with the world through his computer. When everything seems good at home. Corina has been so much more affectionate after Molly's departure. All of that tension among the three of them has disappeared. The new job helps. Hell, after announcing his new job to Corina this past weekend, she put Mason in his crib early and they made love. An aggressive, delicious kind of love like the nights when they were dating . . . before the fire . . . before the baby . . . before all these bills . . . before everything. That's how good things are now.

Jim clicks on a *Fairbairn News* link to a discussion forum about "illegal aliens destroying communities," and sees a thread about one man blaming an "illegal alien neighbor" for his stolen Honda Accord. The man muses about proving it by just opening up their garage and finding his vehicle. He knows those "goddamn bastards" have taken it. This thread also morphs into another one on a stolen F-series pickup, and another commentator mentioning the truck's popularity with thieves. Jim types: "Is there a place I can check whether a pickup has been stolen, with Texas plates? How do I do that?" In five minutes, a link has appeared in response to his comment, and that link leads to a Texas website for reported stolen vehicles and that link to another link of Texas owners of stolen vehicles.

Jim punches in the Texas plate of the double-cab Ford pickup, which he can see in one of Molly's photos. Nothing comes up in the first link. At the second website, he leaves the details of the license plate in a new thread along with an uploaded, cropped photo of the license plate of Molly's blue pickup. She will be calling again any day now, as long as everything is all right, and maybe Jim can give her some news, if he finds anything, before her ride with those Mexican boys turns into deep trouble. How can kids like that own such a gorgeous truck? It doesn't make any sense. And why are they driving across the country? They are like his boss Manuel: maybe they aren't thieves or drug dealers, sure, but what's going on, why are they here? Molly's stubborn independence, not seeing what's in front of her eyes, trusting everybody and anybody who comes into the store, all of it has put her in this situation. Jim knows his sister, but what he has never loved about her is her naiveté about the world, her carelessness even when she would prefer to camp alone immediately rather than wait to go with someone she trusts. Molly calls it "believing in the world." But Jim thinks a fool is someone willingly blind to how the world really works.

"Dinner's ready!" Corina texts him from the kitchen. She is really obsessed with texting, but in this case Jim has to hand it to her. This way they can keep the baby asleep and maybe steal another evening for themselves. He logs off the discussion forum and *Fairbairn News* and turns off his computer. Tomorrow he'll check the website again to see if anyone has responded to his questions about the truck.

Suddenly, as he looks around, the world seems much smaller in their bedroom and through the window overlooking the pines of Steelville, Missouri. He can detect no sound outside on his property.

CHAPTER FOURTEEN

El Hijo de Huerta listens to a song on an old iPod as he sits overlooking desolate St. Vrain Street near el Segundo Barrio in El Paso, just across the train tracks and Paisano Drive in one of the many apartments his boss Don Ilan keeps for the friends of the Guerrero group. Rusted bars interrupt the light from the window. In front of the Gedunk Bar across the street, a drunk writhes on the pavement radiating the June heat, his dried vomit at his feet. In his ears, el Hijo hears these words:

Muñequita	*Little doll,*
le dijo el ratón	*the mouse told her,*
ya no llores tontita	*don't cry, silly one,*
no tienes razón.	*you have no reason.*
Tus amigos	*Your friends*
no son los del mundo	*are not those of the world*
porque te olvidaron	*because they forgot you*
en este rincón.	*in this corner.*
Nosotros no somos así.	*We are not like that.*
Te quiere la escoba y el recogedor.	*The broom & the dustpan love you.*
Te quiere el plumero y el sacudidor.	*The duster & carpet beater love you.*

Te quiere la araña y el viejo veliz.	*The spider & old suitcase love you.*
También yo te quiero,	*I, too, love you,*
y te quiero feliz.	*and I want you happy.*

A tear drips across el Hijo's cheek as he replays Cri-Cri's song "La Muñeca Fea/The Ugly Doll." A mattress sags on the cracked linoleum floor, and one chair and a table are next to a barred window. The sharpest of bowie knives, with a serrated second edge, lies next to the mattress. El Hijo sits on the wooden chair, spilling over it like an adult squatting in a third-grade ladder-back school chair. The chair is a normal size, but el Hijo is huge. His thick thighs rock and lift the table—they don't quite fit underneath it—and his muscled forearms could smash the table in two, surely, if he loses control, if that tear unleashes anger or terror or something worse. No one remembers his real name, Victor Huerta, and of course he is no relation to the brutal Mexican reactionary of the revolution. But that never mattered in grade school, when they pummeled him. It only began to matter when he fought back and how he fought back—when he abandoned school for the streets after his father was found with his neck broken and his eyes with school pen-cils jammed into their sockets . . . and other family members, well . . . Like an evil gust of wind one cannot keep out, "El Hijo de Huerta" became words whispered on dusty street corners if one crossed the wrong people. A truth of this dark landscape. A reckoning.

El Hijo wipes away the tear and stares at the text that buzzes on his phone. A connection inside Dunbar's operation in Clint and Socorro sends Don Ilan and Guerrero the details of the missing navy blue pickup, and Guerrero relays him the information, including the names of the two boys, "Turi and Arnulfo." El Hijo is ready to get the hell out of El Paso before any of Dunbar's men spot him, even though most of them don't know what he looks like even if they've heard his name. He crossed the bridge with his fake United States passport only a few hours ago. No one will ever find him in the States, unless he wants to be found, unless this citizen of Germany, France, Brazil, Mexico, and the United States (or anywhere else he needs to go) is extremely unlucky, unless his current passport does not appear to be valid (an impossibility with Don Ilan's connections), and unless he does something stupid to attract attention from the cops or FBI or anyone else (which he won't do). Only in a room by himself with *La Muñeca Fea*—with this song he has loved most of his life—will he drop the mask of an über soldier for a few minutes. Anywhere else, any other time . . . he will disappear before a soul senses in its bones that el Hijo de Huerta has been there. And if they do sense who he is, even many within the Guerrero group, well, that will also coincide with their last day on this godforsaken earth.

He walks north following the tower of the Hilton Doubletree in the horizon, where he would have stayed under an alias had he been coming to El Paso to see one of his güeritas. After a few minutes he pushes open the heavy doors of the El Paso Public Library in front of the Doubletree. In an isolated corner and using one of the public computers, el Hijo searches for information. He knows the pickup was last seen near Lubbock, and those boys will be heading anywhere but Kansas City, if they half guess what is in the truck. But to find it? That will require an accident or luck, since he doesn't think Dunbar and his men are stupid enough to ever report it stolen.

He Googles the license plate and starts searching through the results, dozens of them. Then he narrows the search not only with the numbers and letters in quotes, but also adding outside the quotes the words "truck" and "pickup" and even "stolen," just to see if he will get lucky. El Hijo follows dozens of links to nowhere and nothing. After going back and forth between his list of results and the links he explores in depth, he clicks on a link to *Fairbairn News* and follows it to the discussion page on "illegal aliens." There it is: first the license plate in a discussion about stolen vehicles, and then, as he scrolls below he sees someone, a "JCrump" from Missouri, has posted a photo of the license plate—the blue pickup's license plate. El Hijo's jeans stretch and creak with a hard-on.

From behind, on his granitelike shoulders, el Hijo feels what seems to be a gentle pecking. When his massive head tilts away from the computer screen, his red-rimmed eyes land on two slender, pale fingers and then on the figure of an Asian woman tapping him again. It's the librarian who handed him the computer when he wrote his name at the reference desk.

"Your time's up," she says, in a tight, willing smile. Her face is smooth like the finest glass.

El Hijo pushes away from the computer, remembering in his head where he was online and how to return to that place. He has not written anything down. He remembers it was *Fairbairn News*, and exactly where it was. He towers over the librarian who is still grinning at him. Her wrinkle-free face could easily fit in one of his massive hands. El Hijo's viselike grip could crush those cheek sockets and . . .

"I'm in the middle of something," the giant el Hijo says in a quiet baritone that sounds as if it emanates from deep within a well. He is standing, trying to back away awkwardly from the table. He can only see the top of the librarian's head. The svelte librarian—in a black wool skirt that drops all the way to her ankles like a nun's tunic—snaps the computer shut and tucks it under her arm.

"You can sign up again at the reference desk. You might have to wait

thirty minutes for the next available computer. Follow me. Let's take a look."
She sashays toward the reference desk, proudly surveying the library floor
and its patrons, one of whom she shushes as she passes by. Another patron
is downloading photos of naked women at a park event. The librarian turns
demurely away, as if shielding el Hijo from that spectacle. He stays at her
heels like a tamed tyrannosaurus. "Oh, good. There's a spot in thirty minutes," she says at the desk, pointing with a bright red nail to where el Hijo
should write his name.

Victor Huerta writes his name on the list. He mutters a baritone "thank
you" under a breath that seems to heave from an abyss within the earth like
a volcanic hiss.

"Victor, you from El Paso?" The librarian's voice has a tinny cheeriness
about it.

"Me?" El Hijo looks at the librarian, now behind her desk, still standing,
still only about chest high to his massive frame. He looks startled that she
would even talk to him. Her black librarian's glasses have cat-eyed frames
with one tiny heart at each upturned corner. "I'm from Juárez, Miss. Long
time ago. I live here now."

"I think this is the first time I've ever seen you in the library."

"Yes." El Hijo is eyeing the empty chairs a few feet away, aching to just
sit down and wait for the computer.

"Let me know if there is anything I can help you find." The librarian
smiles warmly at him, staring intently into his eyes. "I am at your service."

"Thank you." El Hijo stares at her, at this compact body in front of him,
and these incessantly happy dark eyes, and how that chest underneath that
silk blouse might be naked and in his arms, and how her perfect little face
might explode. "Think I'll just sit over there."

"I'll get the next computer when it's ready and bring it to you, Victor. Need anything, a magazine, just let me know."

"Appreciate it," he says, walking away. He stumbles into the chair, almost breaking it as he collapses into it. The wood joints creak, but hold together.

After exactly thirty minutes, the petite librarian—the name tag reads "Miss Akiko"—brings him another silver MacBook Pro and lays it in front of him and opens the screen ceremoniously, which startles him again. El Hijo can smell her jasmine perfume suspended in the air. She returns to her desk. When he stoically looks up to see her sit down, she waves gently at him and waits for him to look away. Eventually he does. It takes a few minutes of searching, and soon he is back on *Fairbairn News*, back to the discussion on illegal aliens and the post by "JCrump" from Missouri with the license plates of the blue truck.

As his breathing quickens, el Hijo imagines he will indeed call one of his güeritas anyway and pay her a visit at home before he leaves for Missouri tonight. Stephanie at Casitas Coronado will always see him without much fuss. Before he calls or emails anyone, however, he takes photos of the URL and IP address of "JCrump" which he is able to track after searching for variations on the name in Missouri. He's even able to find an email address attached to the photo and the comments on the discussion page at *Fairbairn News*. He sends this "JCrump" an email offering a reward for "my truck, which was stolen by my two cousins." He further explains: "I don't want to report them, I don't want to tell the authorities because I don't want my cousins to go to jail. I just want to find them, get my truck back. I hope you can help me." An hour has dissipated into the musky air around him. El Hijo lifts his head from the computer screen and scans the floor around the library. No one looks his way, not even Miss Akiko. No one walks near his corner. He wonders if that's how readers get lost in words, lost so that time apparently stands still for a while, hot inside their heads, souls alive and in pursuit. Their loins warm too, with their imaginations. He decides to return to the El Paso Public Library one day, when this business for his boss Don Ilan is done, and talk to Miss Akiko again. Perhaps she might enjoy having a cup of coffee nearby.

Hey, man. I just need my truck back. Thanks for writing back so quickly. So where's my truck exactly? I don't want to get anyone in trouble. As I said before, my stupid cousins took it.

    VictorH

Okay here's what I know. They were in Ohio and I think going to Connecticut or New York. East Coast. I knew that wasn't their truck. My sister's with them, but she doesn't know. Been trying to call her, but no luck. I don't want to get my sister in any trouble. She was just hitching a ride with your cousins when she joined them in Missouri.

    JCrump

I just want my truck back. Don't worry about your sister. I know she has nothing to do with it. I'm mad at my cousins. They took my truck without asking me in El Paso. They're assholes and I wouldn't trust them. That's why it's better if I get my truck back as soon as possible. I'll meet you in Missouri, I'll be there in a day or so. I could call the police, but then everybody would be in trouble. I don't want that. But I need to know where they are.

    VictorH

Last I heard they were in Salt Fork State Park in Ohio. If I find anything else before you get here, I'll send you another email. But that's all I know. Here's the place where we can meet, just click the link below to get directions. Send me an email about the time. See you soon.

JCrump

CHAPTER FIFTEEN

After two days of driving east from Missouri, Turi, Molly, and Arnulfo exit I-99 and turn south on Route 322/220, driving through Penn State University on their way to Rothrock State Forest.

"I'll be right back," Molly says as soon as their blue Ford pickup truck is stopped in the parking area off Bear Meadows Road at Rothrock. "I'll help you unload." They decide to stay the night. All three feel that in another day or so they will reach Connecticut. Where exactly in Connecticut are they going and why? Will they split up when they reach that little corner on the East Coast? Will they stay together just to share an apartment or a house for a while before they go their separate ways? Who will suggest what first—and when? These are all questions they want to ask each other, but haven't. It's an adventure on the fly, a beneficent cloud that emboldens them until a gust from a merciless wind blows it all away.

Molly finds an open area with a boulder the size of a minivan, climbs on the rock, and takes out her cell phone: she has two bars up there.

"Hey, Jim. It's your little sis. We're near Penn State in Pennsylvania! At Rothrock!"

"Molly? You okay? Everything all right? You gotta get out of that truck! I've been trying to—"

"Calm down. I'm fine. Gosh. Turi and Arnulfo are great. Really sweet guys. Especially Turi. I really like him. Maybe we'll end up sharin' a house or something in Connecticut. Just to start. I want to ask them, but, well, we'll see what happens. They're actually really nice—"

"Listen to me. They stole that truck. I'm meetin' their cousin Victor tomorrow. He's coming to Mizzouruh. Meetin' him after work in St. James, at the China King."

"Victor? This truck? *Our* blue truck?"

"Yes, *that* truck. It's stolen. Victor found me and emailed me. They stole that truck. They're goddamn thieves! They stole the truck. You've been ridin' around with a bunch of truck thieves."

"What? You serious? Who the heck is this Victor? He *found* you? What the heck does that mean?"

"Molly, please, I'm dead serious. Listen to me. Remember those photos you sent me? I posted a JPEG of the license plate on the Internet. I asked where you could find out if a truck with Texas plates was stolen. This Victor emailed me. Said they're his cousins. His cousins stole the truck. He's tryin' to get it back. Doesn't want to report it to the police and get them in trouble. I'm meetin' him tomorrow."

"Jim, really? You're not shittin' me? Come on!"

"Yes. Get out of the truck. Doesn't matter where."

"Jim, okay. Let's say you're right, let's say what this Victor says is true. He's not reportin' it to the police, we can get to Connecticut first. Right? Then he can have his truck back."

"Molly! You out of your mind? You listenin' to me?"

"Get out *here*, in the middle of nowhere? Is that what you want? In Pennsyl-freakin'-vania? No. I want to talk to them. Is this your way of drag-gin' me back to Steelville?"

"Molly, they stole the truck. This is *not* about gettin' you back to Steelville! What the hell you doin'? You're gonna be an accessory to stealin' a truck! Is that what you want?"

"You don't even know what that means. And if he's not reportin' the stolen truck to the police, if he's family, then we have at least another day, right? Tell him he can have his truck back in Connecticut, what's the problem?"

"Molly! They're dirty thieves! They've stolen a truck! You're ridin' with them! What the hell's gotten into you?"

"Jim, please, stop hollerin' at me. I want to talk to them. Want them to have a chance to explain themselves. And please, stop callin' them names. They've been nothin' but excellent boys. *Period.* Maybe this cousin Victor isn't tellin' you the truth. Maybe he did somethin' to them and they stole his truck. You ever think of that? And here's another fact. Arnulfo and Turi aren't related. They've never mentioned it. Why would they bother not sayin' it? They never knew it would matter one way or 'nother, or that you would post the damn license plate on the Internet, or that this Victor would contact you. Cousins, my ass. This Victor is lying. I want to talk to them."

"Goddamn, Molly. You're crazy. What if they get violent once they know you know? What if they beat you up, rape you?"

"Please god. Not again. Please. These boys aren't like that. They're not. I know they're not. What are you thinking? Maybe they did somethin' wrong. Maybe they're runnin' away from this Victor. I mean, Turi, he has some bruises on his ribs, right? Maybe this Victor was the one who beat him up. Maybe this bastard Victor is the reason Turi got the hell out of El Paso. Turi is the nicest, most intelligent boy I've ever met in my life. That's who he is."

"Molly, please think. Think, goddammit!"

"I am. That's exactly why I want to talk to them. I'll talk to them right now."

"Please be careful. And keep your goddamn cell phone on!"

"Okay. Bye."

Jim turns on his computer and glances at the alarmist headlines on *Fairbairn News*, a giddy habit that he can hardly contain. Then he signs on to his email and writes:

> *Victor, just got a call from my sister, Molly. She's fine. But they're in*
> *Pennsylvania near Penn State. At Rothrock, which I looked up in Google*
> *Maps: Rothrock State Forest. See you tomorrow.*
> *JCrump*

Molly sits on the rock, glancing at her cell phone. She's thinking of what she will say, who she should believe, and what she should do. She walks back to the parking area off Bear Meadows Road at Rothrock. Two other families are unloading gear at the other end of the parking lot, while a little girl is chasing a toddler around a white sedan.

"Hey, Molly! You hungry?"

"In a minute. 'Nulfo, can you come over here for a second? Turi, stay here. Have to talk to both of you. 'Nulfo, please come over here, stop unloadin' that stuff just for a few seconds. Sit down, please. Okay, here's a question. Are you cousins?" At the other end of the parking lot, the two families are within earshot, piling coolers and tents next to their cars, the kids still chasing each other and flinging pinecones behind them. A Labrador retriever leaps after the kids.

"Cousins? You mean, me and Arnulfo?" Grinning, Turi stares at Molly. Arnulfo looks at Molly and then at Turi as if they were both insane.

"Arnulfo, is Turi your cousin?" Molly's lips are pursed. Her face is hard for the first time this trip, almost painful in its immobility.

"Do we look like cousins? No, Turi's not my primo."

"Turi, look at me, I'm serious. This is important. Is Arnulfo your cousin?"

"Molly, no. What's this about? What happened?"

"Okay, just remember, you need to tell me the truth. Right now. Don't lie to me. Or I'll walk over to those two families right now and leave you. So don't lie. You guys steal this truck?"

"Molly. Please. What happened?" Turi stares at Molly. Arnulfo almost stands up, but doesn't as soon as Molly's eyes are on him.

"The truth, Turi. Look at me. Did you guys steal this truck?" Her blue eyes bore into Turi's, and they seem to anchor him too, but he also seems to want to hold her hand, to stare back and not be afraid anymore.

"Turi, no le digas nada. Por favor. Te dije que era un error traer a esta mujer." Arnulfo stands up, shaking with anger and fear, as if deciding whether to sprint into the forest or lunge at both of them.

"Move an inch and I'll scream," Molly says, staring down Arnulfo. "Turi, what did 'Nulfo say. Tell me."

"He said—"

"Shut up, Turi. Just shut up."

"He said not to tell you anything, that it was a mistake bringing you along." Turi exhales and continues, "Arnulfo, sit down. I'm gonna tell her everything. Sit down and take a deep breath. Come on."

"Pendejo. It will be worse, it will be worse, oh my god . . ."

"Calm down, please. Everybody calm down. Okay, Molly. Yes, we did steal this truck, but it's not what you think."

"From who?"

"Arnulfo and I were working together on this farm on the border, that's where we met."

"From who?"

"Molly, it's complicated and I'm trying to explain what happened. Just hear me out. Arnulfo was going to be a driver with this old guy who owns the truck—or maybe his boss owns the truck, the owner of the farm."

"So how long have you two known each other?"

"I don't know, a few days. We met a day before Arnulfo signed on to be a driver with this old guy. I don't want to lie to you, Molly, I don't want to lie anymore. You don't deserve it. I'm sorry."

"Pendejo, she's ruining everything! She's gonna turn us in! She's using you! It's a mistake, Turi, a mistake . . ." Arnulfo fidgets on the dusty ground, his shoulders square, his fists clenched, his face in a grimace as if shaking away a foul mist.

"Arnulfo, shut up. We're telling her everything. How'd you find out?"

"Just talked to my brother. Somebody's looking for you."

"What? Your brother talked to them? That's impossible! How?"

"First, tell me everything."

"My family died. I was living with my aunt Seferina and her husband—that asshole Ramon—that's who beat me up. He hates me—"

"Is that how you got those bruises on your side?"

"Yes, he hates me, and I hate them, and . . ." Turi stammers, at once not able to see in front of him as tears blur his vision, ". . . and I just wanted to get away. I wanted to get away from them, from my awful family. They wanted to send me to Juárez. I had to work like a dog. I had no one. I don't have a family, really. I was working at the farm when I met Arnulfo."

"And? How did you get the truck, Arnulfo?"

"This old man, Juanito, he said he would give me a ride to Kansas City if I helped him drive. He needed to get this truck to Kansas City, he said he was visiting his son . . ." Arnulfo says, still half-angry, challenged every second by Turi's stare.

"But that old man Juanito was lying," Turi interrupts. "I saw him give money to an immigration guy at a checkpoint, to an ICE—"

"What? Wait a minute. Wait. Back up. Like a bribe?"

"Yes, a bribe. Juanito handed the officer an envelope of money at the checkpoint. Arnulfo didn't even notice it, I had to tell him, he was almost asleep—"

"Wait a minute. Back up again. How did you get a ride with them, Turi?"

"Ramon beat me up 'cause I had used his gloves at the chicken farm. He kicked me . . . they were going to send me back to Mexico to my great-aunt . . . I just showed up to get a ride with Arnulfo and Juanito let me in, I just wanted to get away from Ysleta. Juanito said I could help drive this blue truck too."

"After that, that's when you got to the checkpoint and this old guy Juanito gave a bribe to the officer? A police officer?"

"Yes. No. I mean he was an immigration officer. Not a cop. 'Nulfo, sit down, we're gonna tell her everything. I'm sorry, Molly, I'm sorry we didn't tell you. We should have told you. We were scared and it just happened so quickly, when you asked for a ride. We were scared. We needed help."

"Then what happened?"

"At a rest stop near Lubbock, we planned it—I think Juanito was going to kill us in Kansas City—we told him we had to pee, Arnulfo locked himself in the truck by mistake, and when we returned from the restroom, I pushed Juanito into a ditch, we took off in the truck, and . . . well . . . we met you."

"So you stole this truck from this Juanito. And he's lookin' for you? Why'd he bribe the immigration officer? 'Cause Arnulfo is illegal?"

"No, no, no." Turi stares at Arnulfo. Arnulfo looks at his knees as he squats on the dusty ground, smoldering. He sways back and forth as if he were a buoy at sea. Is Arnulfo about to pass out, scream at them, or punch him? "Honestly, Molly, I think it's drugs. I think we're carrying drugs in this truck. That's my guess."

"Pendejo. Let's just get out of here. Please. What are you doing? You're gonna get us all killed. All for this girl."

Molly glares at Arnulfo, but then turns to face Turi.

"So when you let me hitch a ride with you, when you were chattin' me up and bein' friendly, and all of that shit . . . you knew!"

"Molly, please. I'm sorry. Tell her, Arnulfo. Tell her you're sorry too, goddammit."

"Sorry."

"Molly, please don't cry," Turi pleads, wanting to touch her hand, but not daring to come close to her. His own tears well up in his eyes. He doesn't bother wiping one away when it drips down his cheek. "Molly, we like you. We were scared. I like you. I am so sorry. We were going to dump this truck as soon as we got to Connecticut. We just needed the ride, that's all. We thought you could help us get away from those bad people. I thought you could help us."

"You lied to me! And who the hell is my brother seeing tomorrow?"

"What? You mean Juanito?"

"I sent Jim photos because he was worried about me. One of them must've had the truck's license plate. Is my brother in danger? This man, he says he's your cousin. That doesn't sound like an old man, like this Juanito."

Turi and Arnulfo stare at each other, panicked. Finally, Turi says, "Molly, tell him not to meet with him. Whoever he is. Tell him not to meet this man. Juanito's an old man. Maybe it's Juanito's boss or someone he sent looking for us. Tell your brother not to meet with him. Please."

"What if my stupid brother doesn't listen to me? What if he thinks you're lying to me again? Why should I believe you now?"

"Molly, please. I am really sorry. Please forgive me." Another tear streaks down Turi's cheek. He can't take his eyes away from Molly's painful blue eyes. Perhaps something passes between the two of them. Something hard, but also something true. It seems as if Turi is about to hold her hand again, but he doesn't. He doesn't dare. "Molly . . ."

Molly looks around, desperate, as if struggling for air, looks away, not wanting to let her eyes settle on Turi or Arnulfo. Especially Turi. She notices that the man, perhaps the father of one of the families at the other end of the lot, is staring at them for a few seconds, watching this threesome as they sit together in serious, subdued conversation. From that distance, can he see the tears in their eyes? Is he about to come over? Molly forces a smile in the direction of the families at the other end of the lot, to keep them away. Soon enough the man turns to pick up one of the coolers on the pine-covered ground.

Arnulfo glares at both of them in disgust.

"Look at me, both of you, look at me right now," Molly says in a hushed, raw voice, like a bell sharply ringing near their faces, forcing them to pay attention. "Are you freakin' lying to me again? Right now, hey, look at me!"

"No, Molly. I'm sorry. We should never have lied to you. Please, we know that. I know that." Turi stares at the ground.

"No. Qué chingados estamos." Arnulfo glares at both of them.

"Turi, what the hell does that mean, 'sheen-gado sta-mos'?"

"It means, 'No, but we're all screwed.' No, we're not lying anymore. But we're in a mess."

"We are in a mess. I have to call my brother right now. This Juanito's an old man?"

"Yes, but I think he's a drug dealer or like a mule for the owner of the farm, this man who always wears a cowboy hat. He's the boss. He's Juanito's boss. Please, Molly, tell him not to meet with him, whoever he is."

It takes about an hour before Molly comes back from making her phone call. Turi and Arnulfo sit apart from each other, not one more item has been unloaded from the truck, and it looks as if they have had an argument, their faces red, stony. But it is done. Now they aren't talking to each other too much, yet they also have nowhere else to go. No one else who would take them. No one else who would want them. For the moment, all of them are stuck together.

"I told him, I begged him, but I'm not sure he'll listen to me. Jim thinks you're lyin' again, just tryin' to prevent your cousin from gettin' his truck back. He told me to report you to the police. If anything happens to him tomorrow, he told me to report you to the police."

"I told you this was a mistake, cabrón! Stupid güey!" Arnulfo glares at Turi.

"Let me guess, 'Stupid asshole?'"

"Molly, your brother can't meet with this guy, whoever he is. They're dangerous. They're narcos. Didn't you tell him that?" Turi says.

"My brother doesn't necessarily listen to me. He thinks both of you are liars. And yes, I told him you were tryin' to get away from this Juanito, told him who this Juanito was—told him what happened—and I warned Jim about gettin' mixed up with this drug dealer. But he thinks you're just lyin' again, watchin' too many movies, tryin' not to get caught. Are you?"

"Well, yes, no. We don't want to get caught by them. We got mixed up with the wrong people. Molly, that's the truth. But we're not like them. We're not. Let's just drive for one day, starting right now, through the night, get to Connecticut, and get rid of this truck. We get rid of it, maybe we tell them where it is, some way they can't find us. A secret letter or something. We get rid of the truck far away from us, so they can find their truck but they can't find us. They'll leave us alone." Turi searches Molly's face for a response.

"That's just it. That's the problem. That's what I've been thinkin' about. Whether I should even get in the truck with both of you anymore, and if I do, what we do then, what we do in Connecticut, or wherever we end up. This thing needs to be far away from us, that I know. After we use it, this thing can't bring them back to us."

"But you've been telling them where we are, haven't you? You tell your brother? Has he told them?" Arnulfo yells at both of them, finally bursting with anger. "And you're thinking whether *you* should get in the truck? This ruca has fucked us, Turi, don't you see?"

"I don't know what my brother has said to them. I hope he hasn't told them much, or anything at all . . . I won't—"

"So why is he meeting with them tomorrow? Turi, say something! Stop taking her side all the time! She's the one leading them to us! I told you it was a mistake bringing her! I told you! We're going to end up dead because of her!"

Molly's face is bright red. After glancing at her, Turi can only look down at the ground.

"I won't tell my brother anything else about where we are. I'm sorry too. I think—I think, Arnulfo's right . . . I'm at fault too."

"Look, I hope your brother's okay," Turi finally says.

"Yes . . . and I hope my brother's okay tomorrow. Thank you, Turi. 'Stupid gway!' Is that the right way to say it?"

"Yes, that's it," Turi whispers, his eyes lowered to his feet again, as if he's descending in an abyss. A wave of shame and anger and despair engulfs him.

"I wasn't calling *you* an asshole, I was callin' my thick-headed brother an asshole."

Turi's eyes plead with her. "It's okay. I know. I deserve it anyway."

"Jim doesn't listen to anybody, not even his Corina."

Arnulfo glares at them one more time. "Pinche pendejos. Come on, let's get out of here!"

CHAPTER SIXTEEN

Jim Crump arrives at the China King thirty minutes early before meeting with Victor Huerta. He sits in the front, near the windows facing the strip mall parking lot so he can check everyone entering or exiting the access road on Route 8, which runs parallel to I-44. The China King is less than five minutes from his work at the St. James Winery. Jim has already seen a few workers from Redtec arrive, including Manuel Aguirre, his crew chief. Manuel waved at him, and Jim nodded the most imperceptible of nods. Why should he be friendly toward Manuel? So what if Manuel has taught him how to install extra electrical sockets after demo and how to perfectly apply grout to new tile? Jim doesn't exactly trust him. Moreover, it strikes Jim as weak that Manuel will still smile at him even as Jim constantly remains cold in return. What exactly does that man want from Jim? Amid the bustle of the China King, Manuel's clueless smile is in Jim's face again, with those two broken teeth and dark brown skin, as if mocking him.

Why has he agreed to meet with this Victor Huerta in the first place? What if Molly isn't lying and this guy is connected to drug dealing? Jim knows those two with Molly are up to no good, and maybe they made up the "drug dealer" story to prevent their cousin from getting his truck back. Jim knew that wasn't their truck as soon as he saw Molly's photo. He has been right all along. He has followed his instincts, Jim thinks, and has never trusted those teenagers. Victor . . . Molly's dorky friends . . . nobody. "Liars, all of 'em," he mutters to himself as his wontons arrive. The waitress smiles at him as she also leaves a cold glass of water.

Jim has warned Molly to get away from her friends, and if she is too stupid to get out of that truck and avoid trouble . . . well . . . that's on her. Jim has tried to protect her, but Molly listens to nobody but herself. He will tell this Victor the little he knows about the blue truck, where it probably is and where it is headed. He will keep his sister Molly out of it—it's not her fault she hitched a ride with two liars—and maybe that will still give her a couple of days to come to her senses. He will have a quick conversation with this Victor. He will leave and make sure he isn't followed. He will walk around to the back of the China King, get in the maroon Impala, and be done with this business once and for all. That is Jim's plan. He will help this Victor get back his truck and nail his thieving cousins, and that will be that. Jim fidgets in his seat.

"You Jim Crump?" Jim hears above him, from a hulking giant in cowboy boots standing next to the window and blocking half the light.

"Yeah, that's me." Jim tries to make out the face in the painfully white backlight, but manages only to tug at his black Metallica T-shirt. He wrote in his latest email he would be wearing that T-shirt at the China King. "Sit down. Can't stay long. Let me give you the info."

"So you saw my motherfucking cousins where exactly? Here?" Victor barks in a too-loud baritone that turns a few heads toward them at the China King. As Jim's eyes adjust to the light and Victor settles into the seat in front of him, Jim takes the stranger in: the man is thick limbed and massive, like the great Tongan rugby player Jonah Lomu from New Zealand. For once, Jim feels small in front of another man—their table a puny square that rocks unsteadily between them as Victor drops his elbows onto its surface. The face, that's what Jim will remember most of all. In an episode of *The Simpsons*, Bart once pries open a crate with a giant Olmec head in it, and that's what Victor's face looks like, square and stonelike, dark, eyes bulging from their sockets, a thick scar across one cheek, and the hair gleaming with sweat. Beyond a scowl, the face possesses an eerie, lifeless calm. The black eyes bore into Jim.

"No, not here. And I actually didn't see them. My sister did. I saw a photo of them in the forest. Not far from here. In the mountains." *Why am I stammering?* Jim thinks to himself. A few patrons at the China King stare, or try not to stare, at Victor and the wolves and what looks like a doll's head tattooed on his preposterous arm muscles.

"You saw them or you saw them in a photo?" Victor snaps, not quite angry but impatient. The massive torso of the giant radiates a latent, ready-to-explode energy.

"I saw them in a photo. My—my sister met them. I guess they were camping for two days, not far from here. They said they were going east. My sister hitched a ride with them." Immediately Jim feels as if he should've never mentioned his sister to Victor. But it's too late.

"Why the hell she take their photo?" Victor ignores the bustle of the restaurant and keeps his eyes on Jim.

"I don't know. She just sent me the photo. I noticed their nice truck in the photo."

"I want my damn truck. East? Where exactly?" Victor says loudly enough to turn the head of a customer walking past them. His black eyes stare unwaveringly at Jim. Their waitress stops at the table, glances behind the bar nervously, and asks Victor if he wants anything. "No, thanks, don't want anything. Just water." Victor waves the waitress away with an arm that swipes heavily through the air like a giant meat hook.

"Connecticut, they said. Last I heard they were in Pennsylvania. Sorry they stole your truck. My sister has nothing to do with it. She didn't even know your truck was stolen when they offered her a ride in Missouri. Just trying to help you. I knew they had probably stolen it. I imagined they did. Once I saw the photo."

"So your sister's been telling you where they are?"

"Well, she was. But once I told her the truck was stolen, she left them in Pennsylvania. She's not with them anymore." Jim tries to stare back at Victor, but Jim grabs his glass of water instead. He swallows hard.

"What's your sister's cell phone?"

"I told you, she's not with them anymore. She has nothing to do with it. But they were driving to Connecticut apparently. Two guys. 'Too-bee' and I think something like 'Ari-nulfo.' Strange names."

"Yeah, those are my cousins. Turi and Arnulfo. Sons of bitches. Wait 'til I get my hands on 'em. Where in Connecticut, they say?" Victor clenches a massive fist on the table.

"Just Connecticut. That's all my sister heard before she left them. Don't think they knew exactly where. Just east. To Connecticut. That's all we know." Behind the bar, Jim catches a waitress, not their waitress, staring at their table, at their feet, strangely. That's the moment when he notices Victor's steel-tipped black boots.

"How'd the truck look? Hope they didn't mess up my truck."

"It looked fine. Brand new, or almost brand new. It didn't make sense those two boys owned that nice truck. That's what I always thought as soon as I saw the photo."

"Little assholes."

"Why not just call the police? Teach 'em a lesson? I mean, why drive across the entire country to get 'em yourself?"

"I'm gonna fuck them up when I find them, that's why." Victor stares at Jim for what seems many long minutes, a stare that doesn't waver from Jim's eyes, that seems like a warning not to move, not to call the police, not to flinch a finger. "My stupid family also doesn't want them in jail. I don't want my truck impounded forever by the goddamn cops. I just want to find them." The waitress leaves the check on the table and hurriedly walks away.

"They're probably in Connecticut by now. That's all I know," Jim says, not moving his face, trying to mirror the stoic in front of him. But one thought is replaying in his head. *What if Molly is right and this Victor is a drug dealer?* He can't give him any more information. He should've never even mentioned Molly.

"You live around here?" Victor says. He shifts forward in his chair and grips the table with both hands as if he is about to lunge at Jim.

"Yes, in St. James," Jim lies. He glances at the empty wonton tray.

"And no one else was with them?"

"That's all I know, man. Again, I'm sorry about your truck. Just trying to help." Jim fumbles with his wallet and takes out enough money to cover his bill and a tip. Without missing a step, the waitress strides by, swipes the cash and bill, and never looks either of them in the eye. Jim immediately stands up, ready to leave and escape Victor's black eyes, which seem to be drilling right into his soul, through the privacy of his silence, as if any secret in time will be revealed to Victor whether Jim wants it to or not.

"Wait a minute, one last thing. How long ago? When'd your sister get a ride with them?" Victor is still sitting down, not moving except for the slightest tip to his massive Olmec head. In slow motion, a sinister grin that isn't really a grin forms on Victor's thick lips, as if a lion has broken through brush and discovered a gazelle trapped in mud. For the first time, Victor surveys the patrons around him, and the few who were looking his way quickly turn their heads away from his eyes.

"Two or three days ago. More or less. I hope you find your truck, man. I'd call the police. That's better than just driving around half the country trying to find your cousins."

"Thanks."

As Jim pushes through the double doors of the China King, he feels the need to go to the restroom, but he ignores it. He marches around the corner, eager to leave. Jim glances back for a second or two, sure that his paranoia about being followed is just that, crazy feelings. His legs keep moving quickly, pumping harder around the back of the restaurant. It's daylight outside, a few cars are coming or going in the parking lot, but the area is nearly deserted. The hair on the back of his neck stands up, and he feels a sudden shiver ripple through his body like an electric shock. For some reason, the St. James Winery, Steelville's water tower, Corina with the baby as she cooks dinner in their home, all of these images flash in his head: what he wants to return to, what he should never have left.

Jim looks at the sky, imagining a plane with everything he loves crashing in the horizon in front of him. He shakes his head clear, scans the area around him again. Nothing is there. He jogs to the Impala, which is next to a dumpster in the far back of the restaurant's parking lot. As another shiver climbs up his back, Jim climbs in, but the car won't turn over. It is dead, with not even a whine as he turns the key.

"What the hell," he says to interrupt the eerie silence. He calms himself down. Jim climbs out and pops the hood, and that's when he sees it: the two cables to the battery have been pulled off their posts. *The China King*, he thinks. *Not possible. How early . . . ?* "What the—"

For a half a second, Jim thinks he glimpses a moving shadow, one beyond the hood's darkness at his feet, a shadow behind him, when a massive hand grabs his hair and slams his face onto the radiator of the car. "Hey, hey, hey . . . ?" Jim collapses, stunned, and vaguely sees the cowboy boots at his feet. Blood gushes across his face. The shadow again whisks around him, grabs his hair again, and slams his face into the Impala's bumper a few feet from his eyes. Bright lights flash in front of Jim's eyes. A kick from nowhere smashes so hard into his ribs that Jim gasps, inhaling deeply, trying to find his lungs, inhaling and unable to take in air. A heavy cowboy boot suddenly is in his face and presses across his neck like a giant log. His blinking eyes in the sun, in and out of the shadows of the Impala's hood, Jim lies on the asphalt and can see only a vague outline through his tears and blood: the Olmec head.

"I don't have your damn truck," Jim gasps, suddenly his voice lost, his neck compressed, his chest heaving in spasms, trying to inhale any air amid these shadows and flashes of sun.

"What's your sister's cell phone number, motherfucker?"

"I—I can't . . . she has nothing to do with it. They were going to Connecticut. That's what your freakin' cousins said. That's what she told me. What the hell, what the hell, man . . ." Jim is in and out of consciousness, his head pulsing. But he is still there. He flails his arms and swings them at the air, hitting what seems like a tree stump next to his face.

For a moment—when he thinks it is over, this attack, the boot still jammed against his neck, his lungs on fire and not working, his head feeling as if dunked under water—a hand like a fleshy vice grip grabs his wrist. Another hand grabs a finger. Jim tries yanking his hand away, kicking and squirming. But he hears only the sickening sound of his finger snapping back like a broken twig. His chest and throat lurch with vomit, a white-hot pain explodes through his hand and wrist and up his arm. His heart jumps out of his chest. He hears himself scream, as if someone else is shrieking in agony. Jim can't see this, but an impassive brown face, like a face carved into a tree, stares at him.

"I'll ask you one more time, hijo de puta. Then another finger. Her number! She still with them?"

"No. Connecticut. Son of a bitch! You goddamn son of a bitch! Please, my god. She has nothing—"

"Her number!"

"No, goddammit! Don't, don't know where your cousins are! I don't know—she doesn't know, my god . . . You son of a bitch!"

A savage punch hits Jim's face, and it feels like a cinder block has been smashed against his skull. Jim kicks feebly and struggles to get off the ground. Blood covers his eyes. His consciousness seems to float just beyond him. Another punch almost knocks him out. Shadows and stars are everywhere. Jim thinks he sees the wheel of the Impala a few inches from his face, what he thinks is the wheel. The world spins. One hand throbs with a pain so intense it feels alive and wild and voracious for its own flesh.

"Her number, damn it! Where in Connecticut?"

Jim feels his other hand being gripped, the one with the broken finger dropping to the ground, throbbing, useless, like a piece of dead meat that has stopped responding to anything but a tiny sun embedded in his flesh and burning through it. Jim coughs and gasps. Blood trickles from his mouth.

His eyes can't focus, his mind in and out of consciousness. But he can feel his one good hand immobile, gripped awfully, inescapably, as if Jim were feeling an animal's maw latched to the stump of his hand, without remorse, without reason, that brute force advancing, attacking. He is there and not there anymore.

Jim is halfway under the Impala, trying to crawl underneath to escape the blows. But Victor has dragged him out, has him by the one hand. In his massive brown hand, the Olmec separates the finger he wants, the middle one next to the index finger. He smashes a boot heel into Jim's stomach without releasing the grip on the hand. Victor's face is still a monolith as he's about to break another finger. A sudden whoosh seems to come from behind both of them, a powerful sucking of air. Jim remembers his hand being yanked away with such a force that his shoulder was dislocated. But it isn't Victor who has yanked the hand away. Tires spinning not far from both of them. A blur. The roar of a motor. Victor is there one moment, and gone the next. Gravel and dust fly across the asphalt in a cloud. Jim regains a vague consciousness; his shoulder hurts but his good hand is free. A thud— Jim remembers a horrible, sickening thud—and Victor flying through the air like a giant rag doll, screaming.

Across the parking lot and noticing the commotion and making some sense of it all, Manuel Aguirre has come roaring in his ratty yellow Ford pickup and sideswiped Victor, propelling the Olmec twenty feet in the air and onto the black asphalt. Victor writhes on the ground for a few seconds and stops moving, with what later Jim will learn are a concussion, a broken leg, bruises, and scratches. Manuel jumps out of his truck and screams at other Redtec workers, who look at Manuel as if he were the maniac who started the bloodshed behind the China King. Manuel helps Jim to his feet, who keeps feebly swinging at him and babbling nonsense about "Connecticut" and "she has nothing to do with it," as blood and vomit pour from his mouth. His right hand is swollen and sickeningly blue-red. Manuel wraps his thick brown arm around Jim's torso and holds him up, even as Jim keeps struggling to get away, still in a daze and wild-eyed. Manuel never takes his eyes off the unconscious giant on the asphalt, as still as fresh road kill.

Jim is taken to the hospital in an ambulance, groggy and in pain. Later the nurses will hear Jim mutter in the night, "Goddamn thieves . . . lunatics." He is heavily sedated and in his painkiller fog keeps remembering only the tires of Manuel's truck missing his face on the ground by what he thinks were inches, but actually was closer to two feet. He will lurch forward in his hospital bed for no reason.

The police interview and arrest Manuel Aguirre for assault with a motor vehicle. The authorities find out he is an undocumented worker at St. James Winery who may or may not have known Jim Crump. Manuel is sent to a detention facility for prosecution and will eventually be deported.

The six o'clock news reports that the other man on the ground, the one hit with the truck at the China King, will walk again. He is also being questioned by the police. Some at the parking lot report to the police that this man may have been helping Jim with his car. Others say he was hitting Jim for no good reason. Still others claim that they saw them together at the China King moments before the mayhem in the parking lot, before the short and stocky Manuel—whom no one has ever seen do anything but smile his stupid, shy grin—leaped into his yellow truck and gunned it across the black asphalt. Everybody at the restaurant remembers the steel-tipped boots, unusual for a man in Missouri.

The news further reports that the big man with the broken leg, well, he is from Italy apparently—or also Mexican but with an Italian passport—only a rental car in his name, and his identification not yet confirmed. Why he was talking to Jim Crump, well, one can only speculate, and reporters are waiting for an interview with the manager of the St. James Winery . . .

CHAPTER SEVENTEEN

Sometime around two in the morning, Don Ilan is alone as he walks the shores near Barra de Tecoanapa in Guerrero. In public, day or night, he wears a mask, this time el Blue Demon. The sparkly blue glints in the moonlight, but the silver highlights around the eyes and mouth are what evoke a ghostly, disembodied face in the night. Two of his men have descended the villa with him, but they know on these middle-of-the-night excursions never to come within thirty yards of him, never to interrupt his phone calls as he stares at the Pacific Ocean, never to disturb him in any way. Knowing it is Don Ilan, the boss, keeps them away, but his masks are always what unnerves them. His personal bodyguards are to remain alert and ready and as silent as they can be. Like dark, frightened angels watching over him under the stars. If he sits three hours on the shore at night, they sit three hours on the shore with him. Don Ilan fingers the new scar on his neck and even the bloody scratch hidden underneath the mask and across his face. For her last day on earth, he allowed her to see his face glistening with sweat. Tonight has been a bad night. *Vieja cabróna*, he thinks to distract himself from his real problem. *She was delicious, a true artist at her gorgeous peak. No se dejó. Fought with her eyes open, until she couldn't. At least she will know my face in eternity.*

But that is not what has truly kept Don Ilan from sleeping. El Tapado called him just after Don Ilan thought his night had ended in bliss. It was a brief call in which el Tapado demanded to know about his precious shipment to Kansas City, when it would be arriving, what the delay was. El Tapado was one of the few people who could be blunt with Don Ilan, and el Tapado was indeed blunt: "If I don't get the shipment soon, Ilan, you need to provide a substitute. I don't care how you get it. From Pushchino, Changsha, or Siberia. That's your responsibility and you know it. No more payments on any items, including this one, until this item is delivered. We discussed how important it was. You agreed to do it. You have been paid a significant amount of the money already." When Don Ilan protested that these blood samples, with Marburg-B, were impossible to find, and next to impossible to ship overseas, and how months of planning had been necessary to get that product across so many borders, el Tapado cut him off. "Replacements or the original product in one week. We are businessmen. Even your distributor Dunbar is a businessman, although I like him less and less every day. And I have, as you know, unlimited resources and an army of followers. So let's not get into threats or anything so nasty. That's beneath both of us. *One week.*" When Don Ilan's encrypted cell phone cut off, he left the bedroom, showered, abandoned the shelter of the villa, and sat down next to the waves, appreciating their relentless force, imagining their casual brutality against sand and rocks, knowing how water would wear out and destroy even the most jagged coast, with time.

His cell phone rings.

"Don Ilan, it's Victor."

"My friend. Where the hell are you? I was thinking of calling you for a report on our errand. This problem is getting worse."

"In Missouri, Señor. In a hospital, but I'm about to get out."

"Qué chingada? Missouri?"

"I met a man who was in contact with the two boys."

Don Ilan deeply exhales and stares at the sea. Perhaps this is the news he has been waiting for. "Go on."

"They're going to Connecticut, Señor. I don't know what city. This man had contact with them in Missouri. Briefly. That's what he told me. As I was trying to get more details, ya sabes Señor, and he wasn't being cooperative, otro cabrón hit me with a truck. Broke my leg. Knocked me unconscious. The police have interviewed me. I'm getting out of the St. James hospital tomorrow morning. Before more questions are asked."

"Victor. Connecticut. Are you sure?"

"Yes, Don Ilan."

"Come back to Chilpancingo. Let me see what I can do with this information."

"Con todo mi respeto . . . no, Señor. I want to finish the job. I can walk more or less. My face is scratched and one side of my body has an asphalt burn. But they just set my leg in yeso. I have crutches."

"You are a soldier, Victor. El verdadero Hijo de Huerta."

"I'll report back as soon as I get to Connecticut."

Don Ilan hangs up the phone. The scratch underneath his mask itches terribly. If he scratches it, he will bleed again through the blue fabric.

He stares at the moonlight dancing on the waves as the surf crashes a few feet from his legs. This night has been a wave of good news, followed by one of bad news, followed yet again by another with some (possibly good) news. But what will el Hijo be able to accomplish in his condition and how long will it take him, especially without knowing what city in Connecticut? *We can never allow our deep admiration for a Wild Beast to cloud our judgment, even a wounded one,* Don Ilan thinks.

The cell phone is in his hands, and it feels like it's burning its shape into his palm. Because Don Ilan knows what he must do. Because he doesn't want to do what he must do. The starlight dances on the waves, but now these lights seem like tiny needles jabbing at his eyes, penetrating his skull, torturing him. He knows what he must do.

No es nada, ese pinche Dunbar. The hell with him. He works for me! He thinks being on that side of the wall can protect him. What a mistake! Those gringos have been thinking that for centuries! He will ask questions, I know. He will probe, and I will say nothing, but he will figure it out anyway. That's who he is. Too much like me. Que se vaya a la chingada!

Don Ilan knows that nothing, even his anger, can stand in the way of their common purpose: satisfy el Tapado's request immediately, at all costs. He picks up the phone.

On the line, Don Ilan hears the phone ring. He hears breathing, a thump, and then, "Just one minute, Don Ilan." After the sound of a door locking, he hears after another long minute, "I'm here."

"I have news."

"Yes?"

"John, I have news about the truck. It's going to Connecticut," Don Ilan says, closing his eyes to avoid the starlight, to shut out the world, to retreat deeper behind his mask, to concentrate. Even the warm breeze from the beach now disturbs him.

"How—"

"John, it's going to Connecticut. That's all I will say." Don Ilan hears a shift of the phone, from one hand to the other, what sounds like a ring on a on the phone's plastic.

"Connecticut," Dunbar repeats softly, without conviction, perhaps with a sigh. At least that's what Don Ilan thinks he hears over the encrypted international phone line. "And you know this for a fact?"

"Let's stop playing games. We have a common purpose. El Tapado wants his product and wants it now. In a week or less. Period. I would never lie to you, John." His eyes closed, Don Ilan smiles to himself.

There is a long silence on the other side of the line. "I'll get my men there right away."

"Exactly," Don Ilan says, still smirking in the moonlight.

"I want what you want, Don Ilan. You understand that?"

"I do. That's exactly why I shared this important information with you. To satisfy el Tapado and move on from our situation."

"And you don't think I should know how you got this information?" Dunbar says on the phone line. Don Ilan frowns in silence again, in his head repeating the sound and sensibility of the tone of this last overheard sentence, before responding. Dunbar continues: "It doesn't matter."

"It's Connecticut, John. Do what you must do." Don Ilan clicks off the power of his cell phone and stares again at the waves now washing up to his toes.

Tomorrow morning he will make sure his spy in Clint keeps him informed about what Dunbar actually does. *Sometimes*—Don Ilan thinks as he shakes the sand from his sandals—*information is more valuable than anything we move across the border.*

As Don Ilan stands in the wet sand, he can see his dark angels stand too, in his peripheral vision. They follow him as he climbs the steps to the villa. After he closes the glass door that he often uses to step outside to the beach, he hears the low voices of his men as they ask each other questions, or decide to get replacements so that they can get some food. He takes off his mask and applies more ointment to the nasty scratch. Don Ilan hears his men's faint footsteps on the parapet of the roof, and he imagines that they are mice, murmuring mice, out to protect him. The opposite of Wild Beasts. At least these sounds and imaginations in his head help him to create that nighttime fantasy he needs to close his eyes and finally relax for the night. But it is the cool air on his face that soothes him to sleep.

After Dunbar hangs up the phone, he looks around at his darkened study in Clint, Texas. The desert moon glimmers through one of the barred windows, and all is quiet. The two-feet thick adobe walls capture a silence he has never experienced anywhere else in his life. The silence of a fortress. *El Hijo is on this side already, and perhaps others are with him. I do not have much time. My contacts in Chilpancingo have failed me.* He and Don Ilan do have a common purpose, but as always, once el Tapado receives his product and unleashes chaos, Dunbar will plan to take advantage of the chaos, just as Don Ilan is planning right now. Their endless chess game to survive and to free themselves of the other.

Dunbar thinks: *All the preparations for the zero hour must be finished—the fortifications, the electric monitors are particularly important. The food supplies in the warehouse. For those who will remain here. And Costa Rica. Perhaps one call in the morning to my friends in Chilpancingo to see if they have more information from Don Ilan's men. Let's give them a last chance to redeem themselves and see if they can be of any use to me anymore.*

Did el Hijo, or whoever gave Don Ilan the information, tell him and the Guerrero group everything? Connecticut? I need to know everything, goddammit!

I'll send Chucho, Eduardo, and Juanito—those three Mexican musketeers—to our friends in Hartford to wait for my next move. That's where the truck will be, somewhere nearby, if that bastard Don Ilan is not lying to me. But why would he lie? He didn't want to call me. That was clear. He had to call me. Don Ilan had no choice. We're attached to each other like two scorpions with their claws interlocked. Only when el Tapado unleashes chaos will one of us be able to deliver a death blow. And if I catch those goddamn kids with the blue truck in Connecticut . . .

El güero stands in his study and looks at the semidarkness and grabs his cell phone again. He dials Chucho, who is half asleep and tells him they are somewhere near Oklahoma City. Dunbar can hear Juanito in the background, but not Eduardo. "Get to Hartford, Connecticut. That's where it will be. Somewhere near there. Get there as soon as you can. Twenty-four hours. Drive all night if you have to. I'll call you later with more instructions. I'll know soon enough where that truck is. Then I'll let you know. You know who to contact in Hartford? Yes. That's right. Exactly. Call me when you get there."

Dunbar looks out the window into the darkness. Outside swirls of dust are in the air, reaching toward the moon like ghosts. He searches for a file— deep inside his metal cabinet where he keeps such items as his will, house insurance, titles of properties. One bright yellow file contains Anna's and Hugo's school reports, report cards, his daughter's meticulous drawings of horses and a cowboy (supposedly "Daddy") on a horse with a Miró-like sunset and weird geometric shapes floating in the background. Dunbar's firstborn, Hugo, ten years old, has never been as creative or as intelligent as little Anna. Another file contains twenty-year-old photos of Mrs. John Broaddus Dunbar, aka María Carolina Terrazas Zaragoza of Chihuahua City, Chihuahua, a radiant debutante. Finally there is the folder he is looking for. Dunbar stares at the documents for a moment and reviews the thoughts in his head. *Yes, that's the only way.* Tomorrow morning, as soon as the office opens, he will pick up his regular phone, what he uses to order farm equipment and chicken cages, and dial a number in El Paso.

This is what he will say: "Yes sir. My truck's been stolen. I was on a business trip. Came back. My truck's gone. Yes sir. Texas plates. I've got the VIN right here . . . ." As Dunbar will wait to get connected, he will think about cities in Connecticut, the ones he knows, Hartford, Stamford, New Haven. Those will be next. The police departments in every single one of them. Connecticut state troopers. With a good story about why he thinks his truck will be in Connecticut. How to contact him. Photos of the truck. That desperation mixed with hope in his voice, which will not be too hard for him: it *is* his goddamn truck. Anything these flunkies find, if they ever bother to find it hidden in the door after impounding it, well, that will be the responsibility of those Mexican kids who stole the truck for their evil purposes—that will be whatever nefarious connections they have in Juárez or even deeper in Mexico. He is just a businessman, a chicken farmer, a husband and a father, from the great state of Texas. Six generations of his family have lived and died on the United States–Mexico border. One ancestor even succumbed at the Alamo.

CHAPTER EIGHTEEN

"A McDonald's parking lot? No, this is *not* what I'm thinking about when I'm thinking about Connecticut. What city is this again?"

"Danbury, Connecticut," Molly says. "Let's go have a cup of coffee—I don't want to eat here—and then we can decide what to do." She jumps out before getting an answer from Turi and Arnulfo.

"We need to get rid of this truck," Arnulfo says quietly to himself as Turi slides out and follows her.

They can all see the navy blue double-cab Ford pickup through the wall of windows from their booth at McDonald's. Turi and Molly sip their coffees, and Arnulfo drinks a Coke.

"So when you say 'Connecticut,' what did you expect?"

"Molly, I can get McDonald's anywhere. I wouldn't have left El Paso if I was looking for stupid McDonald's. Come on!"

"Okay, so I'm trying to understand what you mean, why you wanted to go to 'Connecticut.' We're here, aren't we? I mean, I don't have a problem with it, I'm just trying to understand what you're looking for."

"It's hard to explain. Not sure I understand it. It's something in my head."

"Ese, it does look greener than El Paso," Arnulfo interrupts. "I'm sure I'll find work here. But we need to get rid of this truck." One of Arnulfo's legs is bouncing up and down underneath the table, like a piston, which causes the table to tremble. He keeps looking out the window at their blue truck.

"Is that what you mean, Turi? Greener? Think it gets cold around here in the winter. You have a thing for snow?" Molly leans on the table, closer to Turi, her cerulean eyes, clear as the sky, locked on his. She is wearing her blond hair pulled back in a ponytail, which Turi finds adorable.

"No, I don't have a thing for snow. But snow's okay. It'd be different from El Paso, that's for sure. I saw pictures once . . . and movies. It's kind of embarrassing."

"Movies? What movies?"

"You're gonna laugh. It's stupid, really." Turi's chestnut eyes scan the restaurant briefly and come back to Molly. He shifts in his chair.

"Come on, we're friends, aren't we? Aren't we, Arnie?" Molly turns to Arnulfo for a second, a slight smile on her face. Again she focuses on Turi.

Arnulfo shakes his head at both of them. He looks at the truck again. He can't keep his eyes off it for more than a few seconds.

"'A Charlie Brown Christmas.' Also another one called 'A Charlie Brown Thanksgiving.' That's the one I liked most. It's stupid, I know."

"You mean," Arnulfo says, "that big-headed kid, the cartoon?" He snickers. Arnulfo looks again at the truck through the window. "Este güey."

"Charlie Brown. Yes. Okay. Happy?" Turi says, feeling embarrassed.

"I liked Lucy. She was always my favorite," Molly says with the biggest of grins on her face. Turi wonders if she is also teasing him. "But why Connecticut? Were the cartoons set in Connecticut?" Arnulfo shifts in his seat and frowns at both of them, exasperated by the conversation. Molly smiles warmly at Turi—he decides she isn't teasing him—and scans his face and shoulders, as if she is seeing him for the first time.

"No—it's embarrassing, I'm not sure—I don't think so. Just watching them, these kids, with backyards, playing baseball. I liked it. I saw 'A Charlie Brown Thanksgiving,' and something about the leaves, and playing in the leaves, it reminded me of being outside, having a place where I could be happy. I imagined crisp, cold air and leaves. The seasons. I guess that was it. The seasons, and being outside with all that color. The opposite of El Paso. But I like the El Paso desert. I just didn't like where I lived. I wanted to find a new home." Turi looks around, looks everywhere, looks at Molly as if sneaking a peek through the corner of his eyes, yet she is sitting in front of him. He is thinking: *Why have I told her what I've never told anyone else?*

"But those cartoons are sometimes sad," Molly says. "Charlie Brown's always kinda lonely. I mean, those specials are sweet in a way, but Charlie Brown is always . . . well, an outsider. Alone."

"Well, maybe. But after I saw the specials, I asked Mrs. Garcia about them, about the leaves, about where—what kind of place would be like that. She gave me a big book about New England, with photographs of churches with white *white* steeples. I mean, these things looked like needles poking into the blue sky. Mountainsides full of color in October. Wooden bridges, rivers, forests, and pumpkins. The stupid pumpkins reminded me of Charlie Brown's head, and the Halloween special, the Great Pumpkin, the one Linus thinks is a god. I always thought that was so funny. My favorite photos were from Connecticut. Just so beautiful. I thought, maybe, I could be happy there . . . here. But not at a McDonald's in Danbury. It's Connecticut, but not what I mean."

"Okay. Maybe I get it. Well . . . we need to find this 'Connecticut.' Your Connecticut."

"Really, you mean that? I hope this isn't a joke, Molly." Turi finally meets Molly's stare and faces her without fidgeting.

"Look at me, Turi, do I look like I'm I joking? I'm not." Molly stares back at him with fierce blue eyes, and Turi thinks he will melt if he looks away and he will melt if he doesn't. So they keep their eyes on each other.

"Both of you are crazy! We need to get rid of this truck. We need to get going. Connecticut's okay, but have you two forgotten who's after us? Those narcos will never stop!" Arnulfo turns nervously around to look at others in the restaurant to see if anyone else heard him.

Turi and Molly ignore Arnulfo for a moment. No one says anything while all of them scan the restaurant for a few seconds.

"Molly, I'm sorry I lied to you. I think it's the worst thing I ever did. Hope you'll forgive me."

"I have. Kinda. Just don't do it again. I'd rather you leave me alone, I'd rather you leave me at a crappy McDonald's, if you're gonna to do that again."

"I won't. I promise."

"Don't know anybody here either. I'm startin' from scratch too. I know you guys. Let's find this 'Connecticut' together. Whatever it is, wherever it is. That's where I wanna be too."

"Okay, it's a deal."

With a scowl, Arnulfo studies them as if they were visitors from another planet, beyond puzzled and impatient, trying to understand what is happening and what they are saying. A cold look lingers on his face as he stares at Molly, as if blaming her for something he cannot quite name.

"Molly—"

She stands up abruptly and marches to the wall of booths at the opposite side of the McDonald's and starts chatting with a middle-aged couple reading newspapers and having coffee. Turi and Arnulfo are dumbfounded. What is she doing? Arnulfo glares at Turi as if demanding an answer. They hear laughter and thank-yous, and the man points outside, toward the freeway while apparently giving her directions. Molly walks back to them, grinning, with a magazine in her hand. "Why not ask the locals, right?"

As she slides into their booth again, she drops a copy of *Yankee Magazine* in the middle of the table.

"What's this for? What—"

"Route 7 North. That's where they said we should go. Goes right through Danbury. Takes you to the most beautiful places in Connecticut. Look at the magazine, guys, come on!"

Turi picks it up and reads the cover article from last year: "The Best Towns for Fall Foliage." It focuses on a place called the Litchfield Hills, and towns with names like New Milford, Kent, Cornwall, Warren, Washington Depot, Goshen . . .

"A magazine is gonna tell us where to go?"

"You have any better ideas, 'Nulfo? This is actually pretty good. Look at these pictures. Wow. Reminds me of the book Mrs. Garcia showed me. Molly, gosh, thank you. La Molly Milagrosa."

"They're a very nice couple. Oh, here they come." The man jams a baseball hat on his head as he wends his big body through the tables and chairs.

"You all from Missouri too?" the man says, his wife standing behind him, to one side. His temples are gray, and wiry gray hairs protrude from his hat. A pouty, harrumph-like frown rests between his rosy cheeks.

"Mike, let's go."

He ignores his wife behind him, staring intently at the two teenage boys, waiting for an answer.

"We're from Texas," Turi says, forcing a smile, trying to douse the blue fire he sees in the man's eyes.

"What part of Texas? Him too?" The man looms over the table, taking a step toward them.

"El Paso. We're both from El Paso." Turi has stopped smiling and looks blankly at Molly in front of him, trying to gauge what she is thinking, and at Arnulfo, whose eyes seem cold and knowing.

"Bet you are. That's basically in Mexico, isn't it? Why don't you boys go back to where you came from?"

"Excuse me?" Molly says sharply.

Puzzled shock blooms across Turi's face. He leans back against the hard plastic seat as if absorbing an invisible blow. Arnulfo's leg suddenly stops pumping underneath the table.

"Missy, if I knew you'd be giving *them* the magazine, if I knew you were with *them*, I would have kept it. Stay with your own, goddammit."

Before anyone can open their mouths, before anyone can respond, the man and the woman march toward the glass doors, which swing shut behind them a second later. Turi watches the older couple lower themselves awkwardly into a metallic grey sedan, not saying a word to each other, while Molly stares at Turi and Arnulfo, who scan the restaurant again, empty except for a few people in the food line. Nobody has turned to look at them. Nobody is paying them any mind. Turi thinks about the sound of his voice in English in Connecticut, that stilted border accent he never realized he had in El Paso, the dark caramel complexion of his skin when compared to Molly's glowing, light tan and to the faces of the other diners. Turi examines Arnulfo, who looks like a brawny Tarahumara Indian compared to him. Turi remembers this strange feeling repeated throughout his life: who he thinks he is in his mind is sometimes not who others see or imagine he can be. This gap never seems to go away. Sometimes this secret self is comforting, for its privacy. Sometimes it is amusing, when he witnesses what crazy assumptions others have of him. Too often this gap is dispiriting, a prison inside of him without any means of escape.

"Stupid, fat idiot. I should've said something, I'm sorry—"

"Molly, come on. It's not your fault. How would you know what he was gonna do?"

"It is her fault, ese. She went to talk to them. She's not Mexican. She doesn't understand."

"What the hell does that mean?" Turi glares at Arnulfo, and for the first time during the trip wishes 'Nulfo were not with them.

Molly glances between Turi and Arnulfo nervously.

"She doesn't know what it's like, how people see us, especially los güeros. Maybe not all of them, but enough—enough to make it dangerous for us."

"You think it's better to hide? Not say anything? Not try anything?" Turi says, not wanting to stop this argument, both forearms on the table, glaring at the squat Arnulfo in front of him, as if ready to pounce on him.

"Yes, for me. It's better for me."

"Guys, let's—"

"Molly, wait please. This is important. 'Nulfo, it's not better."

"Because you're an Americano, Turi. That's why you think that way. You don't care if you attract attention or get into a fight. You don't have too much to lose. I do. Imagine the cops—"

"The cops? Who's calling the cops, by the way? And you think the police are gonna treat me better because I'm brown but American?"

"That guy was just a racist asshole," Molly says to both of them.

Silence. Arnulfo looks out the window. The couple has indeed driven away. Their blue truck is still there.

"I don't even want to look at the stupid magazine anymore," Molly says quickly into the silence. "Who the hell does he think he is?"

"I disagree, Molly Milagrosa. I definitely disagree. He gave us the magazine. That piece of paper didn't do anything to us. I still like the photographs and I want to drive around this Litchfield. I'm sure not everyone around here is like that. Let's get out of here and go north on Route 7."

"Finally. Vámonos. Pinche gringo," Arnulfo says, staring at Molly, sliding to the edge of the plastic booth bench.

"Hey, that's like 'stupid white guy,' right? What a jerk."

"Let's just get out of here." Arnulfo stares at the magazine between them as if it were a tarantula crawling on the table.

"Who's driving?" Molly asks.

"I just drove for four hours, güey," Arnulfo says, turning to Turi and ignoring Molly.

"I'll drive. It's my 'Connecticut' we're looking for, right?" Turi grabs *Yankee Magazine* as he stands up.

They drive on Route 7, first past I-84, across it, and finally into an area with empty grasslands on one side and faraway rocky hills on the other. It is at this moment, as Turi is driving, that they cross the turnoff to Route 202 and enter a part of Route 7 not on the truck's GPS screen (and not on their map). On the screen, it appears as if they are flying through the air, an unmapped part of Route 7, with rock cut sharply to create a path for the new highway, a jagged wall of granite on one side and a small, man-made lake on the other. *It's like a portal,* Turi thinks, *a pathway to a new beyond.* After a while on the GPS navigation screen, Route 7 rejoins the smaller, parallel

Route 202, a local road. Everything seems decidedly small-town on this northern side of Route 7, away from the roar of I-84: a neighborhood with an Agway, another with a tractor store and a nursery. The Walmart, Home Depot, another McDonald's and a Starbucks seem interlopers, surrounded by pizza joints, a firework stand, antique shops, and a singing society's storefront. New Milford teeters on the edge of becoming a Big Town. They are driving in the right direction, Turi feels. They just haven't gone far enough. He keeps driving north.

Route 202 splits right, toward a metal bridge crossing the Housatonic River, and they continue on serpentine Route 7. Again, the world keeps shrinking. A road to a neighborhood appears, but next to it are fields of green. A diner is next to the now two-lane road but no houses are nearby or within eyesight. The river appears and disappears through the trees on the right. They pass what looks like a hot dog stand. Apparently—Turi notices by glancing quickly at the GPS screen—they are following the Housatonic north. Route 7 bends and curves to match the river. He imagines that maybe two hundred years ago this road was nothing but a dirt pathway for pilgrims with their wagons and horses guided by only the Housatonic River.

"You know, I have a book in the back called *The Mystery of the Mighty Housatonic River.* I finished reading it in Missouri. Mrs. Garcia also gave it to me. I kinda forgot about it, so many things have happened . . ."

"You mean, that river next to us?" Molly asks, putting her face right up against the GPS screen, squinting to read the tiny lettering, and comparing it to the map on her lap. "Wow, that's weird."

"I know. It's weird, but gosh, I mean, I'm here. It's not a book anymore. I was reading about it . . . and now I'm here. It feels strange, like I've entered my own story."

"No one'll find us here," Arnulfo says, staring through the passenger's side window at the glimpses of the river through the trees. The dark greenish waters rage over huge boulders in the middle of the river. Sunlight glimmers off the water and through the trees on the riverbank. "I wonder if there are farms up here. Not chicken farms. I'm sick of chickens. But other kind of farms. No se parece nada a México. Pero esta precioso."

"Okay, I heard 'nada' and 'Mexico' and 'perro,' you mean, like dog? I don't get it, please explain."

"He said, 'It doesn't look at all like Mexico. But it's beautiful.' 'Pero' is 'but,' but 'perro' is 'dog.' Molly, okay, I want to hear you roll your r's, come on!"

"Rrrrr. Rrrrr. Rrrr."

"Wow, that's pretty good. Where'd you learn to do that? You sound like a lawn mower."

"My dad. 'Ferrocarril.' That was his favorite word. He didn't know a lot of Spanish, but he could roll his r's. 'El ferrocarril de perros.'"

"The dog railroad? Try this one: 'El ferrocarril de perros tiene arrugas.' See how fast you can say that!"

"El ferro-carril de perr-os tie-ne arr-ugas. El ferrocarril de perros tiene arrugas. *El ferrocarril de perros tiene arrugas.*"

"Están locos. What nonsense are you two talking about?" Arnulfo scoffs.

"El ferrocarril de perros tiene arrugas."

"The railroad of dogs has wrinkles! Hah, hah, hah. I don't know if I like it better in Spanish or English. I love it, Molly. You are so good."

Turi and Molly exchange mischievous smiles. Arnulfo shakes his head at the window.

"Oh, shit!" Turi says suddenly, glaring in his rearview mirror. Both Molly and Arnulfo turn around in unison. A Connecticut state trooper's patrol car is racing up behind their blue truck, its police lights on. Turi slows the truck down and pulls it over to the side of Route 7. No one else is on the narrow, two-lane road. Arnulfo swivels his head wildly, trying to escape the truck cab like it's metamorphosed into a cage. His leg is jumping up and down. Molly takes a deep breath. Turi's hands grip the steering wheel. He watches as the patrol car speeds across the double-yellow line and zooms past him. As they watch through the windshield, the siren's lights fade down Route 7.

All three seem to exhale at once. Turi turns the blue truck back onto the road.

They keep driving north. What strikes Turi is how the Housatonic River, just before Kent, switches from their right side to their left, or rather, how they have almost imperceptibly traveled over a short bridge disguised as an innocuous overpass. What strikes him, too, are the dramatic green hills on one side of the river in Kent—a backdrop that seems to hold this hamlet in place and give it a focus. The grassy fields lead to more hills in the opposite horizon. This sudden shift in perspective, this frame of hills and river, all of it urges him to stop, to look around, to absorb the panorama. After reaching the one-stoplight town, Turi turns into a parking lot, following an SUV in front of him, and stops behind a few small stores in what looks like the center of town.

The trio walk up and down Main Street, or Route 7, which splits the town of Kent in two. The most popular place for lunch, it seems, is a diner called the Colonial Settler, with big red umbrellas right on Main Street. Turi's stomach grumbles. He notices, too, one of the waiters serving customers outside is a stocky, muscled, dark-skinned man with a crew cut. A Mexican in Connecticut? Maybe Turi can talk to him and learn about this place called Kent. As soon as they sit down inside the diner, Turi notices the papel picado crisscrossing the walls, colorful cut paper with elaborate designs, Mexican folk art. He reads the small stand-up menu on their table announcing "Mexican Night" on Wednesdays. The people behind the counter, the cooks flipping burgers and tending the omelets, all of them seem to be Mexicanos. All the customers are güeros, or Anglos as they say in El Paso, but the people who run this place are Mexican. A few customers waiting to pay for their meals shake hands with a genial, mustachioed man in a black T-shirt, also short and sturdy like the waiter outside. Amid the lively cacophony and conversations, Turi hears the name "Rudy" several times, but he isn't sure.

Turi tells Oscar—the waiter Turi first saw outside—that they are from El Paso, that his parents are from Juárez. Arnulfo starts speaking Spanish with Oscar, and Molly can't stop grinning at both of them—that's when Rudy comes over and introduces himself. Oscar is Rudy's younger brother. Mimi, Rudy's wife, is behind the counter. His son and niece take turns at the cash register. His sister-in-law is a waitress too. "Miguel over there, you see him, he's our cook. Son de Juárez, Miguel! He's also Oaxaqueño," Rudy says, his eyes dancing with joy. Miguel waves at Turi, holding a spatula up in the air. Rudy Fernandez, merry and somewhat of a punster, is the owner of the Colonial Settler. In a diner in that small town in the remote Northwest corner of Connecticut, Turi finally feels at home. Molly is in front of him with a smile that won't stop. Arnulfo relaxes for once. That is exactly the moment when Turi decides he'll stay in Kent. He isn't sure what he'll do, or how he'll do it, but that is the clearest thought in his mind. Kent can be his new home. Not far behind is how to ask Molly to stay with him.

CHAPTER NINETEEN

"So what's a 'thru-hiker'? That's what Rudy thought we were. Thru-hikers. He gets them all the time at the Colonial Settler."

"No se. Don't know what he was talking about. I think he felt sorry for us, el funny Rudy. Muy chistoso."

"I think they're people who hike through the Appalachian Trail. We have the Ozark Trail, which I think they're trying to connect to the AT. Over 2,000 miles, from Georgia to Maine."

"Where should I put all this stuff, this backpack, Molly?" Arnulfo says, balancing between his two legs uncertainly. All of them will be in the small room, at least for the next few days. There isn't much space to walk. They'll have to all sleep in the room, either in a sleeping bag or on the blankets Elodia handed them when they knocked on her door and introduced themselves. Outside one window, in the distance, a sprinkler from a Kent School soccer field sprays jets of water into the sun. They could have walked from the Colonial Settler to Elodia's house across the river on Route 341 behind the school. The blue pickup is parked on the tree-lined gravel road in front.

"Anywhere's fine. Okay, so, thirty, thirty, and I'll put in forty today. We'll just take turns puttin' in that extra ten. Here's mine. Great. Should I give it to her, or do you want to, Turi? Arnie?"

"Go ahead. Ask her if we can take showers right away, will you?"

"I think that's why Rudy felt sorry for us. Apestamos. I haven't taken a shower for days."

There is a knock at the half-opened door, and a smaller, female version of Rudy appears. She has apparently been listening to them from just outside the room, and smiles, but not a real smile, a forced little gesture that to Turi indicates she is more than happy to get their money immediately. Turi walks up to Molly, who seems startled by Elodia's presence, and gently takes the money from her hand and hands the bills to Elodia. Whereas Rudy is irrepressibly friendly, a harried restauranteur oh-so-happy with his customers, his older sister Elodia seems to want to bolt from her spare bedroom as soon as the money is in her hand. *Do we smell that bad?*

"I'll go get the rest of the stuff in the truck."

"I'll help you, güey."

Elodia stuffs the money in her jeans. At that moment, she looks exactly like her younger brother. Her dark, almost black eyes jumping from backpack to backpack, she doesn't leave the room, but stops to stare carefully at Molly.

"Hi, Ms. Fernandez. Thank you for letting us stay here until we get settled down."

"Well, you're paying me—Molly, is it?—*so thank you.*" Her English is mannered and perfect, as if she were repeating English enunciating lessons, very different from Rudy's heavily accented, quick, half-laughing cadence. "My brother told me on the phone there was a young girl with two boys. Not too many girls hiking the trail. But you're not even hikers, right?"

"No, we're just traveling. We like Kent. We're looking to stay, maybe. Don't know yet."

"And you're okay traveling alone with two boys?" Elodia's brown eyes turn to the scene beyond another window, with an angled view of the front of her house, the blue truck, and the boys.

"Turi and Arnie? Sure, they're nice. We wanted to see if we could use your shower right away. We appreciate it."

"Well, yes, you mean you first, of course. Of course."

"Thank you, Ms. Fernandez."

"Before they come back. Just another word. It's just something I have to say, even when I have two boys staying in my home by themselves—imagine that! Certain rules. And now, well, two Mexican boys with a güerita. Well, Molly—right?—you know, no relations in this room please. I hope you understand."

"'Relations'? Oh, you mean like sex! No, of course not, it's not like that. We're just friends. Really, just good friends. Or at least I think we are. Well, you never know. But, of course, no sex."

"Thank you," Elodia says, her lips and cheeks puckered as if she has sucked on a lime. "The shower's to the left. Just outside your door. Let me know if you need anything else. My brother Rudy opens at seven in the morning, for breakfast." Elodia rests the sporty, wraparound glasses on her white blouse as she fingers one of the wirelike loops around her neck.

"Okay. Thank you."

When Turi and Arnulfo walk in with more gear from the blue truck, Molly is just leaving the bedroom for the shower with her change of clothes and a towel in her hand. She smirks at them as she rounds the corner to the hallway.

CHAPTER TWENTY

"Hi Corina. It's Molly. Can I talk to Jim?" Molly says. She is surprised, but not too surprised, Corina is answering Jim's cell phone.

"Wait a minute. I need to step outside." A few moments go by, and Molly can hear Corina tell someone softly, "I'll be right back." A door closes. "Do you know Jim's in the hospital? It's all your fault!" Corina half screams, half whispers into the phone.

"What—?"

"That cousin of your drug-dealing friends attacked him at the China King! Where the hell do you think I am? Jim's down the hall with a concussion, broken ribs, a broken finger. The bastard broke his finger to find out where you are! It's all your goddamn fault!"

"Oh my god! I didn't—He's not Turi and Arnulfo's cousin! He's not! I told Jim not to meet this man! I told him! My brother's fine? You're with him now?"

"Been at the hospital all day! Yes, he's pretty beat up. My poor Jim. They're taking care of him now. You hitch a ride with two boys driving a stolen truck? You get mixed up with drug dealers? What the hell's wrong with you? You know what you did to him? You know your brother's face is black and blue? That son-of-a-bitch almost tore off Jim's finger! If it wasn't for that crazy guy in the truck, some guy named Manny, if he hadn't helped Jim. My god, Molly! It's all your fault!"

Molly is sobbing into her cell phone. Finally, she says, "Corina, I told Jim not to meet with this man. I told him. He's—he's not their cousin, he's not! My brother will be okay, you sure? Can I talk to him?"

"You kiddin' me? No, you can't talk to him! No! He can barely move his mouth! That's what you did! What the hell, Molly? Look, stop, okay? Stop cryin'. Your brother . . . He'll be okay. He'll be fine. At least Redtec is paying for his medical bills. I don't know who the hell you're with, Molly, or what this is all about. The police interviewed Jim. The police, Molly!"

Molly can't stop sobbing. Even after she hangs up the phone, she sits shaking on the wooden bench outside the Kent Memorial Library.

"I'll take the truck," Arnulfo says, exasperated. "I just want to get rid of it. Didn't you hear? Didn't you just hear what they did to Molly's brother?"

"He's fine," Molly says, in a quavery voice. "He's goin' home today. And the guy was deported already. Or, I think, someone tried to help him. Not sure. Another guy's in the hospital with a broken leg."

Turi reaches out to hold Molly's hand. They are at a window table at the Colonial Settler. She doesn't pull her hand away. Her cheeks are flushed, streaks of tears crisscross her face, and strands of her blond hair tremble like tendrils in the wind. Her hand relaxes inside of his. After calling Jim to tell him where she is, Molly returned disheveled, shaking, in tears. No one has touched their omelet, breakfast burrito, pancakes, or cups of coffee. Rudy's wife, Mimi, glances warily at them from behind the counter.

"I'll take the truck, I'll get rid of it," Arnulfo repeats, his leg pumping underneath the table in another frenzy. Tiny waves of coffee quiver against the insides of the cups like a mini earthquake. "Dios mio."

"Molly, I am so sorry. Oh my god. Did you talk to Jim, did he tell you what happened exactly?"

"He's fine, he's safe. The bad guy's gone. The police are there. Only talked to Corina. If she didn't hate me before . . ." Molly cries softly, rubbing Turi's hand.

"Molly, please. It's not your fault. Who was this guy?"

"He said he was your cousin. He said he wanted his truck back. My brother, he told him what he knew. Then this man attacked Jim in a parking lot! Why the hell didn't my stupid brother listen to me? Told him not to meet with him. I told him!"

"Molly, please. Molly, look at me. That man's not our cousin. We, 'Nulfo and I, we're not cousins. That man, he's probably with these people who want their truck back."

"The drug dealers," Arnulfo blurts out and immediately regrets it. Mimi suddenly turns toward their table, and now she seems to be actively trying to listen to their conversation. He whispers: "I'll take the truck somewhere right now."

"Why didn't he listen to me? Why?"

"It's not your fault." Turi squeezes Molly's fingers. For so long, he has wanted to hold her hand, but not in this way, not under these horrible circumstances. He feels he has taken a right step that is wrong somehow. Her hand is so warm inside of his.

"I know that, I know that, I know that . . . He's fine. That's what matters. He's fine." Her other hand wraps itself around Turi's hands as he caresses her, so that both of her hands envelop his.

"We should have told you, Molly. We should have told you at Mark Twain. It's, it's—it's our fault," Turi says, staring at her teary blue eyes. His eyes are burning—inside his head—his eyes are burning.

"Turi, no. Stop crying. Stop it, please. Jim's fine. It's not your fault. I warned him. I told him not to meet with this man, and he didn't listen to me. Look at me, Turi. I'm glad you lied to me. Please, stop crying." She squeezes his hands even more tightly, holding them as if they were precious jewels. "I'm glad you lied to me, because if you hadn't—if you hadn't, I wouldn't be here right now. I would never have met you."

"I just, I just wish . . ." Turi stares at her, perplexed. "I don't know what to do."

"Get rid of the troca." Arnulfo's deep voice interrupts their one-on-one. His leg is still pumping underneath the table.

"'Nulfo, you're right. That's the first thing. Of course. I'm just so sorry we got mixed up in this. I'm not sorry I met you, Molly. That's the best thing that's happened to me." Turi is unafraid, staring at Molly, who stares right back at him. They are still holding each other's hands, but in a different way, softly, caressing each other's fingers, almost playfully. Their hands are together, because they want to be together.

"Look, you two stay right here. I'll take the truck, drive it to New Milford, or somewhere más lejos, and dump it on a road far away."

"And how exactly will you get back, walk?"

"Turi, there's a train. This morning Elodia told me about a train that passes through Wingdale, not far from here, across the New York state line. That train goes all the way to New York City," Molly says, wiping one side of her face with her shoulder.

"Let's look at our map, let's see exactly where it is. You sure, 'Nulfo?"

"Of course, you two stay here. I'll get rid of the truck, take the train back. That's the plan. Easy." Arnulfo glances for a moment too long at their hands, which seem to belong together.

"There are probably taxis at Wingdale, they could bring you back to Kent. We can check. We'll split all the costs, everything three ways."

"Look, if you cross here at the covered bridge, Bull's Bridge, just south of where we are now, follow 22 to 22/55 and go south, you go right by Wingdale. Keep going and eventually that goes all the way to New York City on 684. That 22/55 follows the train tracks. Anywhere there, just leave the truck at a train station. There are also other stations on 684, Goldens Bridge and Purdys, anywhere there. Then just take the train back. You see? You sure about this, 'Nulfo?"

"Of course. No problem. I would've done it yesterday, but then, we wouldn't be in Kent, we wouldn't have found Rudy and Elodia. We wouldn't have found our 'Connecticut.' Elodia, she told me her brother needs another dishwasher or waiter right away, 'cause one of their workers is going back to Oaxaca. To take care of a sick mother."

"Arnie, I'll write it down, so you won't forget. You can also take the map."

"You think he would hire me? He seems like muy buena gente." Arnulfo's face brightens through his dark features, as if a small light glows under each dark brown cheek. His lips part just enough, almost in a smile, to reveal his front gums, a look that has always struck Turi as carefully kind.

"'Nulfo, of course he would."

"She said Rudy wouldn't care if I didn't have any papers. Their brother Oscar doesn't either. Elodia said she and Rudy passed their citizenship test two years ago. That's all I want. I want to work. I want to live here. That's my dream."

"Okay, 'Nulfo. Just leave it at one of the train stations. Which one? You know which one?"

"La más lejos. Goldens Bridge on 684. The far one from Kent. I'll be back in a few hours. No problem."

Without another word, Arnulfo stands up and straightens his bulky frame in a confident manner that seems to make him suddenly older than seventeen, leaves fifteen dollars on the table, and walks out the door to the blue Ford pickup parked in front of the Colonial Settler. Through the window, Turi and Molly watch him make a quick U-turn at the Kent Memorial Library next to the diner and drive south on Route 7. They are still holding hands when Arnulfo and the truck are out of sight.

"I like you, Molly." Turi's heart thrums inside his chest.

"I like you too, Turi."

After a few minutes, after they start eating their food again, Turi and Molly stop holding hands. But things are different between them. They stare at each other and smile for no reason. Now they know more or less what the other is thinking. No gap exists between them. They are happy together. Now they need to figure out the rest. In this "now," nothing else matters—the world another world, beyond their world.

"I'm really sorry about your brother. I hope he's okay. I'd like to get to know him better."

"No, you wouldn't. Turi, I mean, really. He's my brother. He'll always be my brother. And I don't want anything bad to happen to him. I know he'll be fine. But—but . . . I don't know if I like him. He's stuck in his ways. He won't ever leave Steelville. I wanted to leave so bad."

"Just like I wanted to leave El Paso."

"Well, and maybe that's why we like each other. We both wanted to leave where we began. We both wanted to choose our hometowns. Not be stuck. We have family, but they're not really 'family.' Know what I mean?"

"Yeah."

"*A Charlie Brown Thanksgiving*, huh?"

"I know. It's really corny."

They laugh so hard that Mimi turns to their table again. At least they aren't crying anymore.

"You see the library next door? Can this place get any better?"

"I know. I was gonna ask you if you wanted to check it out."

"On our first date?" Molly asks with a wink. They laugh again.

"On our first date. It's so corny."

"Well, maybe we're just a couple of geeky corncobs. Of course, I'd love to go! You kiddin' me?"

"Corny geeks. Or geeky corns."

"Corneeks!" They laugh with simultaneous snorts, so loud that more than a few patrons at nearby tables turn their way. Mimi forces a smile and leaves the check on the table.

When Turi and Molly walk out of the Colonial Settler, they are about to turn right to the library, but for some reason Turi glances left, south on Main Street, toward the lone stoplight at the intersection of Route 7 and 341. He notices a commotion. A traffic jam. Cars stopped both ways on the two-lane road through town. The red lights of a state trooper flash in the distance. Somebody has already sprinted into the Colonial Settler, and Rudy bolts out, a towel in hand, also stretching to see what is happening down the road. As Rudy starts walking briskly toward the scene, so does Turi. "Molly. Let's see . . . oh my god. I think it's—"

"The blue truck. Turi. I think, is that . . . ?"

"Oh my god. No, please. Dear god." Turi starts running down the sidewalk. He can hear Molly right behind him, breathing as hard as he is, matching his stride. On the other side of the street, others have also half-sprinted toward the commotion, and stopped suddenly, as a small crowd gathers. Gawkers. Mothers pushing strollers. Kids with ice cream. A few onlookers sit in front of the House of Books, while others are still eating lunch at Kingsley Tavern, turning to look at the action. The town's Fourth-of-July banners flutter in the breeze. No one seems alarmed. But everyone's eyes are on the blue Ford pickup, a gray Audi SUV, and the state trooper. In the middle of the road, everyone is standing, everyone is okay, and the trooper is talking to the young man next to the blue Ford pickup. Turi finally gets close enough to see, a few rows of people in front of him: the young man, Arnulfo Muñoz. Their friend. Turi thinks he is going to vomit.

Suddenly a hand is on Turi's shoulder. He thinks it's Molly, but it's Rudy. Rudy aims a steady, uncompromising stare at Turi, as if to say silently, "Wait, don't do anything, see what it is." Molly is behind Rudy, her mouth wide open, stretching to hear what the trooper is saying to Arnulfo.

The pickup and the SUV do not appear at first glance to be damaged. But the truck has veered across the double yellow lines, into the oncoming lane, while the SUV is half-out of a parking space on Main Street, just behind the truck. Both are facing south. As Turi works through the crowd to get a closer look, he notices that the SUV has scraped the back part of the truck and that the SUV's front bumper is dangling from one of its hinges. An older man—stout, hair completely gray, in a yellow polo shirt and plaid shorts, his face red with anger or embarrassment—fidgets in the Audi with the door open. The trooper has already put his hand up toward the man squirming in the Audi, again, to indicate for him to stay in the car, to wait. Rudy and Molly sidle up to Turi as he tries to catch Arnulfo's attention. The state trooper is interviewing Arnulfo, who seems frightened by the chaos around him.

In the crowd, Turi, Molly, and Rudy hear:

"The stupid Audi pulled out too fast. It's his fault. What's he yellin' about?"

"Didn't see him? The truck was right there. Where it's supposed to be. The idiot pulled out too fast and sideswiped him. God, if that had been my truck—just look at that beauty!—I'd be pissed as hell. Pissed."

"I mean, why doesn't the trooper just get the cars off the road. It's a fender bender. Ridiculous. They have no sense of the traffic jam they're causin'. Here comes another one. Two troopers for this?"

"Yes, confirm, 2401," the radio cackles loudly on the trooper's vest.

"Oh, shit," someone else hisses behind Turi. "That's a stolen vehicle. On my ham radio, I hear it all the time. That kid stole that truck."

Someone else in the crowd audibly gasps when the trooper turns Arnulfo around and places handcuffs on his wrists. More mutterings surround them. "What the hell is he doing?" "The kid's not at fault." "Stolen?" The trooper slowly leads him into the patrol car and locks him inside, as the other trooper starts directing traffic around the mayhem. Through the car's window, open about two inches, Turi can see and hear Arnulfo softly sobbing and shaking in the backseat. Turi lunges through and around the people in front of him, toward the patrol car. A hand grabs his shirt and pulls him back. Two buttons pop off his shirt. Another hand grabs him by the shoulders and pulls back harder. Molly and Rudy.

"Turi, please, *think*," Turi hears a sharp, harsh whisper in his ear like a blast of air. It is Molly's voice, strained and choking. "We'll all get in trouble. Please. Stop." He wheels around. A few people watch them carefully. Rudy's smile is bright—too bright, almost strained—if anybody looked close. He pulls Turi's shoulder further back and wraps an arm around him and ushers him away from the crowd. Most turn away, back to the patrol car, but a few peer at them, trying to understand what just happened.

"Go back to the restaurant," Rudy growls in Turi's ear. The fake smile never leaves Rudy's face. He is looking past Turi for anyone else who may be staring at them, following them, as both take a few steps back to the Colonial Settler. Rudy's grip is exceptionally strong, half-a-bear-hug around Turi's waist. Turi cannot go anywhere. Rudy is almost lifting Turi off the sidewalk and "walking" with him in tandem. "I'll find out what I can."

As soon as Rudy's arm releases Turi, Molly's arm is around him, replacing Rudy's hug, yet hers is gentle around his waist. She keeps leading him down the sidewalk. Rudy stands facing them on the sidewalk as they walk away, still forcing a smile, with his hands on his hips, like a sentry making sure they keep going.

"Molly, Molly. What have we done? Oh my god! What have we done?"

By the time Rudy comes back, both Turi and Molly have quietly stopped crying and are sitting in a booth at the Colonial Settler. Rudy walks behind the counter toward Mimi, leads her through the cooking area and passes Miguel and the hot grills, and has a quick, inaudible conversation with his wife. He comes out and sits in front of their booth, his legs straddling the back of a wooden chair.

"Okay. You guys knew about the stolen truck?" he says.

Molly and Turi look at each other. No one says a word for a few seconds.

"Did you know? Answer me, please."

"It was Arnulfo's truck. He said it was his truck." A tear drops across one side of Molly's face and into the corner of her mouth. "But he was our friend. He is our friend."

Rudy stares at Turi, waiting to see if he has anything else to add.

"He was giving us a ride. He was just giving us a ride, my god," Turi finally says, unable to look at anything but the empty table in front of him. "What's going to happen to him? What—what did you—"

"I think he'll get arrested, deported. You know Oscar, you see him out there, my kid brother waiting tables?" With a nudge of his shoulders, Rudy waits for them to look out the window. "He's undocumented too. It's dangerous what just happened. It's dangerous if they come here, asking questions. You understand?"

"Yes."

"He didn't have papers either, right?"

"Not yet."

"That's what I thought. So you understand, I hope, the situation we're in. I'm sorry about your friend. Before the trooper left, before the tow truck came for the blue pickup to take it to the Litchfield Barracks, I got close to the window. The trooper was busy talking to the tow truck operator. I told your friend, Arnulfo, 'Remember to tell them you're seventeen. A minor. Es mejor para ti. With or without papers, less serious for you.' Through his tears, he looked at me and nodded. The poor boy. Then Arnulfo was suddenly shaking his head, like saying, 'No.' I thought he wouldn't do it, but what I hadn't seen, what he had seen, was that the trooper was approaching, and I think he meant, 'Don't get closer. Don't get in trouble too.' He had stopped crying by then. The boy has cojones. Seguro que sí. He might have to spend a few months in juvi and he'll get deported. He knows that.

But it's not the end of the world. It could be worse, you understand? Much worse."

"Yes."

"They could have shot him. He could have tried to run away and they could have shot him. They need only an excuse in their heads to shoot Mexicans."

"Yes. But, the truck, what will happen to him if it's stolen?"

"Well, that's the problem. I'm not a lawyer, I'm not an expert on what happens to undocumenteds who are, you know, who commit a crime, juveniles. Probably jail, I don't know. No idea. But my advice to both of you is to stay away. Listen to your friend. If you don't, you'll get in trouble and you might get me in trouble too. I can't have that. My whole family depends on this restaurant. You understand? I have sympathy for the boy, but you have to understand. That Arnulfo, he's a little soft on the outside, still a boy in a way, but he's got real cojones, I tell you that. From the look in his eyes, I know he'll say nada. He didn't want anybody else to get hurt. That's what a man would do. That's what he's going to do."

"Okay."

"One more thing. It's too late. Everybody in the restaurant knows what happened on Main Street. It's too late to keep it from Elodia. But I'll talk to my sister right now. Just take a walk, don't go to her house for a few hours. She'll want to kick you out—I *know* her—as soon as she finds out about Arnulfo and the stolen truck. She's different from me, she doesn't even talk to Oscar that much, her other brother from Oaxaca. Es un poco dura y malinchista. A difficult personality, a traitor in a way. I'll talk to her. You can stay there as long as you can pay her. I'll make sure of it. Go to Kent Falls or take a long walk on Cobble Road. It will be good for you. Both walks are beautiful this time of year. That pinche Arnulfo, he reminds me of how I was when I arrived in America. A little stupid, a little innocent, a little hard. Needing a few breaks for me and my family. I got them, thank god. But he didn't. Maybe he can save himself, still."

"Okay."

"Mexicans. You know, they want us in this country, they use us for our work, and then they want to throw us away like the garbage. We need to help each other and work together. That's how we survive to belong where we are trying to belong."

"Okay."

"That trooper was really grilling Arnulfo about where he got the truck. I hope he doesn't come back to the restaurant asking questions, talking to people. It's a small town. We don't need any more trouble."

CHAPTER TWENTY-ONE

"Tonight we get the truck. It's in an impound lot in Torrington. Just heard all the details from el jefe," Chucho says, jamming his cell phone into his jeans.

"They found it! Thank god, thank god!" Juanito says, his chest palpitating with spasms. The old man can hardly breathe with his delight. For the last few days they have roamed East Hartford in a working-class neighborhood their friends say is safe for them, waiting for instructions in a borrowed, half-abandoned house. Mattresses line the floor, a rusty, tilted refrigerator, a few bare light bulbs on the ceiling connect to a closed garage that does not fit their SUV. Juanito has not slept much, his nights beset with nightmares of what he imagines awaits him back in Clint, Texas, if he returns to the border without finding the blue truck. In one nightmare, Eduardo the linebacker grabs his neck from behind as they travel across the country. He twists off his head like mercy killing a chicken and tosses it out the window.

"Great." Eduardo huffs from a chair, not taking his eyes from the window, which is about the fifth word he has said in the past four days. The ex-Marine follows Chucho, obeys Chucho—like a lion obeying a ringmaster, snapping his whip with bravura.

"We won't be taking the truck tonight. We can't. He's been notified about where it is, how to get it. Eventually he'll get it, in a couple of days. It was impounded two days ago, actually not too far from here. We need to get to the product immediately, put it on ice, keep it on ice, and then drive it to Kansas City. Eduardo and me. Those are Dunbar's instructions. Juanito, you'll wait for the truck. But el jefe wants the product on its way to Kansas City tonight."

"What about those goddamn kids? Where the hell are they? I'd like to—"

"Shut up, Juanito. You'll have your chance, cabrón. While you're waiting for the paperwork from el jefe to pick up his truck, he wants you to find them and take care of business. Dunbar doesn't want anybody left leading back to him, understand? That's your time limit, two to three days. El güero said they found one of them, the illegal, and he's in jail not far from here. Dunbar knows where he is. Guerrero and Don Ilan probably know too. They're talking to each other now that the truck's been found. They will be sending someone to take care of that son of a bitch in jail. The illegal is not your responsibility. The other one is." Chucho stares at Eduardo for a second too long, as the giant stays mesmerized by the window.

"Can't wait. That goddamn son of a bitch—"

"Listen to me." Chucho moves closer to Juanito sitting next to a crooked table. He leers over him, making the old man tilt back in his chair. "You want to make things right with Dunbar? Do a good job this time, pendejo." Eduardo grins at the old man, and then his eyes go back to the front window. A Lubavitcher family strolls across the sidewalk. Chucho has explained, more or less, who they are, why they are always walking. No machines. No cars. No electricity on the Sabbath. Friday evenings to Saturday evenings are like Sunday for Catholics, except those Lubavitchers dressed in black follow the Old Testament "como chingones," to the letter of God's law. Eduardo has repeated this new word as "Luba-bitchers," his third word the past four days, prompting a wink from Chucho. "He's allowing you to clean up your mess by taking care of the one left behind in Kent," Chucho continues. "The police told el jefe where they arrested the illegal with the stolen truck. You do the job this time, you take care of that Tejano and the girl they picked up, and el jefe will be happy with you again. So don't fuck it up. But the truck is what really matters to el jefe. The product. Period. Eduardo and me will take care of that tonight. You finish this business in Kent."

"Of course. They picked up a girl, huh? Esta bueno. Esta mejor. But on the truck, how are we going to get it out of the door . . . ?"

"Listen, both of you. Dunbar told me how to do it, just get the door open with screwdrivers, undo the panel for the radio's speaker. I'll go in. Juanito, you'll keep watch. It shouldn't take more than twenty minutes, if that. 'Uardo, you're with me. We'll take a look at the impound lot this afternoon, to see where the cameras are, the guard, get a sense of the place and the streets around it. Find where the truck is exactly, before tonight, so we're not just bumbling around like idiotas. Our Hartford friends said they know the place and said it's easy to take something from one of the cars, as long as you don't need to take the whole damn car out of the lot. That's what they're trying to prevent. Not someone taking a piece of one of their trocas. It's the Connecticut State Police who has it too, and not even a local police department."

"Like robbing a junkyard for a spare part."

"Yeah, something like that. Doesn't matter if one of us gets caught. The goddamn product has to be out of there and off to Kansas City tonight. No excuses. That's what el jefe wants without question. If one of us gets caught, we say nothing, Dunbar will get us out. Don't worry about it. But the product has to be iced immediately, and it has to be on its way to KC. Understood?"

"Seguro que si."

Concertina wire crowns the cinder block wall at the lot for impounded vehicles in Torrington, Connecticut. Earlier that afternoon, Chucho has been able to find the blue truck, which stands out among the rows of dusty, mostly decrepit, crashed-up cars like a beauty queen in a laundromat. Through the chain-link rollout fence at the entrance, he spots only one guard booth (no one there midafternoon) and one camera. The gates are locked. No dogs behind the fence, few streetlights outside the lot, and none in the lot itself, except for a spotlight atop the booth. If they use an alley outside the lot at the furthest corner from the guard, and if they walk up to that corner and leave their own truck a block away, they can cut the concertina, heave themselves over to the other side, and easily get to the blue Ford truck in the darkness.

At three in the morning, Eduardo parks their truck, as instructed, at the edge of an abandoned strip mall with only a used furniture store and a piano shop with a vast empty space behind its storefront glass. The Torrington lot is around the corner and about a block away. They have a cooler packed with ice in their truck, plus wire cutters, screw drivers, flashlights, a blanket to place over any wire left on the wall, and pliers. The streets are shiny, dark, and desolate. Far away, a lone car turns a corner and disappears.

"Listen, Juanito. You sit your ass over there . . ." Chucho talks softly as he points to an alley between two brick buildings, ". . . under that light. You can keep an eye on the guard's booth. I don't know if anyone's even there. It looks like a small light's on. He can't see you from there, in the shadows, but you can see him. If he steps out of the booth, if you see anyone pull up to the gates, any activity, you send me a text. I have my phone in my front pocket.

I'll feel the buzz as soon as you send that text. But only if there's a problem. Got it?"

"Yes, of course. It's raining."

"So?"

"Nothing, Chucho. I'll keep an eye on the guard and the gate."

"I'll text you when we jump back out with the product, when we're headed to the truck. You can meet us there. Any questions?"

"No, señor."

"We're saving your ass tonight, Juanito."

"I know that. Thank you." The old man slips away with those words, finds the alley, and tries to scoot toward the wall to sit onto a brick or on a piece of cardboard or on anything but the cold, wet asphalt. But there's nothing but bits of gravel and trash. Rivulets of water run down the brick wall onto the asphalt, in and around where he is. He squats without sitting, yet drops of rain still fall on him. His shoes slowly absorb the puddles of water, and even droplets splash up from the asphalt and into his exposed, hairy ankles. The phone has to be off, but ready. He touches it through his pant legs. Any phone light will be seen, so he can only turn it on if there is a problem. Squatting, or sitting, is best, Juanito now understands, because the slanted light from a street light cuts across the brick wall behind him, about chest-high. If the guard turns to glance across the street or if a police car happens to patrol the area or some busybody drives by and pays the slightest bit of attention, they will see a head, they will see his shoulders, they will see him standing in the alley across the lot. Low and in the darkness, Juanito is wet, but invisible. Not far from him, a dumpster reeks with the stink of a dead animal.

"'Uardo," Chucho whispers as the two of them enter the alley and walk toward the far corner. The lot's cinder block wall is on one side, a warehouse on the other—and after the monolith of the warehouse what looks like weed-infested backyards of a few multifamily houses, which are all dark. The gloom is almost absolute in the alley. With the rain under heavy clouds, it seems even more deserted than the loneliest of alleys in the most forgotten of cities. "You hoist me up, hand me the wire cutters, and then the blanket. Soon as I'm over, give me the bag with the rest of the tools. Can you get yourself over . . . ? 'Uardo?"

"Here."

"Can you get yourself over this wall?" A dog barks a few houses away, but only three times.

"Easy."

"No noise. No one sees us. I'll wait for you on the other side."

Cutting the wire and pulling it back are easy, but one barb does pierce the garden gloves Chucho has bought at the Ace Hardware earlier that day, the reason for his "Shit!" that sounds more like a guttural hiss in the darkness. He can feel the blood trickling down his wrist, inside the leather, as he jumps to the other side, narrowly missing a plastic bumper that has fallen off a car he cannot see. He kicks the bumper away from the wall. He stares up at the top of the wall and waits for Eduardo. There's a scuffle of feet kicking at the cinder block—a darker silhouette vaulting over the wall and flying past him through the night—and a heavy thud a few feet in front of him. The tools in the plastic bag clang softly in the darkness. The dog barks once again, but only faintly, on the other side of the wall. They are in.

"Give me a flashlight, hold my hand."

"What?"

"Hold my damn hand, 'Uardo. I'm not . . . you know . . . just hold my hand. Just don't want you bumping into any shit, making any noise. Only one flashlight on, mine. Keeping it low to the ground so it can't be seen. I know exactly where the truck is. I can barely see you and I know your eyesight's worse than mine. Just follow me. Okay?"

Before he finds the flashlight's switch, Chucho feels a giant paw pat his chest, his shoulder, which he directs to his hand. The light goes on, illuminating their feet and not much else. Chucho squeezes Eduardo's massive mitt of a hand. *Am I imagining this? Eduardo, what are you doing to my hand, vato tan guapo? Is he rubbing it slowly with his thumb? I must be imagining this. Sweet boy ... just ... yes ... just keep ... yes. Maybe I'm in a dream.* They walk through rows of cars, toward the end of a row near the middle of the lot, to the blue truck.

Chucho jimmies the lock and opens the truck's passenger door, which creaks loudly. After he clicks off the overhead light, he jams his flashlight under the seat to point toward the door's inside panel. He begins to work on it with a screwdriver. It's no use trying to get a clear look at Eduardo's face: they are both in the shadows of darkness.

"'Uardo, you see the guard's booth? It's way on your right. 'Uardo, goddammit! Where the hell are you?" Chucho's whispers sound like a screechy hiss. He crouches and works on the door panel, removing screws. A finger inside his gloves stings. He feels the wetness of the blood.

"I see it, kinda. After a couple of rows. Just a little light." Eduardo's voice wavers a bit.

"If you see anything change, any other light, anybody coming toward us ..." Eduardo's muscular body is but a few inches from Chucho's face as he crouches to work on the truck's door. Whiffs of Eduardo's breath waft downward with hints of a scent he thinks is Aramis.

"Okay, okay."

After a few minutes of removing part of the door panel and faux radio speaker, Chucho sees it up close with his flashlight. The first of six slim blue cylinders, about the same size as a tire pressure gauge but a bit thicker, padded and held in place with clamps. More loose padding around the cylinder and clamps, and another blue cylinder next to it, and another . . . Refrigeraton coils lace near and around the neat row of cylinders, like tiny gunmetal snakes slithering around a row of blue cigars. An electrical wire is attached to an apparatus below the cylinders and disappears into the interior of the truck's door. As he exposes more of the panel, Chucho marvels at the workmanship of this custom job, at how perfectly the contraption fits inside the door, how those six blue cylinders and their insulated micro-refrigeration unit seem one of the factory options available for any Ford F-350. He touches the first cylinder, and it is still cool. After he frees each cylinder and carefully lays all six inside the plastic bag at his feet, he hastily jams the panel back in place and tightens the screws. After a few more interminable minutes, he passes the flashlight over the entire inside of the door. It looks as if the panel has never been touched.

"Done. Hold these tools." Chucho stands up. "Let's get out of here. Everything good? Hold my hand."

"Yes, of course."

Chucho thinks only of the warmth of Eduardo's hand as they walk through the darkness.

In a few steps they are at the far corner again. Chucho is about to place the plastic bag with the six padded blood vials on top of the wall next to the concertina, but then he thinks he may inadvertently hit the bag and knock it to the floor as he hoists himself up.

"Hold this carefully and bend down so I can step on your shoulders." Eduardo's hand grabs the plastic bag. Chucho finds the massive shoulder and taps it downward and stands up to place the blanket over the wall again. After he is on top and avoids the strands of concertina around him, he says, "Just wait until I'm over and put the bag on top of the wall carefully, so I can grab it before you climb over. Got it?"

Chucho jumps into the alley, straightens himself, and hears the dog barking, but only a few short barks again. He touches the top of the wall, trying to find the plastic bag. "'Uardo, the bag, care—," he hisses over the top of the wall, but before he can finish his sentence, the bag is there. Chucho grabs it, waits, hears the scuffle of feet hitting the other side of the wall, and then finally sees the giant silhouette of Eduardo on the wall moments before an imposing shadow lands inches in front of him, as if a winged demon has vaulted from the dark clouds. A certain elation fills Chucho's heart as he glances at the other shadows in the alley and marches quickly back to their truck a block away. Remembering Juanito in the alley across the street from the guard's booth, he unlocks his phone as his body splits what seems a dark sea in front of him. He types "Done" with one thumb, not caring about the brightness of the light against his chest. He grips the plastic bag tightly.

It is this elation and its reverberation, an almost electrical effect on his tired body, in retrospect, that keeps Chucho from paying attention to all the details as quickly as he normally would. He the favored leader in Dunbar's group. The one who has been entrusted with this most vital job. The one who often fixes el güero's biggest problems. Pride swells in Chucho's chest. After they reach the truck, opening the cooler packed with ice in the backseat, Chucho will realize one detail and then dismiss it, possibly causing the disaster that will come. Only posterity and a god can guess what exactly happened that night, and how. But when he reaches for the blue blood vials, he finds first the screw drivers and the pliers and one flashlight, all of them mixed in with the vials, Chucho now realizing the bag was too heavy at the wall when Eduardo handed it over. Too heavy in the alley as they walked through the darkness to their escape from Torrington. Too heavy now in his hands as he gingerly places each padded blood vial in the cooler. His palms are bloody from the concertina wire.

That is his blood on one of the vials, isn't it? Posterity and a god can also only guess that perhaps it wasn't that brusque, short walk to their truck that imperceptibly cracked one of the blue vials, but dearest Eduardo himself when he mixed their tools with the vials and dumped the plastic bag on the top of the wall, but how to be sure? And does it even matter? The details— the heaviness of the plastic bag all this time, the blood on one of the vials— Chucho dismisses as he stares for a brief second through the gloom at the waiting Eduardo next to the truck, who smiles back like a friendly skeleton in the shadows of the strip mall parking lot. All teeth and hollow eyes in a macabre geniality. *Eduardo, my friend, you look as tired as I do. Your hands are so warm. So warm.* They have nonetheless finished the job—Chucho convinces himself as he guns the truck's motor. Juanito is in the back already making himself comfortable, and Eduardo jams in his earbuds for the long night ahead. They are on their way to Kansas City after they drop off Juanito in Kent. They are beyond okay: they have been triumphant. The hell with any doubts, the hell with his personal demons, Chucho thinks, almost waving away the darkness in front of them. He has done the job for el jefe. That is what matters. Not his fantasies. Vamonos.

As Chucho, Juanito, and Eduardo head west on Route 202 toward Kent and then south on Route 7 to connect to I-84 West, for the long drive, none of them will recognize any symptoms from their exposure to Marburg-B on the first day. Juanito will immediately attribute a slight fever to sitting in that alley in the rain, along with a few aches, which is normal—isn't it?—after days in the truck, after nights sleeping on smelly mattresses, and after all that tension, all that worry . . . Many days later and far from Juanito, Chucho will be the first to realize something terrible has happened, the most terrible of results. After Chucho and Eduardo have already stopped at many gas stations, motels, and restaurants along the way to Kansas City—their first stop—and back home to Clint, Texas. After Eduardo says to him, out of the blue at a Dunkin' Donuts, "Chucho, you don't have to pretend. You don't have to pretend anymore." Perhaps the elation Chucho feels about what the enigmatic Eduardo truly means—at what Chucho is certain he means—that's what clouds his mind, obfuscates his thinking, and propels him forward to find out the meaning of Eduardo's words in Texas, once this sordid business is done. They press forward in their journey across America, two Johnny Appleseeds, or Juanitos Manzanas, if one prefers, planting the deadliest of seeds—half with ignorance, half with hope—at rest stops and service plazas along the way.

As they near Kansas City to drop off their package, Chucho opens the cooler again at a Citgo gas station, dumps the ice, and replaces it before visiting el Tapado's warehouse, not noticing—or not wanting to believe his eyes—that the infected blood has seeped throughout the ice like a faint, copper-colored fog. They keep moving, trying to get away from a darkness on this earth they will never outrun.

CHAPTER TWENTY-TWO

"Tell me about el Tapado, Chucho. God, I don't feel so good." Eduardo heaves but does not vomit as they approach Kansas City. The giant has been trembling since the morning. Chucho does not tell him about his diarrhea or the blood in his stool. He has a slight fever, but not as bad as Eduardo's. *We're just tired. It's been a long few weeks. But we'll be home in Texas soon. Everything will be all right then. We will be who we are. We will be who we always wanted to be.*

"No one has ever seen el Tapado. No even knows where he is at any given time or where he lives or why he does what he does. But he has enormous power. Beyond money. Beyond secret armies. With the intelligence and ability to kill whoever he wants."

"Secret armies?"

"Sure, that's what I've heard. Rumors are that he's a foreigner, from the Middle East or Africa, and maybe that's why he hates the United States. Another guy from Guerrero also told me that's all wrong. That el Tapado comes from Mississippi or Alabama or West Virginia and that he doesn't hate *all* the United States, just what it has become. Too feminist, too multicultural, too Constitutional, not Constitutional enough. Those pendejos probably don't know, but they guess."

"Constitutional? I have to stop again . . ." Eduardo says, turning into an alley. As soon as the truck stops, he opens the door and vomits just beyond it. Is that blood too? Is Eduardo vomiting blood? Chucho sees his companion shaking for a moment just outside the truck. Eduardo shivers as if the weather is Chicago-cold in January, but it's almost ninety degrees in July in Kansas City. "I'm okay. Keep going. Tell me more about el Tapado, we're almost there. It distracts me. I'll be fine, probably just the flu."

Chucho looks at him for a second as Eduardo starts the SUV and maneuvers again into traffic. "I've also heard el Tapado is not one man, but an organization, which makes sense to me. With serious money and connections. An international network. Maybe they want to create havoc and watch everybody run for cover in terror. Maybe they just want to take advantage of the panic and nobody having any balls during a crisis. Maybe 'el Tapado' is just a contact and customer with our boss's boss, Don Ilan, in Guerrero—a figurehead of a vast octopus ready to pounce on Gringolandia after everybody loses their heads, to devour when everyone's confused. Who knows? Maybe they want to create a new government—or at least destabilize the current one." As if a gigantic worm were inside of him, a quiver reverberates through his stomach and loins, but Chucho just gasps and sips more water to hide his discomfort. His fever is not getting better. *Eduardo gave it to me, or I gave it to him. Doesn't matter. We're in it together.* Chucho continues: "I've also heard that el Tapado is just an evil businessman with money—gambling, real estate, kickbacks, extortion—a psychotic, an idiot, a moron who just wants to kill people for the hell of it, a sicko who loves mayhem because it gives him more power. But no one really knows who or what el Tapado is. Everybody respects him. Many fear him. We won't see him, but he'll be there somewhere, watching us. Just keep your cool and let's get through this and deliver the package from Dunbar. Get him off the hook with Don Ilan."

They pull into a warehouse amid dozens of others near the Kansas City rail yards. On the roof, Chucho can see cameras watching their every move and a booth suspended near the ceiling with only mirrored windows. The warehouse door slides open with a ghostly screech and shuts with a thunderous bang. At once the darkness surrounds the cavern inside. The only spotlight is on the pickup and on two of el Tapado's men who are there to receive the package. Through the windshield, Chucho can see that both men don headsets to communicate, presumably, with whoever is in the mirrored booth. Both men wear gloves and masks.

Chucho glances at Eduardo and at himself before stepping out of the SUV and has the feeling that he has vastly underestimated el Tapado, despite what he knows about his reputation. Chucho knows very little of what he is carrying for this madman—perhaps he has been incautious and stupid and overconfident . . . Eduardo asks for a warehouse bathroom, heaving again. Chucho notices that one of the men possesses a sinister grin behind the mask—"Help yourself. It's over there."—while the other one shakes his head and whispers to the headset, as if he and Eduardo are beyond help, clueless and ignorant, what el Tapado expected from his border connections. Chucho, who feels dizzy but hiding it, tries to hand the product in the cooler to the grinning man. But instead of taking it, he leaves it on the ground. They can all hear Eduardo retching through the closed green door of the bathroom. Sweat pours from Chucho's forehead. From above, both of el Tapado's men are instructed to step away from them, the SUV, and the product on the ground. Two more men in yellow hazmat suits enter through a side door and immediately encase the cooler in a kind of heavy plastic and carry it out through the same door. Chucho wonders *What in god's name have we done? What have we done?* Eduardo finally emerges from the restroom.

"You two can leave now," Chucho overhears from a loudspeaker above, in a modified electronic voice that reminds him of an all-powerful computer-god. "Get in your truck and leave. I will talk to Guerrero. Everything is fine. Thank you."

As Eduardo starts the truck and the warehouse doors groan open like the enormous gates of Mordor, Chucho cracks open a window. He knows they can die at any moment, that el Tapado, or whoever is in the booth, can easily order their execution on a whim, because the product has been turned in late, because of Juanito's stupidity, because . . . because . . . for no reason at all but simply to spill more blood and send a message to Don Ilan through Dunbar. But as Eduardo slowly pulls out, Chucho overhears that electronic voice echo behind them in the warehouse, "Zero protocol for that bathroom. Nobody uses it until it's sterilized, all your clothing should be . . ." The rest of the computer god's words evaporate into the Kansas City heat.

At that moment, Chucho realizes it's too late for them. A bird seems suddenly trapped inside his chest, fluttering. *What in the world have we done? If I had been moving the product instead of that damn Juanito . . . but how . . . did it happen? The bag at the fence in Torrington . . . after we left the bag was . . . too heavy . . . the tools must've broken one of the vials . . . the wound on my hand—what an idiot I am—dear god . . . dear Eduardo. Dearest Eduardo. What have we done?*

For hours on the drive home to Clint, Chucho imagines what el Tapado must have been thinking as they departed: *This is better than killing them. That's what they deserve for their incompetence. Let them kill themselves. Let them kill each other.*

CHAPTER TWENTY-THREE

Dear Mrs. Garcia:

Thank you for loaning me these books. I really loved them. Huckleberry Finn *was my favorite. I wanted to return them to you, because I won't be starting junior year at Ysleta High School. I moved to Connecticut, but I shared these books with some new friends, and we really loved them. My friend Molly also loved* Catcher in the Rye, *and I liked it too, but I think she liked it more than I did. There's a prep school like Pencey Prep near where I live now, called the Kent School, but the kids there don't seem as stupid and stuck-up as the ones at Pencey. I see them all the time, the students from Kent, and they're usually nice. I work in a restaurant in the late afternoons and through dinnertime. The kids are friendly when they come in. The parents sometimes seem more like Pencey, but the kids aren't like idiots. They kind of seem afraid of their parents, so maybe something happens when you get old.*

I wanted to tell you that I'm trying to enroll in high school in August. I want to go to New Milford High this fall, if I can get my paperwork and everything. That's another reason why I wanted to send you the books now. I wanted to ask you a favor. Can you get YHS to send me my grades and records for my immunization shots? I think I need a birth certificate to get a Social Security number. I'm working without one now, but I think I'm going to need it later. I think I can get a birth certificate in the mail. I'm checking on that now. If you know how to get that document in El Paso more quickly, let me know.

I don't want you to ask for help from my aunt and uncle in Ysleta. You probably can guess why, but I want to tell you so that you don't ask them to help me. My uncle hurt me. You guessed that already, I think. I just want to get away from them. I'm fine in Kent, as long as they don't know where I am. Really, I don't think they care if I'm gone. In less than one year, I'll be an adult anyway, so it won't matter. If you need an official adult to sign anything, my Tía Romita lives in Juárez, on Calle Rodolfo Fierro 13. I'm sending her a postcard to tell her why you might visit her. I know this is a lot. But I don't have anyone else in El Paso to help me. You can email me (below) when you get the books and this letter. I think it's easier that way. Don't worry, I'm safe in Kent!

Your student (who still loves to read!),
Arturo Martinez
PelegrinoFromElPaso@gmail.com

CHAPTER TWENTY-FOUR

Rudy begged them not to visit Arnulfo in detention. Rudy glanced at Turi's fake driver's license, and yes, it seemed okay to him. Turi would probably pass as an adult. They were at Union Station in Hartford. Turi and Molly were taking a long, two-bus trip to Plymouth, Massachusetts.

Rudy asked them to do one more thing, for their own sake. They agreed, not "fake agreed" just to get Rudy off their backs, but *agreed* agreed with Rudy's idea. Turi will go alone into the juvenile detention facility for ICE detainees—where Turi has found Arnulfo's name in a searchable ICE website meant to locate undocumented immigrants and where they are being held—and Molly will wait nearby, outside the ICE facility, at a restaurant or coffee shop. What is the point of both of them being arrested if Turi's fake ID doesn't work? Only "adults" are allowed to visit detained undocumented immigrants, and all visiting minors have to be accompanied by adults. Molly's fake ID will only increase the chances of both of them being caught. "Well, they won't arrest you, Turi. You're just a minor pretending to be an adult. You're not undocumented. You don't have your birth certificate yet, do you? Well, that's too bad. But your English is perfect. They could consider you a runaway minor, if they question your identification, and send you back to Texas. Is that what you want? I know he's your friend, but let him go. He'll be fine. He listened to me and told la migra he's a minor. That's how he's registered. Arnulfo, he's not stupid. What you're doing . . . well, that is. He's fine, I tell you. Here, both of you put these masks on for the bus ride, or I'm not stopping this truck. I mean it."

Rudy's words are still in their ears as their connecting bus from Boston nears Plymouth. Both are wearing particulate respirators with "advanced air filters." Turi and Molly have been on buses for almost five hours. So much has been in the news about a strange and potent flu spreading in Kansas City, Lubbock, Cleveland, Bloomington, and even Hartford. Hundreds have been afflicted, and news reports say seventy are already dead with internal hemorrhaging, high fevers, and convulsions. Half the passengers on the bus also wear masks of one sort or another. Rudy warned them against making the trip, but they didn't listen. They thanked him for the ride, told him they'd be back when they could get buses back to Hartford Saturday night, or maybe Sunday. He told them to call him, and he would pick them up. Turi knows these trips will ruin Rudy's weekend. But Rudy was adamant about being their ride to and from Kent.

"I could go instead of you. I'm older. I'm blond. I could say he's my boyfriend," Molly says as they amble off the bus and follow their map to Long Pond Road, about two miles away.

"*I'm blond?* Molly, really? I knew him first. I'm going. We're not arguing about this." As soon as they are alone, they yank their masks off and shove them into their backpacks.

"What if somethin' happens to you? What if Rudy's right, and they send you back to Texas?"

"Well, in a few weeks I'm back in Kent. Period. We're together, okay. That's how it is. Nothing's going to happen to me. I'm visiting a friend. Visiting hours for minors in detention are in the evening from six to ten on Saturdays. The ICE website says it takes about forty-five minutes to go through security to make sure you're not carrying firearms or anything else that's illegal. Just wanna tell him we're waiting for him, nothing's changed, when he gets sent back to Juárez. Wanna tell him to cross the border again, to find us in Kent."

"I think he knows that, Turi. I know he does." They hike side by side on the sidewalk, holding hands. A sculpture of a lobster, creamy white and reddish orange, about half the size of a human, stands on its tail as if pointing to the sky.

"Molly, what's wrong? Come on."

"I—I—" She won't look at him, but her hand grips his tightly, almost yanking him toward her. "I don't want anything to happen to you! I don't think you should sacrifice yourself for Arnulfo! Rudy's right. Don't know why we're here."

"Well, why are *you* here?"

"Because I'm with you! Don't you understand? I'd rather somethin' bad happen to me, I'd rather it be me."

"Is that why you said you'd be better at this because you're *blond?*"

"Well, just think about it, Turi, whatever guard takes your ID, they're just going to see . . . you know . . ."

"A Mexican?"

"What do you think? That's what they do. That's the world, Turi. I didn't create this stupid world."

"Maybe you're right. Maybe you'd have a better chance. You are probably right. But I need to do this. Arnulfo, you know, he wasn't like my best friend. I've known him only for a week or so and two thousand miles. We were just helping each other. But I know he's a good guy. Kind of lost. I know what's inside of him. As good as anybody who landed on stupid Plymouth Rock. This is where they started, you know. This town. When it was full of Native Americans. No roads . . . no horses . . . nothing."

"The stupid Pilgrims, I know." Molly kicks the dust with her sneakers and matches Turi's quick stride. "I don't care about those old stories. People came here a long time ago and more people like Arnulfo are still comin' over. It's the same thing and it's also different. But in Steelville, I know so many who hate all Mexicans. Vietnamese. Muslims. Anybody who's not them. Anybody who doesn't look like them. Anybody who works harder than they do. It doesn't matter what you say to them, they won't change, they won't listen."

Saltbox houses—some so small it is hard to imagine more than one person living in them—line the road in front of the cracked sidewalks where patches of grass sprout and form lumps as big as baguettes. No one else is on the sidewalk. No one Turi or Molly can see in what appears to be a partially abandoned neighborhood. A yellowing, warped poster for treating opioid addiction flutters against a crooked metal lamppost.

"Why aren't *you* like that?"

"Because I'm not. Why aren't you blond?"

"Because I'm Mexican."

"Some Mexicans are blond."

"Well, I'm not."

"Well . . . and some blonds are not racist morons."

"Molly La Milagrosa."

"Turi the Texas Tantalizer."

Turi holds Molly's hand. His eyes follow the contours of her face.

"Molly, I really like you."

"I like you too, Turi. More than anybody else I've ever met. We're, like, each other's fan clubs."

They laugh and squeeze each other's hands.

Two blocks from the Plymouth County Correctional Facility, Turi and Molly find a Panera Bread shop in a strip mall along with a Planet Fitness and a beauty salon. Molly agrees to wait at Panera with her phone on for any news. "It could be two hours at least, forty-five minutes through security, other delays, then thirty minutes with Arnulfo. Please don't panic."

Molly wipes away a tear as Turi steps out through the Panera double doors. She feels sick to her stomach. Her phone has eighty-six percent power, the ringer is on the loudest setting. She slips it into her front pocket, next to her thigh to feel the vibration. Panera is empty except for two Goth teenagers in a booth and an old woman talking to herself in a corner. Molly stands up to buy a cup of coffee.

After crossing two streets, Turi steps through the archway of the correctional facility, opens the door, and slowly approaches an enclosed hexagonal booth in the middle of a lobby with thick glass windows at the top and a dark wood base waist high, like a bulgy belt to keep anybody a few more inches away from the police officer inside. A sign at the top of the booth reads: "INFORMATION, INFORMACÍON."

"May I help you?"

"Yes sir," Turi says, his brown eyes discovering through the glass the cobalt blue metal chairs on the other side of the booth with families waiting: two men in T-shirts and a woman in jeans too small for her body. He thinks he hears a word or two of Spanish, rapid fire like a *rat-tat-rat-tat-rat-tat*, but he isn't sure. "I came to visit a friend who was sent here. He's undocumented."

"His name?" The officer swivels slightly in his chair. He isn't smiling, but he isn't frowning either.

"Arnulfo Muñoz. He's a minor and I checked the ICE website and—"

"Wait a sec. How do you spell that?"

"M-u-ñ-o-z. The 'n' has that little mark at the top in Spanish."

"The tilde."

"Yes, I guess that's what it's called." Turi almost smiles to himself: he remembers the first time he met Arnulfo at the chicken farm east of Ysleta, Texas. That seems years ago, although it has been almost two weeks. Turi notices the black gun holstered on the policeman's hip, the cameras aimed at him over the booth, the cameras on the ceiling, other doors and mirror windows, with police officers marching through the lobby. Cops and ICE agents are everywhere.

"Okay, I think I've found him. But no inmate visiting list. That's odd. Why does it have . . . ?" The officer doesn't finish his sentence as he flips up his dark brown glasses and brings his eyes closer to the computer screen.

"Visiting list?"

"He doesn't list anybody who's allowed to visit him. You contact him already? No list, no visitors."

"You mean, he has to list the people he wants to visit him?"

"Yes, that's right."

"How do I get him to do that if I can't talk to him? I've never done this before."

"Good for you. Write him a letter. Here's the address, put his name on top of it. He'll get it. This is really odd . . ." The officer twists in his chair, again putting his nose close to his computer screen, absorbed. "The other problem, by the way, is that after he puts you on the list, this friend of yours, then you have to fill out this Preapproval Request to Visit Questionnaire. You can fill it out now and send a letter to your friend at the post office across the street, to the right. Speed things up a bit." The officer hands him the form, another sheet of paper, a pen, and keeps trying to decipher something perplexing on his computer screen.

"Thank you. But officer, what—what I mean . . . what if he gets sent to Mexico first, before I can come back?"

"Well, that happens sometimes. Give me a sec, I want to keep checking . . . this. You a family member?"

"No, just a friend. Don't think he has any family here. He is alone. His parents are in Mexico."

"Just fill out the form over there. Leave it with me."

"Okay, thank you."

Turi walks around the booth to the blue metal chairs anchored to the floor, to the edge of a row, away from the loud family at one end and two young men, slumped and almost asleep in the other row. He notices the tattoos on their forearms, which strangely remind him of Ramon and his friends on Corralitos. One man's tattoo looks like the conch shell of the Virgin Mary, except the virgin's face is black with two large white eyes. Turi doesn't want to stare too long, so he focuses on his form.

Do you possess a current driver's license? Yes or No. If Yes,

*License # & State of Issue:*_____

Should Turi really write his fake driver's license number and wait for them to check it?

Other questions:

Have you ever been arrested? Yes or No. If Yes,

*List the year and the offense:*_____

Have you ever been sentenced to a Correctional Facility / Prison?

Have you ever been convicted of a crime?

Have you ever been convicted of a felony?

If Turi puts his name down, his real name, will he come up as one of the boys who stole the blue Ford pickup? Wanted by the authorities in Texas? And will they track him back to Kent, especially if he is using his real name to enroll at New Milford High School, with Mrs. Garcia or Tía Romita sending him a copy of his birth certificate from El Paso? But they already have their blue truck. And Arnulfo told them he stole the truck, no one else. Turi's sure that's what Arnulfo did. *What should I do?*

He glances at the information booth and then around to the doors he came through. There is only one way out of this lobby—and only one way in. Behind him, beyond the waiting area of lumpy blue metal chairs, are what appear to be doors and more offices, and behind glass even more police officers working at desks, secretaries, men and women in suits marching through the lobby. What if he doesn't fill out the form? What if he just walks out? What if instead of leaving anything there, Turi first writes to Arnulfo and waits for his response? That will be better than getting himself (and maybe Molly) in trouble right now. What if he walks right by the officer at the information booth, who was staring at him before for a moment? What if Turi just walks out? Will he be stopped? Has he just gotten himself into another mess? Escaping Juanito in Lubbock was one thing, but escaping this situation, the police—well, even Ramon would never be so stupid as to get himself caught at the police station.

Turi stands up from the blue metal chair whose bars have been pressing against his back and starts marching toward the door. He won't look anywhere else. He will just walk straight ahead . . . through the door . . . to the street . . .

"Hey. Sir. *Sir*," Turi hears behind him, a metallic voice that later he understands came from a speaker atop the information booth. "Sir." Turi, his heart thumping inside his chest, wants to keep walking, but he doesn't. He turns around. The police officer is standing inside the glass booth, waving his hand for Turi to come back. The eyes behind the Buddy-Holly brown glasses, which are in turn behind the thick glass plates of the booth—Turi can see and not see well through the reflections—these eyes seem insistent, aimed at him. Turi walks back toward the officer, even as his mind urges him to sprint toward the door.

"First, my pen. Don't forget my pen."

"Oh," Turi says, staring at his hands as if they weren't his, and marveling that they hold a pen and two sheets of paper. "I'm sorry." He slides the pen through the metal slot and exhales.

"You're a friend, right? Of Arnulfo Muñoz?" The officer is still standing inside the booth. One hand is on his holster, as if resting but also ready on the black leather.

"Yes sir. I'm his friend," Turi says, a million thoughts bursting in his head like fireworks, but one in particular lingers, the shine against the floor from the sun's rays piercing the glass of the outside door, that brilliance almost blinding him like a sudden, yet vague memory. He thinks about Molly waiting for him at Panera. He wants only to be with her. He wants only to return to her. "I'm a friend of Arnulfo Muñoz, sir."

"I need, well, your contact info. Before you leave."

"I was going to fill it out later. I—I . . . I was going to write to him first."

"Son, this friend of yours, Arnulfo Muñoz—I finally got the notes on him, some people around here don't know how to type—anyway, I confirmed the right info, it was entered oddly, wrong—your friend, sir, he passed away. He died yesterday."

"What? How—?" Turi's knees feel weak underneath him, the shine from the glass booth, the shine on the floor, all of it seems to come up to his chin at once like errant and evil waves of light.

"Another inmate attacked him, stabbed him. It's been a mess around here for the past three days. We also had an outbreak of that plague from the Midwest in another cell block, some prisoner extradited from Kansas who arrived with a few others about a week ago."

"Arnulfo's dead? I—I don't understand."

"Yes sir. They've isolated the perp, a real badass from one of the drug gangs. I think there was a little confusion about who goes where with the infected Kansas prisoner, the quarantine of an entire cell block, all members of that group, roommates. Half of them have died too. In the mix up, in the transfers of prisoners from one area to another, your friend was attacked. I'm sorry, sir."

"I—I can't, oh my god. How is that . . . ?" Turi wants to sit down, but only the linoleum floor is below his feet. He feels dizzy, his palms are suddenly sweaty, and he grabs hold of the thick wooden bulge around the booth just to keep himself steady. Near his hands he sees a piece of paper coming through the metal slot, and that ICE pen again. The entire room seems to tilt in a sickening fashion.

"He's got no family here, you say? He's from Mexico?"

"Yes, that's right." Turi scribbles on the blank piece of paper, trying to concentrate, his hand shaking.

"Just your name, address, phone number, email. Just in case anybody has questions. They'll ship the body back to Mexico, I guess. Or just cremate it here. I don't know. I'll put your info in the database, just in case anybody has any questions about who he was. I'm sorry, son. Sorry I had to be the one to tell you. You should get vaccinated ASAP."

"Officer, Arnulfo, my friend, he wasn't part of any gang. He wasn't like that. He wasn't like them, he wasn't *with* them. He . . . he . . ." One of Turi's tears drops just beyond the paper he is writing on.

"Never met him. Again, I'm sorry about your friend."

"Thank you, officer. I appreciate your help." Turi slides the paper and pen back to the officer through the metal slot. In Turi's mind, the world tilts, as if in a slow, cataclysmic earthquake. The young man who is so far away from his hometown of Ysleta, from the parents he loved and the family he hated, Turi struggles to stay steady and find again the light of the door to the outside.

On the paper, Turi has written his name, no phone number, Elodia's address, and an email he created for what he hopes will be his occasional correspondence with Mrs. Garcia: PelegrinoFromElPaso@gmail.com

"Take care," Turi hears somewhere behind him.

He stumbles through the doors of the Plymouth correctional facility, into the bright sunlight outside.

Rudy arrives to pick up Turi and Molly in Hartford, surprised they are making it back Saturday night, a few minutes before midnight. He was expecting them back tomorrow on Sunday. Ten hours on buses, from Hartford to Boston to Plymouth, and back. One long day. A rough trek for

anyone. Rudy has often told them how he admires their youthful tenacity; it reminds him of how he was back in the day. They trudge toward Rudy under the streetlights and the grime and exhaust and other stragglers in shadows in and around the buses. Both of them are exhausted. Their faces deathly pale, even when they climb into the truck's cab. Up close, their watery, red eyes confuse him, alarm him. Both teenagers have been crying. After Turi tells him what happened to Arnulfo, what the police officer said, the almost unspeakable news, no one says another word on the ride back to Kent.

Turi and Molly don't tell Rudy how they stayed at Panera, shocked by what they were trying to understand. Molly stifled screams ("They killed him! They killed him! I don't know how, but they killed him!"), and Turi did not even try to stop her, just held her hand, he himself deep inside an abyss. He first told Molly, "We don't know that! We don't know! Maybe just some bad guy in jail killed him by mistake!" but now he's not so sure. Maybe she's right, somehow. Maybe they know where they are.

In any case, Turi believes Arnulfo should have been with them. Arnulfo should never have been in that jail cell alone. Arnulfo should never have gotten into the truck to get the danger away from them. His friend should never have been the one to give them a chance in Kent. Arnulfo, goddamn Arnulfo, all he wanted to do was work. All he wanted was to pull himself from la nada into the good life. Arnulfo had been like Turi's parents, those Mexicans from Ysleta, who wanted another America, who took risks and remade themselves to have a better life, who loved the United States, even if they didn't quite belong there, at least not yet, but in time they would— only to be crushed within sight of their dreams. When the assistant manager came over and told them they would have to leave Panera, because someone complained, because he didn't want any trouble, Turi and Molly staggered onto the sidewalk of the strip mall, refugees again, and wandered without thinking, and arrived at the bus depot again as if in a dark trance.

It's near midnight. They drive west on Route 202 through Avon, Canton, and Torrington. The dark empty streets in front of them are a reflection of what's inside Turi's head: the street lights mindlessly blinking yellow at corners, no lights inside any stores, no one out anywhere, nothing. The nothingness called to Turi. He'd like to open the truck's door and succumb to the river of glittery black asphalt coursing underneath them. Molly's hand keeps him from doing it, Molly's warmth on his hand, Molly's head on his shoulders, the scent of Molly's breath wafting around his neck, she mercifully asleep . . . Even Rudy's grim face, as Turi glances at him, his fierce eyes that never stray from the road, and his two tears, half dry on that cheek of brown granite. All of these images keep Turi from yanking open the truck's door and jumping into the night.

CHAPTER TWENTY-FIVE

Rudy solves their biggest problem. First he held off his sister Elodia from kicking them out of her house immediately. But then, after what happened to Arnulfo, that week, as Molly is finishing her shift at her new job at the Colonial Settler, Rudy mentions it to her, this "accessory apartment idea."

"She's charging you too much. You know that. One hundred dollars per day! I wouldn't pay that!" Rudy says.

"So what's this 'accessory apartment'? You live in somebody's house, here in Kent?"

"No, not quite, it's something they're doing. These affordable housing people. I know Ken who comes here all the time. I donated tamales for a fundraiser he had. They couldn't build enough affordable apartments. They have about thirty on South Commonplace. You know, for people who live in Kent, but don't have a lot of money. The workers. Julio who cooks on Tuesdays, Wednesdays, and Thursdays, he and his familia got into one of those. But only thirty, and they went fast."

"I don't—" Molly will still intermittently cry at the back of the diner after work, just a few tears, for no reason. She looks like she is about to start crying now. She sits on the bench behind the kitchen of the restaurant, her shoulders slumped, her blond hair in a tight bun for work. Sometimes the thought still slips into her mind that she has the job Arnulfo would have had.

"Just hear me out. Turi will be back tomorrow, right? I can't give him another day off. You talk to him. Tell him this, Molly. You live in someone else's house in Kent, in a little apartment above the garage. A person who's alone, or who only visits their house on weekends. These rich New Yorkers. That's the idea. More affordable housing without building it. Ken was telling me about it. I called him yesterday and he told me one's available. Perfect for you. On Segar Mountain. I told him about both of you."

"Really? Why are you helping us? It's—it's—"

"Of course I'm gonna help you. Of course! Why wouldn't I? We help each other, right? You talk to Turi tonight. This is a great idea for the two of you. Don't let Elodia hear you. Ken's coming in tomorrow. You can go look at the place. About six miles from here on 341. He said it's a nice retired couple, a professor and his wife who have a small garage apartment in their house. They would love somebody there, to take care of the place when they're traveling. It's an affordable housing program, these apartments and everything. Ken said there are rules. The couple signed up with him, with his program. It's perfect for you and Turi. And not $100 per day! I can't believe my sister Elodia. She's not like the Marriott."

Strands of Molly's hair are matted against her forehead after working eight hours straight, from six in the morning till two in the afternoon. Her dirty apron is still on her lap as she sits on the thick wooden bench and leans against the wall beyond the kitchen at the back of the Colonial Settler. A few feet away, a skillet sizzles with burgers. The hum of the lunch crowd, including many students from the two local prep schools, undulates in a formless, unending rhythm.

"Thank you, Rudy. Gosh, thank you."

"Everything's gonna be fine. You hear me, Molly?"

"Yes." She finally looks up from staring at her hands. A crooked strand of her blond hair with a blue streak dangles oddly over an eyebrow and in front of her mouth.

"You're going back to school too, right? Just like Turi?"

"We decided he'll go first to New Milford High. He's six months younger, but a grade ahead of me. He can start in one month, in September, as long as he gets all his paperwork in. I'm too old to be a sophomore at a regular high school, but I can go to an afterschool GED program they have at New Milford, at night, after five p.m. I can go after work, as long as I can find a way to get there."

"Oscar can drive you after work. He lives in New Milford. I'll tell him."

"Rudy—"

"Molly, don't give me those eyes. Nobody helped me when I got here from Mexico. At first. Then Mr. Johnson gave me a break at the White Horse Tavern. I worked hard. Then I got promoted to cook. Then I took the test and became a citizen. Then I started my own place. I'm gonna help you and Turi, so don't even bother with your protestas. That's how it's done. That's America. Okay? You talk to Turi tonight. Talk to him about Ken and this idea. Accessory departamentos."

Molly stands up to leave. Her knees buckle. It is her first time sitting down in eight hours. Although she has worked in Steelville, Missouri behind the register of the country store, that work was never close to the non-stop controlled chaos of the Colonial Settler in mid summer, with bikers touring the Litchfield Hills, students in summer music or sports programs with their parents, weekenders visiting their favorite diner, and cranky locals at the counter reading the *Litchfield County Times* or the *Republican-American*—all of them trying to act normal in these abnormal times. But

Molly overhears their whispered conversations about what is happening beyond Kent. Once in a while she even sees a few faces covered by surgical masks. Rudy has given all his workers surgical masks, and some wear theirs every day. Molly only wears her mask whenever she gets a warning from Rudy or another worker about a customer potentially infected with the virus. "I'll talk to Turi when he gets home from registering. Hope they didn't have any problems."

"Mimi's done it before. For our kids. She knows the people there. Turi even looks like her a little bit. Same forehead and eyes. With what his aunt sent from Juárez, that should be the only documents they need. What's another 'cousin' in the family! Molly, before you go, can I ask you a question?"

"Of course."

"You and Turi. I'm not a metiche, but you know, are you guys together?"

"I don't know. I think so. Meh-tee—?"

"I'm only asking because I like both of you. I want you guys to be okay. I had it hard when I started out. I was alone. Many times I wanted to give up, until I met Mimi. You two, I hope you stay together. It's better that way. It's how you survive."

"Yeah, I know. Thank you, Rudy. But, that word . . . meh-tee . . . ?"

"*Me-ti-che.* Nosy. Snoopy, but not like the dog on TV."

"Hah," Molly says almost in a whisper to herself. "It's a Charlie Brown Thanksgiving." Rudy waves at her as he marches into the kitchen and returns to work.

She starts to prep the tables for the next shift, when she notices an old man sit at a table booth next to the window, the lunch crowd almost gone. She smiles, brings him a lunch menu, and starts clearing a couple of empty tables of their dirty dishes, napkins, and a child's seat. The old man keeps staring at her—she sees through the corner of her eyes. This wouldn't be the first time an old guy was a little lecherous. Molly ignores any inappropriate comments or stops smiling at anybody getting too creepy and that usually works. But in the booth by the window on Main Street, the old man is also coughing up a storm, all over his water glass, and seems permanently hunched over as if he's suffering stomach pain. Molly reaches for her mask in her back pocket, puts it on, and looks at Rudy, who is busy ringing up customers in a small line at the front of the restaurant. She almost feels sorry for the old man in the booth. Molly is certain she has never seen him before at the Colonial Settler. But he keeps staring at her every move, wherever she is, with black, shiny eyes. She also notices a tattoo of a snarling black dog or a wolf on the old man's forearm. Again she glances at Rudy, but he is still dealing with customers paying their bills.

"So what can I get for you?" Molly stands at what she thinks is a safe distance from her customer, without being too rude. She keeps remembering what Rudy has repeated many times each morning, "I don't care if it's the First Selectman of Kent ordering his burger with caramelized onions: if he coughs, if he sneezes, watery eyes, put your mask on, keep away. Get me and I'll deal with anybody who's sick."

"Thank you, señorita. A cup of coffee. The turkey melt with avocado sounds delicious. I noticed on the menu you have 'Mexican Night' on Wednesdays. Looks like the cooks and the man behind the register—excuse me, please, excuse my . . ." The old man starts coughing so hard, the table shakes as he grips it with both powerful hands. He coughs toward Molly's apron, even as she takes two steps back. "I apologize. Just sick with maybe the flu. The regular flu. Not anything else, really. But just so sick, but . . .

well . . . oh, yes . . . so there are Mexicans in this little town of Kent? I'm Mexican, you see, señorita." Molly sees the tattooed wolf on the old man's forearm twitch as if it's about to leap out the dark, coppery skin.

"Yes, sir, the owner is Mexican. His family. I work for them. I'll bring you more water in—"

"Pardon me, miss. Just one more question . . . don't have a lot of time, I think . . ." The old man seems to lose his train of thought, and his eyes roll back in his head as if he's about to pass out in the booth.

Molly looks at him, turns again to get Rudy's attention, but Rudy's already looking at both of them. Molly guesses by Rudy's worried look that he's thinking how to get this patron out of the restaurant as quickly as possible just in case he has that dangerous virus that's been affecting areas in Hartford and New Haven and all across the country. Rudy's kicked people out before, but not often. He often reminds all of his workers to stay as clean as possible, to wash every apron, to scrub every dish, and even to don thick plastic gloves when picking up dishes of patrons who have exhibited flu-like symptoms, just in case. No one at the Colonial Settler has gotten sick yet. Molly turns back to the old man. His dark, unblinking black eyes remind her of a mongoose. Those eyes focus on Molly again.

"Any other Mexicans in Kent, señorita? I miss being around my people."

"Of course. I have a friend who just moved here from El Paso. Sir, you okay? Let me get your order in." Molly is only thinking of getting Rudy and getting away from this old man, but she doesn't want to be rude.

"Thank you, thank you. Yes. El Paso. I know the place very well—" The old man stops as he ends with another coughing fit. "What's your friend's name, if I may ask?"

"Turi. Short for Arturo. I'll be right back."

The old man's eyes follow Molly as she picks up the dishes at a nearby table before heading to the kitchen. Rudy meets her there and tells her to have her apron washed thoroughly, to wash her hands, and even to make sure all her clothes go directly into a plastic bag for the dirty laundry when she gets home. Rudy tells her he'll take care of the old man. "Molly, go home. I got this."

The stocky Rudy talks to the old man from a measured distance of a few feet, and asks him to leave the restaurant. The old man fakes a smile revealing his crooked golden teeth, waves his arms in mock submission and a bit of anger, and gets up and shuffles out the front door onto Main Street. Rudy stands guard by the window to make sure the old man leaves the premises.

CHAPTER TWENTY-SIX

Juanito lurks near the Colonial Settler for a few seconds and sees the squat pinche Mexicano staring at him through the window. He shuffles away, thinking of where he can go to keep an eye on the restaurant, to wait. He crosses the street to a complex of shops and thinks about finding a secluded spot to wait for Turi. *After I find him, after I kill that little bastard, my boss will find a way to take care of me. Dunbar will trust me again. Dunbar has the money to help me. But without him I'm a dead man. I have to finish the job.*

On a bench hidden behind some trees, Juanito remembers the last communication with his boss in Clint, a text message before cell service stopped working: "Get home, Juanito, bring the truck back after you finish the job. And get home. It's getting nasty out there." Dunbar's blue truck is parked behind the shops in a corner where it won't be seen by anyone, including Turi. It was more than easy to retrieve it from the Torrington impound lot once his boss had delivered the papers and permissions to the Connecticut State Police. This time Juanito will take care of business for Dunbar.

On the bench, under the trees, Juanito's cough seems to recede. Just a slow wheezing rises from his chest. He doesn't believe he has the deadly virus—Chucho and Eduardo have the blood vials, don't they? It's just a coincidence he got the flu after he retrieved the truck from Torrington. It's a run of bad luck that will turn into good luck as soon as he finds Turi.

But instead of his target, Juanito spots another stranger, a man with one crutch heavily swinging on the sidewalk on the other side of Main Street, an odd, hulking man walking right past the Colonial Settler to the liquor store a few doors down. *Could it be? How in the world? Here in Kent?* Juanito sits on the edge of the bench and waits for the wounded giant to exit the liquor store. He searches his memory. He remembers the article from *El Sol de Chilpancingo* about the decapitated police force, the famous photo of barrels with heads on top of them, the one with the mask of Mil Máscaras. In the background was a hulking man with just the slightest smile, a man everyone ignored since the focus was on the gory barrels. Juanito always wondered if that was the only photo of el Hijo de Huerta in existence. The same build. The same hunch to his shoulders. The face, although blurry in the photo, was massive like an ancient stone from a pyramid. Juanito kept that photo for months on his phone. El Hijo de Huerta. The executioner of Chilpancingo. The Babe Ruth of narcos. The famed soldier of his boss's boss, Don Ilan, el Luchador from Guerrero.

It would make sense, Juanito thinks, as he waits for the giant to exit the liquor store. It would make sense if Don Ilan has sent el Hijo to Kent to find Turi. It would make sense that Don Ilan and Dunbar, his jefe, would be talking to each other, maybe sharing information about the truck, to finish the job. To get rid of that little bastard. But why hadn't Dunbar told him about el Hijo in Connecticut in his last text? Maybe Dunbar doesn't know el Hijo is here. Maybe Don Ilan is trying to get rid of Dunbar, as the rumors have often indicated. Maybe el Hijo—if it is el Hijo—has been sent to kill Turi *and* him. To begin the move against Dunbar. Is that what's getting "nasty" out there? Juanito is certain his boss would have told him to watch for el Hijo in Kent. If Dunbar knew.

The giant exits the Kent liquor store and shuffle-sways down the sidewalk with a bag gripped awkwardly in one arm. Juanito gets up from the bench and marches into a side alley to get an angled view of the man in crutches. The adrenaline rushes to his legs, he starts walking fast, the wheezing seems to have stopped completely. As he exits the alley and stands discretely behind a fence, Juanito sees the profile of the man in crutches, not only a Mexicano, it is clear, but that ancient stone-face, and those powerful arms. The same blurry face in that photo Juanito stared at for months. El Hijo de Huerta. As odd as discovering a black rhinoceros ambling down the picturesque Litchfield Hills of Kent. Juanito follows him.

If I kill him . . . if I kill him . . . Dunbar will be more than grateful. He will take me to Costa Rica with him. He will save me if I am really sick. I will have recovered his truck. I will have killed that damn kid and finished the job. And I will have eliminated el Hijo de Huerta. Ese maldito. My boss will love me again. The hell with Chucho! I will be Dunbar's number one. I will be el mero mero. The one who finished that wounded animal, the pride and horror of Chilpancingo, El Hijo de Huerta. But how?

Late at night, by the side of isolated Cobble Road in Kent not far from Main Street, Juanito coughs and coughs, an uncontrollable cough that thunders inside his chest like a cyclone. The old man feels he'll cough his brains out through his nose and mouth. No light is visible on this road, no house lights, no streetlights. This is where Juanito has slept in his quest to find Turi in Kent, where the old man has rested after he staked out the Colonial Settler during the day, and where he has tried to sleep tonight after he found el Hijo de Huerta on Main Street. Even in the desert of El Paso, Texas, Juanito has never seen so many nights like these: the absolute rural darkness of northwest Connecticut, the ominous quiet in the trees, a hole in the fabric of the earth. The cyclone cough ripples through his chest again. He reaches for the truck's cab light in the front seat, punches it, and grabs a white paper towel from the passenger seat. On the towel, speckles of blood, mixed with phlegm, cover the surface.

I am dying, I am dying. I don't know how—goddamn Chucho—but I am dying. Why fool myself? In Dunbar's truck. In this Connecticut nada so far away from home. But I know where he is, el Hijo. I can do him in at least. And if I find that little bastard from El Paso, I will do him in too. I might still get back to Dunbar, he might still help me, but only if I return with these prizes. Only if I do the job. Only if I do more than my job. Only if I ...

Juanito looks at the knife tucked away in a sheath on the floor of the backseat. He stares at the white paper towel with his blood. He knows what to do. It is three in the morning. He starts the truck and drives slowly through the dark rural road back to Main Street, on the other side of a hill from Cobble Road. At the corner of Main Street and Route 7, he can see the bright yellow house that reminds him of a toy house, the place where he last saw el Hijo, shuffling inside with his package from the liquor store. There's only one car in the small gravel parking lot in front of the toy house: that must be el Hijo's rental car, with Arizona plates. Not a single car on Route 7. Nothing, not even a cat, on Main Street. At three in the morning, Kent seems like an abandoned ghost town in the middle of a forest. Juanito parks by the side of the darkened road and steps out.

This is how he will get the job done tonight, he thinks. This is the easy way, for that monster and enemy of his boss. In front of the car with Arizona plates, the gravel crunching under the old man's work boots, Juanito forces a wheeze through his chest and coughs blood and phlegm right on the driver side door handle. He smears the mess in and around the handle with the paper towel, as the warm summer night releases a breeze at his feet. Juanito's black eyes stare at the yellow toy house. All the windows are still dark. Nothing is on the roads tonight. He walks up to the entrance of that toy house. On the front doors, again he forces a wheeze and coughs directly on the doorknobs and rubs the blood and mucous everywhere a human will touch to enter that ridiculous yellow house.

If I am going to die, they will all die with me.

CHAPTER TWENTY-SEVEN

The stillness at night in Kent reminds Molly of rural Missouri and camping out in the Mark Twain National Forest, whereas the same quiet reminds Turi of rural Ysleta and meandering next to cotton fields when he wanted to escape for a few hours from Corralitos. Molly and Turi are still awake, lying on their twin beds at Elodia's. They can't see each other. All the lights and soft noises that enter through the bottom of their closed door have ceased. Elodia is probably asleep and not spying on them for a few minutes as she often does at night. They always know she is there. Sometimes they whisper extra softly when they hear that first, faint creak of the floor. Molly and Turi stop whispering for a moment and hold hands across the gap of darkness between their beds. They do it every night before falling asleep. Almost like a good night kiss.

Turi tells Molly about getting registered for high school for the fall semester, which will start in about six weeks. Mimi knew everybody at the registrar's office, and her kids—Rudy's kids—although not necessarily stellar academic students (or so complained Mimi) have been well behaved and well liked, one a starter for the high school soccer team. The registrar accepted all the documents sent by Tía Romita via Mrs. Garcia at Ysleta High School in El Paso: the transcript, the birth certificate, the certified letter indicating the "family relationship" with Mimi. A nurse gave him the antiviral vaccine immediately, a requirement for all registered students.

Everything happened so fast. The sudden end of the process shocked Turi when they were walking out. In Mimi's Chevy on Route 7 back to Kent, he cried, and not because of the shot.

Turi doesn't relate this part of the story to Molly, but she wouldn't have been surprised.

He thought about his parents and Arnulfo, he remembered living in the shed in the back of the Alvidrez house, and everything that happened to them as they drove across the country. From news reports, he has heard about the river of death created by the strange malevolent virus affecting thousands in the Midwest, particularly cities. Will it ever reach rural Kent, and how? Will a sporadically produced vaccine contain the flames of infection? So much, too much, crashed upon his shoulders inside that Chevy with Mimi as they were driving back home. Turi has often imagined his seat-of-the-pants survival like a bridge collapsing behind him, a bridge between where he began, where he has been, and where they are now. He imagines it as a version of the scene in *The Lord of the Rings*, Gandalf's epic battle with the Balrog, the bridge in the Mines of Moria falling behind and around the wizard as he runs to escape. Ysleta and the Alvidrez house on one side of the imaginary bridge—Kent and Molly on the other side of that bridge. In between, in the abyss: the blue Ford pickup, the narcos, the virus and its river of death, and Arnulfo. Yet Turi does not think he is as brave as Gandalf, nor does he think he is as lucky as Frodo. Turi is only exhausted. This day, Mimi helping him for no reason at all, this help miraculously working to register him again in school—all of it has overwhelmed him.

Now it is Molly's turn. Across the darkness in Elodia's spare bedroom, Molly tells him about Rudy's idea, the accessory apartment, and getting out of Elodia's, and how it will be cheaper, and how they can save money. Maybe they can buy two cheap bikes, for the six miles to work at the Colonial Settler. Tomorrow they can see this garage apartment, and she mentions Ken, how he is a friend of Rudy's. When Turi says nothing in the darkness, Molly swings her arm toward his bed until she reaches part of his blanket or the mattress— she isn't sure—and at that same moment Turi's hand reaches for hers and their hands clasp together in the nothingness. All she hears is, "That's great. Tomorrow we meet Ken? But, but . . . why are they helping us? Why?"

Molly doesn't say a word for many minutes, their hands still together, his fingers tracing hers, as he moves closer to stop straining toward her in the blackness, to easily hold her hand. Molly feels a sharp, gentle tug. She slips off the bed and sits against it on the floor. Turi is already there, Molly can't see him, but she touches his knee in front of her, as he squats against his own bed. They have done this a few times before, facing each other in the pitch black, whispering, listening for any creaks in the hallway in case Elodia wakes up. Their beds are almost like invisible, heavy ramparts against the night and the outside world, against any possible spies. The space in between their beds is their warm corner within a cave of darkness.

"Don't know why. Maybe they think we're damaged," Molly says to the darkness in front of her. She pats in front of her until she finds Turi's hand again. It is warm like hers.

"Young and damaged. That's who we are. Los perdidos."

"Per-dee-tos. Per-ree-dos? What?"

"Sounds like it, but not little dogs. Perritos. But *perdidos*. Per-*dee*-dos. The lost ones."

"The invisible ones, right now. That's who we are."

"Here, 'see' me with your hand, here." Turi takes Molly's hand and brings it to his cheek. She caresses his face and runs her fingers through his hair, and lingers her fingertips around his ear. He shivers.

"Here, now you can 'see' me too." Molly brings Turi's hand to her cheek, and he brushes his fingers across her skin and touches her neck, and one finger lingers near her lips, and she kisses it. "Wait," Molly whispers, "give me your hand again," after Turi pulls it away and rubs her knee in the gloom. "Just here. Just keep it here." Molly brings Turi's hand to her left breast. He seems to pull it away quickly as soon as he realizes where his hand is, as soon as he senses what he has touched. "It's okay, it's okay," she repeats. "I want you to."

"You sure?"

"Of course." Turi's hand lingers and gently strokes her breasts. After a few moments, she feels him slide across the floor closer to her, next to her, and every touch seems to change the night, just that one hand lightly touching her, exploring this new country. Molly cannot hear him breathe anymore. Turi is perhaps holding his breath.

"Molly, thank you," he whispers.

"You can stay there, if you want. I like it."

"Oh, Molly. You're so beautiful. I like it too. Can I tell you something really corny?" he says toward the sweet scent wafting toward him—Molly's breathing—which has always reminded him of salty caramels.

"From a fellow corneek? Yes, of course."

"I wanted to do that for a long time."

"So why didn't you?"

"I—I . . . Okay, I wasn't confident. I still see myself as a stupid . . . chubby Mexican kid with bruises on his body."

"Well... you're not chubby." After a few seconds, she continues, "Gotcha."

"Molly, I wanted to do that ... every time ... when I felt sad ... when I just wanted to give up, I ..."

"You what?" Molly whispers, an octave lower, entreating him to keep explaining.

"Well... I looked at your breasts. I love looking at your breasts. They give me hope. That's not creepy, is it?"

He hears a sharp snort from Molly, and he imagines her face grinning, chuckling, at the brink of mirth, and her lips with the widest of smiles, and then, "Really? My breasts?"

"I know. That sounds really stupid."

"You got *hope* from staring at my little boobs?"

"Please, I know. It's idiotic. And they're perfect, by the way."

"And now?"

"Molly, they're wonderful. Touching them. My god. I can't see them, but touching them, it's—it's just beyond what I ever imagined. Better than magic."

"Okay, here. You get some hope right now. Tantalize me, right ... right ... exactly, *yeah.* Right there. Happy to be of service."

"Molly. Thank you. I ... I ..."

"Shhh. No words. We ... just ... just ... yeah. Give both of us a little more of that hope, a little more of that magic. Yeah."

CHAPTER TWENTY-EIGHT

Cosio and Miriam Torgerson walk Turi and Molly around their twenty-one-acre property on Segar Mountain, about six miles from the town center of Kent. The Torgersons are relieved to have their first tenants for their "accessory apartment" under the town's affordable housing program. The four walk down their long gravel driveway into a hidden clearing between two hills, about a fifth of a mile from Route 341. An ancient stone wall—its rocks greenish-white with dried moss—appears and crumbles into the landscape.

"About ten years ago, we found that old tractor tiller when we cleared the side yard—you see it over there on top of that rock? Jorge our Brazilian landscaper thought it looked good, like an art object, on that slab of black mica. Brilliant move," Mr. Torgerson now says as they keep walking the property, in a clear-as-a-bell voice that often hits a high, almost whiny note. He lurches in heavy, deliberate steps, as if he is about to start trotting for a 70-and-over marathon. While Miriam's hair is still sandy brown, with a streak of gray on one side, her husband's hair is as white as the belly of a squirrel, his face ruddy red.

"I know Rudy at the Colonial Settler," Miriam says as they circle the back of the house, where a small creek meanders into Lake Waramaug. "About the only people of color in town. Poor souls."

"You pay for your own long-distance calls. Maybe do a few chores around the house. Empty out the dehumidifier in the basement, I'll show you where it is. About once a day. Clean out pond filters, feed the fish. Every other day. Very easy stuff," Cosio says, still marching around the gardens, not even glancing back at them.

"How old are you two, by the way?" Miriam asks. Ken had told the Torgerson's that Molly and Turi were teens, but he mentioned that they weren't typical: they worked for Rudy, and a friend of theirs had recently died.

"We're seventeen," Molly says, the slightest of smiles on her face as she turns to Turi.

"Older than Romeo and Juliet," Cosio says, swatting away a mosquito as he makes a U-turn for the forest-green backdoor of the garage.

"Your parents know you're here? In Missouri and Texas?"

"We're both orphans," Turi says without hesitating. "My parents died in a car accident in Chihuahua when I was little." Turi follows Miriam and Molly and Cosio into the three-car garage. A mixture of odors—gasoline, oil, fertilizer, cedar mulch, and split wood on a long storage rack—greets them in the cool shadows.

"Mine died in a fire in Mizzouruh. Not too long ago. About three years."

"Orphans and seventeen," Cosio says in their kitchen, waiting for them as they enter through the mudroom behind him. "That's tough. That's even worse than how I grew up in Denmark after the war. Don't end up like Romeo and Juliet, that's all I have to say. You ever read John Womack, the historian? A Harvard man."

"No, sir," Turi says. Cosio Torgerson leans forward even when he's not walking, as if he might topple into them or push through them at any moment.

"*Zapata and the Mexican Revolution.* It's in the study. You're welcome to use it. Best goddamn history book on Latin America I've ever read. You're Mexican, right? 'We just need a man with his pants on, to defend us.' Remember that line."

"Yes, sir."

"You have a study, sir?" Molly says, her eyes widening.

"Just around the corner. I'll show you in a minute."

"We both recently finished reading *Catcher in the Rye,* sir," Turi says quickly, returning Molly's smile.

"Overrated. It's good, but not great. I like the real—history, philosophy, economics. You hear that, Miriam?—that's too much milk, honey; keep it for yourself—we have *readers* here."

Miriam hands her husband a new cup of coffee and winks at both Molly and Turi, as if they have passed an important test. "Let's show them the apartment above the garage. It's not much, but it's cozy."

"It's about as cheap as you'll find in this town of wannabe blue bloods!" Cosio snaps behind them, climbing the stairs with what sounds like stomps.

Before the Torgersons leave for their apartment in New York City, they tell Turi and Molly stories about Manhattan's Upper West Side, a world which seems to be in another dimension from rural Kent. It is not just the largest city in the United States—not just the expense and the crowds. He is a retired architect and professor and Danish expatriate, and she a retired school administrator whose Jewish ancestors were founders of an important Manhattan synagogue and Houdini's rabbi. Cosio and Miriam shake in their seats, half with fear and half with fury, as they tell of the City's unraveling.

"We've lived on the Upper West Side for almost fifty years, but this is different," Miriam says at the kitchen table, cleaning out a drawer stuffed with receipts, pencils, pens, four pairs of cheap plastic sunglasses, and all manner of operating instructions and warranties for different appliances. "Yes, when we were out of school, the area around Columbia University, it was dangerous. Morningside Heights. You needed 'mugging money' just in case you got robbed on the way to classes or to the grocery store."

"Penny-ante stuff. Poor people robbing to make a living. Mostly young Black kids from Harlem."

"Well, I'm not sure I would say that. Puerto Ricans too. Poor whites from Bensonhurst. But it was just *crime*. But last week, groups of men slaughtered twenty-eight people in one weekend. One weekend! The police are nowhere in sight. At night, groups of kids, Staten Islanders—who knows?—roam Broadway, Amsterdam, even Columbus. More windows are broken every night. People scream racial epithets at each other—or retaliate for an attack from another group. Or simply assault someone alone—like our friend Patricia—because, why not? Twenty-eight murders in one weekend, that's *normal* now. Something's happening to New York, to the government, they're overwhelmed."

"It's that disease. That virus. The hospitals are overflowing. Too many people in too small a space. Like infected rats crowded in a box," Cosio says. "They say they have a vaccine. But people don't listen. Poor people don't get the shot. We're not poor, and we haven't gotten it. Our doctor has never received enough vaccines. He keeps running out. We thought the homeless were a problem, hah! That was years ago. Now, in the subway, people are vomiting. Defecating on the benches. This pestilence is everywhere. It's not even safe to ride the buses, not in the City. You don't know if they are being cleaned properly." Turi does not tell the Torgersons, although Molly knows, that he was recently vaccinated at New Milford High School.

"You wear plastic gloves and a mask, even to go to the bank. That's the new normal," Miriam says, gripping the kitchen table with both hands as if she might float away, a little hill of pea pods in front of her. She has shown Molly and Turi her garden, her passion, where she has often planted dozens upon dozens of tulips every year, but now focuses on vegetables. "You can't eat vegetables from any grocer in the City. People do, but I wouldn't. You don't know if the bodega workers are infected. They have signs, guaranteeing this or that. The restaurants too. But are you going to risk your life for a cucumber? To eat a pastrami Rueben? Of course not. We wouldn't anyway, not before we get the vaccine. The restaurants and grocers are closing by the dozens. I thought it was bad when the Upper West Side had a few empty storefronts because landlords demanded ridiculous rents. That was nothing! Now *entire blocks* are empty. A lot of people have gotten the vaccine. A lot of people haven't. I'm not even sure if they know if it works for everybody. They rushed it through."

"But there's only one place that has a Memorial Sloan Kettering. So I have to return to the City, vaccine or no vaccine," Cosio says softly, a tone that startles Turi and Molly because they haven't heard it from him.

"We have to return," Miriam responds, her eyes glistening. "And we will survive."

When Cosio and Miriam finally pull out from the garage and wave goodbye, their big colonial house in the woods is deathly silent.

Turi and Molly's room is a large loft with a pullout couch for a bed, an extra TV the Torgersons had in a box, and boxes of books and papers from their New York apartment and from their old offices. They watch a few minutes of the news on TV, but it is bleak too. The apartment over the garage is on the opposite side of the house from the master bedroom, "for privacy," Miriam winked at them before she left. She reminds Molly of Minerva Mcgonagall from the Harry Potter movies.

That night, the high ceiling above them is like another sky.

CHAPTER TWENTY-NINE

It's deep in the night when Turi imagines he hears a vehicle pulling into the long driveway and a flash of lights against a wall, but then nothing. He is still half-asleep and keeps his head up for a second or two to see if he will hear the garage open underneath them. Perhaps the Torgersons have forgotten something. But nothing. No other sound or light. Only a slight ringing in his ears. Only Molly's soft breathing next to him. She is asleep. Turi attempts to go back to sleep, but he drifts in and out of a shallow sleep. After a few minutes, Turi is startled by what he thinks is glass breaking. That wasn't a dream.

"What—?"

"Molly, stay here. I think someone's in the house. Someone's broken in."

"In the house?"

"Don't turn on any lights. Get the phone and call the police."

"Don't turn on any lights? But maybe the lights will scare away whoever is inside," Molly whispers, already sitting up. There is no sound in the loft, but on the other side of the house they hear a faint creaking sound. Someone or something is definitely walking inside the house.

"Okay, turn them on. But call the police! I don't know how long it will take them to get here in Kent. We're in the middle of nowhere. 9-1-1, Molly. I'm gonna go see what it is."

"No, Turi, stay here!" she says, turning on the lights in the loft. The second floor hallway is still dark. The second, smaller staircase from the loft, next to the garage, is dark too. She finds the phone and dials. "Stay here!"

"Molly, I'm going to find out what's happened. The lights are on. He knows we're here, maybe he's left. 554 Segar Mountain Road. Call the Torgersons too, if you can. Maybe it's an animal, for all we know," Turi says, as he hears Molly talking on the phone, repeating the address to the police.

As he steps quietly through the dark upstairs hallway leading to the main part of house, Turi hears Molly saying, "We're staying at the Torgersons. We rent the loft. Please come right away. How far is the Litchfield Barracks? Please right away. Two of us. I'm five-foot . . ."

On the second floor, Turi crosses into the darkness of the upstairs second bedroom that connects the loft to the main part of the house. The central stairway leads down to the study, a living room facing the back-yard with sliding glass doors—what they call the 'Striped Room' for its wallpaper—and a dining room that faces the front of the house and the kitchen. The first floor is a warren of large rooms and open archways. On the second floor, the master bedroom is on the other side of the main stair-case. He stops at the staircase. The carpeted floor has creaked, but not too much. Turi listens. He hears nothing below. In the darkness, he can see a few shadows from the nightlight of the upstairs bathroom, but the stair-case is a black abyss in front of him. A faint breeze seems to blow from below like the breath from a deep cave. Still he hears nothing. As soon as he walks down, the stairs will creak loudly, as he remembers they did when they were first touring the house with Cosio and Miriam. If someone is still down there, that someone is not moving at all, as far as Turi can tell. He turns on the stairway lights, both on the first and second floor. He still hears nothing. "We've called the police! They're on their way, if anybody's down there!" he shouts before slowly descending the staircase.

As the wood on each stair groans loudly, Turi listens for a moment before taking another step. No other sounds. No more glass breaking. No footsteps. Did they imagine these sounds? He wonders what Molly is doing in the loft. He hopes she is hiding somewhere. Was she able to find the Torgerson's New York number taped on the desk in the loft? At the final step, he peers around the corner to the dining room to his left. No one seems to be there.

As Turi steps around the staircase to his right to check the sliding glass doors of the Striped Room, he hears a familiar, growly voice from behind: "You fucking little cabrón, you think you would get away with it!" just as a powerful forearm with a wolf on its leathery skin grabs his neck. Without thinking, Turi whips his elbow around and strikes Juanito in the face and steps away from him. The old man dangles a knife in one hand. Turi suddenly notices he is bleeding from a gash on his arm, the pain like an echo after the slash.

"How—"

"I'm gonna kill you once and for all, you little bastard!" As the old man teeters toward him with the knife gripped in one hand, Turi notices Juanito is injured, or walking strangely, as if he can't stand up straight. Juanito moans with pain, grabbing his stomach, and sweats profusely. Turi can smell something rancid, what seems to be feces in or around Juanito's pants.

"Fuck you! We've called the police!" Turi steps back and away from Juanito who is following him slowly, painfully, into the hallway that leads to the kitchen.

The lights suddenly, miraculously, go on in the kitchen. As he faces the lurching Juanito, Turi hears Molly shout behind him, "It's the old man from the Colonial Settler! He must have followed us!" She has probably come down the second stairway from the loft and peered into the kitchen from the bottom stair. Turi thinks he hears her running up the stairs again.

"Molly, stay away! Stay up there!"

"After I kill you, cabrón, I'm gonna kill her. But I'll have some fun first," Juanito growls in the full light of the kitchen, swaying as if he's drunk, his eyes yellowy and almost teary. The old man looks like a decrepit, mean hobo about to pass out from exhaustion or liquor.

"Hide, Molly!" Turi yells, not daring to turn around to see if Molly is behind him anymore on the loft stairway next to the mudroom and kitchen. Turi's eyes stay on Juanito who keeps walking, stumbling toward him, barely able to stand up. "We've called the police! We don't have the truck! Get the hell out of here!"

"I have the truck, you little asshole! I don't give a fuck about the police! They can shoot me dead! That idiot Eduardo... and Chucho, mother-fuckers... I would kill them too if they were here. If the cops shoot me, if they—who cares!—just look at me, goddammit! I'll be dead in one or two days anyway!" Juanito lunges at Turi with the knife, but misses. Turi is quick enough to shove Juanito's shoulders as the old man slowly swings the knife, then stumbles to one knee in the kitchen.

Juanito has soiled his pants: the putrid stench of uncontrolled diarrhea finally hits Turi's nose. The old man seems to have shrunken from what Turi remembers. But that powerful musky smell still lingers. The forearm with the wolf's tattoo is still weirdly muscular like the still-dangerous dark claw of a crippled black scorpion. Rivulets of blood drop onto the kitchen floor.

Turi grabs a cast-iron Le Creuset top from a large blue soup pot Miriam always keeps on the stove and flings it like a Frisbee right into Juanito's chest as the old man awkwardly straightens up. Juanito stumbles backward, gasps, smashes his back against a counter top, and drops to both knees. For a moment, the old man looks like he's praying; his eyes roll backward in his head and refocus. Turi grabs the bottom of the pot with both hands.

"Turi, the police, they're almost here! Come up here! Turi!" Turi hears Molly's voice behind him, from the loft stairway above him. He keeps his eyes on Juanito, who now is on all fours, breathing heavily, like a wounded animal.

Just when he thinks Juanito has had enough, the old man lunges again. The knife slashes into one of Turi's thighs as he jumps backward. In the same moment, Turi brings the Le Creuset crashing down onto Juanito's skull. The old man crumples flat on the ground, still breathing, barely conscious, the knife still weakly gripped in one hand. Turi steps on his hand and kicks the knife away as Juanito tries to grab Turi's leg but misses. Without taking his eyes off Juanito, Turi backs up closer to the stairway where Molly waits at the top. Turi's leg suddenly feels weak: he turns his eyes to stare at his thigh. Blood has covered the skin on his leg like a red one-legged trouser. More blood is dropping in splatters onto the mudroom floor. Molly is safe, Turi thinks. Molly is safe. "They're here! They're here!" he hears behind him, Molly's voice. Somewhere in his mind he thinks he hears the wail of a siren, but he isn't sure. He is lightheaded. Turi stumbles back onto the stairway, as Molly sprints past him to open the mudroom door and the garage for the police. The last words he hears before he faints on the stairway are Juanito's words. Breathing in gasps, the old man is conscious, but not moving from his prostrate position between the kitchen and the mudroom.

"El Hijo knows, cabrón. El Hijo de Huerta."

CHAPTER THIRTY

"You're not infected," Molly says to Turi after they have left New Milford Hospital. Turi is walking with a slight limp. His arm and thigh have been stitched up. The doctors have told him to rest. He lost some blood, but he will be okay. The Torgersons returned immediately from New York to help clean up the mess in the kitchen and mudroom—to have the house thoroughly disinfected. "You're not infected, thank goodness."

"I—I—I'm glad you're safe, Molly," Turi says, still shaken, noticing the hospital seems eerily empty, half vacant. "What are we gonna tell Cosio and Miriam? I mean, about Juanito?"

"That was the old man you stole the truck from?"

"Yes, in Texas."

"He found you. He found you through me. I'm so sorry, Turi."

"Molly, gosh," he says as he waits for her to open the Volkswagen in the parking lot. Oscar from the Colonial Settler, Rudy's brother, has lent her the car after they found out what happened, after Turi was taken to the hospital. Everybody has helped them. "I'm the one who should be sorry. You think the state troopers will ask any more questions? They think he was just an intruder. A crazy, sick person. I don't like lying to them."

"Well, I'm glad we did. We don't want to get into any more trouble. Let's get all of this behind us. Juanito's dead, you know that, right?"

"He was almost dead when he broke into the house. Like a zombie. Yes, the trooper who talked to me this morning told me. He said I didn't kill him. He said it wasn't my fault. Several times. He told me Juanito was already in the late stages of the viral infection that's everywhere. He told me I was brave, but I don't feel brave. I was angry and frightened. He was surprised I wasn't infected. A miracle."

"You were brave. And maybe lucky."

"I certainly don't feel lucky. I almost got you killed. I did all of this. Me and Arnulfo. And look what happened to him. Look what almost happened to you."

"But you're not infected. I'm okay," Molly says. "Don't forget we have to get your antibiotics in New Milford before we go back to Kent." She turns the Volkswagen south onto Route 202, which Turi notices. "I hope we can find a drugstore that's still open. When I told the guy in the ambulance that you already had the vaccine, he told me a few days wasn't enough for the vaccine to work, to protect you. You need at least ten days, two weeks."

"The ambulance took forever. That trooper saved my life. Trooper Everett. With the tourniquet on my leg. The hospital seems weirdly empty, doesn't it?"

"Turi, we can't tell the Torgersons anything about Juanito. We tell them the same thing."

"We're lying to them too?"

"That old man was an intruder and you stopped him. Period."

"You don't think they'll connect him to us, to me?"

"The Torgersons?" Molly asks.

"No, the state troopers. Somehow . . . maybe they could."

"Don't think so."

"But—but . . . Juanito said—" Turi is exhausted. He puts his head back against the seat and closes his eyes. The painkillers are still working, more or less.

"Said what?"

"Before he passed out, he said, 'The son,' or 'His son.' And something else. I don't . . . I don't know what he was talking about."

"Weird. Was he talking about you? Or just delusional?"

"Well, I've been thinking about it and at first I thought he was talking about God. But Juanito, I would never expect him to believe in anything, certainly not God. You know, like the 'Son of God' in Spanish, or something like that."

"He thought you were his son?" Molly asks, turning the Volkswagen south on Route 7 in New Milford, even further away from Kent but toward more commercial areas. Many storefronts have been boarded up. Many streetlights are either out or blinking as if it's midnight, even though it's the middle of the day. Route 7 is mostly empty as far as the eye can see.

"No, that's ridiculous. Never really talked to him before I got into the blue truck with Arnulfo in El Paso. Maybe Juanito was losing his mind. Maybe he was so sick he didn't know what he was saying. Also thought maybe he said, 'Mi'jo,' which is like a nice way to call your kid, 'My child. My son.' But that doesn't make sense either."

"Okay, here we are. This place is still open, thank goodness. Must be the only drugstore still operating in New Milford. Give me your prescription."

❧

After two days, the Torgersons tell them of their immediate plans. Mr. Torgerson is walking briskly through the house, but he has a more noticeable slump forward, almost a bow, at all times.

"Molly, St. Louis is particularly bad. But you see it in New York, the beginnings. Albuquerque. Los Angeles. I think it's fear. We need to get ready," Miriam tells them, as Cosio is clearing out the garage for where they will put their supplies. "We should've started earlier . . . we delayed because we thought it would never get to Kent . . . but now with this intruder, this attacker . . . we should've started earlier."

"Mrs. Torgerson—I mean Miriam—I don't understand, ready for what?" Molly says, looking at Turi who looks at her, both of them expectant, but neither one knowing exactly what to expect.

"It's getting better. In some places. But other cities . . . no, it's worse. Just be ready for the worst in two, three months. Ready for winter. We want to make sure you're prepared."

"Is it like that everywhere?" Turi asks. His leg is still sore, and visible on his arm is an ugly gash with neat stiches, which looks much worse that it feels. His limp is almost gone. He has noticed that *The Litchfield Journal* and the *New Milford Spectrum* have not printed editions recently. Should they believe the few bits of news they have heard and seen on the television and radio? They know, but they also don't want to know. The Torgersons were shocked that a deranged person with the virus had broken into their weekend house.

"Let's go! Only a few places, Hannaham's, a Home Depot north of Torrington, have what we need!" Cosio Torgerson speaks a bit too loudly through the mudroom door. No trace of the bloody spectacle remains. The faint smell of Clorox still wafts through the air. As they enter the garage, he wipes the saliva off his lips with a wild-eyed look.

They buy three gas-powered generators, and then ten red plastic tanks—all the stock at that Home Depot—to store gasoline. They fill up the tanks at a gas station in Torrington and bring back everything and line it against the wall of the garage, where Mr. Torgerson has cleared a space. Turi's hands stink of gasoline, and a few drops have also fallen on his sneakers. They have told him to stay home and rest, but he repeats he is okay, just sore. Secretly, he feels guilty about lying to them about Juanito. Again, they go out.

"It's just in case we can't come back to Segar Mountain for a while, so that both of you will have what you need," Miriam says, trying to hide her frayed nerves. She gives a concerned look to her husband, which Turi does not miss.

At Hannaham's, they buy what Molly and Turi think are enormous quantities of canned tuna, canned soups, cases of Cup Noodles and granola bars, even more bottled water. They pack load after load, from Costco, Hannaham's, Walmart, until their Toyota Highlander is stacked inside to the roof. First hundreds of dollars. Then more than one thousand dollars. Molly and Turi are shocked. "It's always better to have too much than not enough. Some of it we'll take to New York. But we have most of what we need there already," Miriam says.

When they return from one of these trips back to the house on Segar Mountain, Turi notices that their Brazilian landscaper is already there at one end of the Torgerson's property, with a machine that is splitting small mountains of wood from their woodpile. Mr. Torgerson waves at Jorge, goes over with an envelope from the house, and returns for another trip to buy more supplies.

The next twenty-four hours is the same. The Torgersons instruct Turi and Molly to accompany them to stores, sometimes forty miles toward the

Berkshires in Massachusetts, in search of storage bins for diesel this time and for food Turi and Molly want that doesn't need to be refrigerated, plus boxes of matches and candles. The phone rings, yet there is no one there. Half the time, the outgoing calls are also dropped, with a warning that "This call cannot be completed at this time." No other explanation. Nothing. The house on Segar Mountain has also started to lose electricity for hours at a time, for no apparent reason, but this is already happening throughout Kent.

"Diesel works with our oil tanks, in case the oil runs out. This is where you put it in," Mr. Torgerson instructs Turi and Molly outside, in front of a pipe that sticks out from the house's foundation next to the American flag by the front door. "But the two tanks in the basement are full. Just in case. I'll show you the gauge in the basement to see how much oil is left. Don't let it run out, or the pilot light will die, and you'll have no heat the rest of the winter." The Torgersons keep a calm and determined veneer. Turi notices that their Highlander is always kept at or near a full tank, but sometimes they have to wait in long lines at gas stations to fill up on gas. Jorge has stacked one side of the three-car garage with what must be hundreds and hundreds of pounds of firewood, a mountain of wood that partially covers the garage windows.

The night before the Torgersons leave for New York again, Turi and Molly overhear them in the kitchen.

"We've done everything we can for them, Miriam. Everything and more. The boy is fine, you see how hard he works? I need to be in New York. They've attempted to ransack the Guggenheim!"

"What do you think you're going to do? In your condition?"

"I'm going to help. I'm going to fight. I'm certainly not an invalid! I don't care what happens to me."

"*I* care what happens to you. I care what happens to me. The treatments are working. You will be fine. Maybe we should go to St. Petersburg with Sarah. She says everything is okay in Florida. The state has many good hospitals. Maybe we can get the vaccine more quickly."

"I am not leaving New York to those monsters. These kids are ready. Look at how they handled that vagabond, that scoundrel! I for one am glad he's dead. I don't care what anybody thinks. It's time to go back."

"They are so young. And alone."

"But not stupid. Not helpless. They will find a way. Just like we will find a way."

"Everything written down? Everything?"

"Yes, everything. How to work the fireplaces and woodstove. Issues with the furnace. Saving water in case the electricity is out for days. Melting snow for drinking water, in case of an emergency. As much as I can remember. I have also left them this much, in this envelope. In the drawer."

"We won't be able to come back before the New Year?" Turi and Molly can hear the fear and uncertainty in her voice.

"I don't think so."

"We'll tell them tomorrow before we leave. Jorge also has to take care of his family. It's remarkable you haven't lost any of your hair yet. We have another appointment at Memorial in the afternoon tomorrow. How do you feel, my dear? Any nausea?"

"No, not at all. Feel as strong as a Swedish ox."

"They will be on their own. Poor souls."

The phone rings twice, Miriam picks it up, but apparently no one is on the other side of the line.

CHAPTER THIRTY-ONE

"Victor, your breakfast is ready," el Hijo hears from somewhere down the narrow hallway connecting the main house of the bed-and-breakfast in Kent with what was the small carriage house where his bedroom and study are. The outside of the carriage house is canary yellow, with ornate wooden roof gables that remind him of the elaborate dollhouses in the main house. Anne (she has never mentioned her last name) is an avid doll collector, and that's what drew el Hijo to this place three days ago as he tried to find out exactly where to find Turi and Molly, Jim's sister.

"Victor, your breakfast, saynore," a woman comes up to his door, which he left slightly open after using the shower in the main house. Victor's lone crutch rests against the doorframe. Blondish Anne is about sixty years old, a recent divorcée, new owner of the three-story main house and carriage house next door, with a need to make it on her own, and children in their mid- to late-twenties. All these details she told Victor within their first ten minutes of meeting, details which she often repeats over breakfast (included with the carriage house room). El Hijo often thinks about how quickly he could snap her slight, pale neck in his massive hands if he hears again how happy she is to have her first "Mexican client."

"Thank you, Miss Anne. I will be there in a minute." Victor suppresses a cough.

"I want to show you my Martha Jenks Chase doll after breakfast, if you don't mind," she says cheerily through the slight opening in the door and coughs hoarsely, which leaves a slight ringing in his ear. El Hijo can see her blue eyes trying to scan inside his room. He thinks she has given him this deep cough that kept him awake for two hours last night.

"Thank you. I just have to finish this one thing," el Hijo says, his massive Olmec head pretending to smile at Anne to keep her out of his room. He waits for her to walk down the hallway, pushes the door closed, and dials again on his cell phone to see if it will connect to Don Ilan or anybody else. Nothing has worked with any regularity for weeks. Last el Hijo heard: Dunbar has already escaped (temporarily) to Costa Rica with his family; Don Ilan has stopped sending any more shipments to the United States until the disruptions in services, communications, and travel have stopped because of the virus outbreak, riots, National Guard militias . . . So el Hijo is alone in Connecticut. He has never been this far north in the United States. If it weren't for the exquisite dolls that Anne has shown him every morning, el Hijo would have acted on his recent darkest daydream days ago. He stayed too long, and now he is paying for it with this wheezy cough.

From Don Ilan, el Hijo found out about Connecticut weeks ago. From their spies in Clint, Texas, he eventually discovered the navy blue truck was first confiscated by state troopers in Kent. The last orders from his boss? "Make sure no one connects this truck and the blood vials back to me, even back to that son of a bitch Dunbar. We will deal with him later." Victor Huerta, a mountain of a man, stands up in the carriage house ready for breakfast, ready to finish his mission today, and ready to see one of Anne's precious, antique dolls. The shiny wooden floors creak and groan as el Hijo de Huerta brings his things together and packs his Army duffle bag. His rental car is at the front of the carriage house, but he has not used it since arriving in Kent. On one crutch, he has slowly walked around this quintessentially New England town in the southern Berkshires, watching the different restaurants to see who goes in them, keeping an eye on the lone grocery store in town. It has been difficult to remain anonymous in such a small place, but he has not spoken to anyone but Anne at the bed-and-breakfast. On his first day in Kent, he also noticed the thru-hikers from the Appalachian Trail, true outsiders—scraggly, smelly, fatigued—who meandered around town without a notice from anyone. El Hijo has adopted their gear: he bought hiking boots, canvas shorts, a brown camouflage hat with air holes. He does brusquely tell the clerk at SunDog Shoe and Leather that he injured his leg on the AT. No one has given him a second look as he's sat on benches watching and waiting. One day, he saw a young blond girl, with a striking resemblance to Jim Crump, enter the Colonial Settler. Not long after that, as el Hijo sat across the street in front of an art gallery, he saw the back of the head of a young man, maybe Mexicano, presumably Turi, who kissed Molly outside, behind the restaurant, just before she hopped on her bicycle. Now el Hijo knows exactly where they are: the Colonial Settler on Main Street, about three blocks away.

"Victor, good morning. Sleep in today? I hope your leg is not bothering you. Here's your breakfast, two omelets, six sausage links, a bowl of oatmeal, coffee . . . anything else?" As soon as she hands him the plate, Anne turns her face away and coughs into her elbow.

"No, I'm fine, thank you." He sits in the wicker chair, which strains to contain him. The crocheted doily covering the table swings as the table rocks with el Hijo's tree-trunk-like legs—one partially in a cast—inadvertently smacking the sides of the table as he settles next to it. "I will be checking out today, Miss Anne." His flat and unusually wide Olmec face stares at her impassively. She smiles pleasantly back.

"Of course, of course. But before you do, I want to show you this," she says, bringing an item from behind a counter at one end of the cranberry-red dining room on the first floor—el Hijo has not seen another customer in three days, which has been perfect for him. She lovingly hands him a doll from her collection behind glass.

Something breaks within Victor Huerta when he sees and touches the ornate doll in a red ruffled blouse off the shoulders, with a face as round as the moon, and a somewhat sad expression looking downward with brown-black eyes. The nose is scuffed and perhaps slightly broken. The hair is painted onto the skull, split down the middle in coffee-colored strokes. But it's the cheeks still rosy even in the hard-biscuit porcelain . . . that mouth so precious and tiny and pink. The doll reminds Victor Huerta of his mother. Reminds him of something long ago, in another life, perhaps of everything that he has lost along the way and what he has yearned to find again to help bury the pain. "The doll is beautiful, Miss Anne," he says in a deep baritone that seems to tremble the air even as his chest wheezes.

"I knew you would appreciate it. A Martha Jenks Chase from 1883. I have seen how you look at my dolls, how carefully you study them. Victor, it's been a pleasure having you as my first Mexican client."

The Olmec head does not move a millimeter, but bestows all its attention on the precious doll, ignoring Anne as if she were only a gnat between him and what he most covets. The doll has not ever struggled to breathe. The doll has never felt pain. The doll has never bled. The doll is perfect.

CHAPTER THIRTY-TWO

Molly's blond hair is matted against her forehead, and Turi notices she is slouched forward as she walks, as if she is still serving customers. The smell of burgers sizzling on the grills one doorway away, he comes close to her in the storeroom behind the kitchen of the Colonial Settler. He wants to kiss her, but he only settles his hand on her hip. It is Molly who strokes him on the cheek as he dons his apron. She has told him to take it easy, but he says he's fine, only sore. He can smell the work on her—her sweetly acidic sweat mixed with cooking oil—but also still with a hint of clover from her favorite soap. Miguel the cook is glancing at them from the grills, so Turi does not kiss Molly on the cheek.

"Watch the guy in the booth. With his two friends. The motorcycle guys. Rudy knows. See you tonight," Molly says, after she folds away her apron and returns from the bathroom. At one of the two front doors, Oscar waves to Molly and starts walking to his Volkswagen at the back of the restaurant. He will drive her to New Milford. Later tonight, the GED teacher from Cornwall will drop Molly off at the intersection of 341 and Route 7, just two blocks from her bike behind the Colonial Settler.

Turi watches Molly exit a front door. He checks the next order and where it should go. He also sees what Molly was talking about: the shotgun rests inside a long leather sheath attached to a motorcycle saddlebag, and it's pointed downward, next to the booth with three leather-clad men with forearm tattoos who are drinking coffee, eating burgers and fries, and finishing the last morsels of their guacamole and chips. The first time Turi saw a customer with a shotgun, he told Rudy about the "rifle," but Rudy corrected him: "It's okay. Just as long as they don't do anything with it. It's . . . well . . . where we are now. Look at the barrel when you get a chance. Thick and round. The ejection slot for cartridges. It's not a rifle, but an escopeta. A shotgun. I have one in the back too. Don't worry." Turi imagines the shotgun is like a tree limb on Segar Mountain Road: it could kill him, but it hasn't. The trick is to ignore it, to keep going, to always pay attention to every conversation around him. The men seem oblivious to others in the restaurant and even smile at the cashier behind the counter. From the back kitchen window, Turi sees Molly walking toward Oscar's car. Oscar is waiting in the Volkswagen under the dark shadows of an oak tree a few feet away . . . and from behind a dumpster a huge man on one crutch hobbles toward them, a knife in his hand . . .

"Molly!" Turi screams. He runs out the back door.

Oscar jumps out of the car in front of Molly as the man with the knife quickens his awkward steps toward her. She turns around and screams. Later Turi will remember that when he yelled inside the restaurant, the men in the booth turned toward him and must have seen what he saw through the window. They were a few steps behind him.

The huge man lunges at Oscar. He towers over Oscar and grabs him by the neck. Oscar struggles to block and grip the hand with the knife. In shock, Molly staggers away from the melee and runs toward the restaurant. Turi reaches her and runs toward the two men grappling with each other. The crutch has clanged to the asphalt. Oscar grips the powerful arm even as it swings to free itself from Oscar's grasp and elbow him in the face. The attacker teeters on one leg, grimacing in pain, with the knife still in one hand, the other hand punching Oscar in the neck. People rush toward them. Turi grabs the crutch and swings it with all his might into the face of the attacker, which stuns him for a moment. But it's too late: the man plunges the knife into the back of Oscar's shoulder. Oscar screams and drops to one knee. Turi suddenly notices that he and Oscar are wearing almost identical, navy blue polo shirts.

As the knife rises in the air to finish the job, the Olmec-looking giant glares at Turi with teary, bloodshot eyes, stops dumbstruck for a millisecond in midswing, and hisses at him, "You little son of a bitch!" The wounded Oscar is still swinging feebly at the man's waist.

"Turi!" he hears behind him, a second before a thundering blast stuns Turi near his left ear. He stumbles back at the shock. On the ground is the Olmec, bleeding from his chest and neck. A huge hole suddenly is smoking on the giant's upper body. Steadying himself to fire again, Rudy reloads his shotgun.

Turi comes to his senses and pulls the bleeding Oscar away from the attacker on the asphalt. His ears are still ringing. He smells the gunpowder in the air. Others surround Oscar and try to help him. The leather-clad men with tattoos, their shotgun abandoned back in the restaurant during the commotion, help Oscar to his feet. Mimi sobs and presses her hand against his wound and attempts to stanch the bleeding. Turi barely hears Rudy repeating, "You okay? You okay?" and sweating profusely as he shakily points the shotgun at the attacker.

The Olmec struggles to sit up and almost makes it to a standing position before collapsing to the ground again. The flat, wide face in bronze is stunned that anyone would shoot him. The knife is on the ground next to his hand, and blood has dripped next to it, around it, on it. The attacker breathes heavily on the asphalt. "You attack my family, you attack me, hijo de la chingada!" Rudy yells with a nervous crack in his voice. He points the shotgun at the man's massive face. Almost with a life of their own, the attacker's hands feel the ground for the knife, until the Olmec is still. The giant body does not move after one last twitch of the good leg. Turi stares at the carefully shaped cast on the attacker's leg and stares at his own polo shirt and stares at the perspiring Rudy as if nothing makes sense anymore. The gaping wound at the chest of the attacker leaks blood onto the ground, but the blood appears black on the asphalt. The teary eyes of the giant fix a stare at the cloudy Kent sky above the Colonial Settler. With his eyes open, he is dead.

From behind them, one of the leather-clad motorcyclists slaps Rudy on the back—which startles both Turi and Rudy as they stare at the scene, the body—and exclaims, "You are one bad motherfucker, my man!"

"I'm closing the Colonial Settler," Rudy says two weeks after the shooting in the parking lot, while Turi and Molly both sit on the bench next to the kitchen. "We're going back to Mexico, maybe only Texas. I don't think it's safe here anymore. Too much is happening. We'll be gone about six months. Maybe three, I don't know. We'll see what it looks like over there."

"What are we supposed to do?" Turi asks. Molly stares at him, yet she doesn't seem surprised. She looks at her feet, and Turi still doesn't know if she is drained or just defeated. It's 4 p.m. and they don't have much time together before she will leave for her GED class.

"You're supposed to survive. Look, Turi... Elodia, Oscar, all of us are leaving. We'll come back. Elodia swears the only way she'll go back to Mexico is in a casket, so I don't know. You can come with us, but maybe, I was hoping, you'd stay here, check this place once a week, or so. We trust both of you. You can have all the extra food, whatever doesn't spoil. We'll sell some of it, but we'll also have so much left." Mimi is next to him, nodding.

"But, I—I—"

"We'll do it," Molly interrupts, looking at Turi now, almost smiling. Just a corner of her mouth the slightest bit raised, as if it were a joke between them or an idea they secretly shared. Yet Turi doesn't know what she is thinking exactly. "Turi, we'll do it, okay?"

"Okay." Turi presses a smile at Molly in return, trusting her. "Okay." They will be together. Perhaps that is her idea at that moment in their in-between, perhaps that is the reason she smiles slightly, he thinks. Will that be enough? In that moment, Turi doesn't care. He doesn't need anything else.

"On one condition," Molly says, just as Rudy and Mimi are about to walk back to the kitchen, which surprises both of them. That Molly would even talk, as sullen as she seems. Turi is surprised too. "We need a car. Doesn't matter which one. Something that works."

"A car?"

"Yes. A car. You're not giving it to us. You're just leaving it here so we can use it. How are we supposed to check the restaurant? By bike? For six miles and back? How am I, or Turi, supposed to go to school?"

"They are closing the school," Mimi says. "That's what I heard. So many have already dropped out. A third of the teachers have disappeared with their own families."

"It's fine, mi'ja. We have my truck, and your car, and Oscar's. We don't need three. We'll fit in two, and Oscar can't even drive very much right now. I think he told me he was gonna try to sell it. This is better, Mimi, it's fine. I'll talk to him today." Rudy and Mimi turn back to the kitchen, still whispering to each other, something about "think about it" and "pobrecitos" and "that ranfla would never make it back to Mexico anyway."

Turi places his hand on Molly's lap, noticing how her thigh muscles have thickened with her daily bike commute on Route 341. She places her hand over Turi's—it is cold, but warms up in a few seconds—and squeezes Turi's hand hard.

That night on Segar Mountain, after her last GED class at New Milford High School, Turi can tell Molly has been crying, perhaps on the drive home, although she is not in tears as she piles her dirty clothes in the laundry room. But her eyes are bloodshot. She sits in the living room in the dark. Turi sits next to her, caressing her hand. But she won't look at him. Turi imagines Molly wouldn't even look at herself, if she could. She seems to want to lose herself in the darkness.

"Turi, I love you so much. I am so glad you are with me."

"I love you too, Molly. You okay?" He wants to hold her, he wants to pick her up and hug her entire body. But just as that first day at the Colonial Settler when they heard what happened to her brother in Missouri at the China King, Turi thinks only holding her hand is what he should do. He could kiss her. She would smile at him in the darkness now, and let him, but that kiss would seem a betrayal in his mind, not what their kisses should be. "What did they say about your evening class at New Milford High?" Turi asks. Molly is still not vaccinated against the deadly virus.

"Same as what they told you earlier. All classes are immediately suspended for now. The high school is closing temporarily." Molly says nothing for many minutes. Their hands are clasped together in the darkness. "Turi, sometimes . . . sometimes I think Arnulfo was the lucky one. Is that bad?"

He thinks about this for a moment. Looks in her direction and can see the glimmer of tears on her face from the light in the kitchen. "I—I don't think he was the lucky one. He wanted a chance. He never got that chance."

"But a chance for what? Our teacher also told us New York is getting worse, with the blackout and riots. Really bad. Some people are just going crazy. I mean, a chance for what, Turi? I really want to finish high school."

"And you will. Both of us. And college, maybe. With me, right?"

"Okay," she says, but it's only a half-hearted whisper in the darkness.

"We just need to get through these days. Just the next few months, through the winter. Maybe even a little longer. But school will start again, more vaccinations will become available. You'll get one. We need to make sure you get one somehow."

"Okay." Another long silence. "Why don't you ever get depressed? Why don't you ever want to give up? It's so hard, Turi. Everything is so hard."

"I do get depressed. I do sometimes want to give up. But I hide it. I get angry. I want to fight back. Maybe that's the Mexican side of me. When Ramon was beating me up on Corralitos, I hated him. He could kill me, but I could still hate him."

"That helps?"

"Well, not the hate. But it's what you do with it. It's like energy. Stubbornness. Something to throw back against the blows to your face."

"So glad you are with me. You, Turi, you are what keeps me from drowning."

"And you keep me from just being a stubborn Mexican dude." He smiles slyly at her.

"We are lucky. Together, I think we're lucky. You're right," she says and kisses him slowly on his lips, her tongue flickering gently inside his mouth, so deliciously, as if they were falling and falling in a wet darkness into each other. Turi does not want her to stop. He does not want her to ever stop.

CHAPTER THIRTY-THREE

In mid-October, the quiet of the town of Kent has unnerved them to action, the lack of people and cars at the height of leaf-peeping season. No one is there. No one is coming there. The people of this small town have also disappeared or gone into hiding or simply stayed home. Earlier that morning, as they talked about the eerie desolation around them, with little news, Turi and Molly decided they have been late to sequester themselves. Perhaps they are just reacting to the panic of others. Even when the radio has worked for an hour, they cannot find a single station still broadcasting. Forget about the television. They have already boarded up the Colonial Settler. That's a promise they made to Rudy and his family. Next will be the house on Segar Mountain Road.

"Okay, grab it. I think it's loose now," Turi says straining at the edge of their driveway. He takes the shovel and jams it into the black dirt again. Finally the T-shaped wooden post pulls out, with the mailbox attached, and it's surprisingly heavy. They put it in the backseat like an upturned cross. The muddy end still sticks out from the passenger window. They drive slowly down the long dirt driveway. Molly hangs on to the half-open Volkswagen door until they reach the garage. They have not received any mail for weeks.

"I have a story for you. Been thinking about it. You okay?" Turi picks up another shovel and rake from the garage. Molly is already holding Mr. Torgerson's long flat-head shovel, two pairs of garden gloves, and a hoe. Molly has told Turi she agrees with him about what their next task should be. But her blue eyes—Turi thinks—look at times confused, fearful, or even panicky for a moment. What choice do they have? Turi's greatest fear is that Molly's not vaccinated. Until the world stops collapsing around them, she has to be safe. Turi has to keep her safe.

"Yes, I'm fine. This . . . this might take us a while."

"Maybe a few days. My mom . . . she always told me about her mother, my grandmother. My abuelita. I never met her. She was quite a character, apparently. Grew up during the Mexican Revolution." With the crunch of gravel following them at every step, they walk on the long driveway, around the bend in the forest, about one-fifth of a mile, until they reach Route 341, Segar Mountain Road. Under the canopy of trees, the leaves are turning shades of yellow, red, and brown like a living tapestry above their heads. "She—"

"What was your grandma's name? My parents rarely talked about their parents."

"Doña Dolores. Think her last name was Rivero, but that wasn't her name. She remarried. My mother would complain she didn't have shoes until she was eleven years old. They were very poor."

"Wow. Really." They reach the hole where the mailbox used to be. The first thing they do is to cover it up, to make it appear as if it was never there.

"As an adult, my abuelita washed clothes for rural teachers—that was her job. She lived with the teachers, in a shack next to the main house. My grandmother and her three kids. My mother as a little girl had to sell candy, gum, during recess to help make money." Turi glances at Molly, and her momentary panic is gone, perhaps forgotten. She is engrossed in their work; she is deep into the story.

"She wasn't married, Doña Dolores? Did I say it right?"

"Perfectly. No, she wasn't married. Her first husband left, or died, I'm not sure. They lived with the teachers, in a place called El Charco. Literally, The Puddle. In Chihuahua."

"The Puddle? Sounds smaller than Steelville."

Molly and Turi drag logs and dried bushes to the entrance next to where the mailbox was, to cover up the driveway and make it look like part of the edge of forest next to 341. They also drag boulders, whatever they can lift together. Rotten logs are the easiest to carry for two people. One foot at a time, the driveway starts to disappear. Molly rakes in dead leaves from the forest around them, while Turi keeps dragging more branches, or rocks onto the driveway, whatever he can handle by himself. Turi has noticed that Molly turns to glance over her shoulder repeatedly, even if he is in front of her, even if nobody is near them for miles around.

"El Charco is in the state of Chihuahua, and it's definitely a rancho. Tiny, tiny, not even on the map."

"So your grandma was kind of a country girl. A single mother in the middle of nowhere." Molly smiles at Turi, the first smile he's seen on her face today.

After about fifty feet or so, the Torgersons' driveway drops into a small valley and eventually curves and reaches the house. Turi tells Molly their goal that first day is to reach that drop: from the perspective of 341, the more they cover the driveway, the more the entrance to the house will be hidden from anybody on the road. The house is so deep in the forest that without the driveway the house will be invisible in the trees.

The next day Turi and Molly take Mr. Torgerson's sledgehammers with them, and two heavy picks. They realize that the asphalt on 341 still hints at a driveway entering that section of the Connecticut forest, even if the first fifty-feet of the dirt driveway are nearly covered up. So they spend the morning breaking up any asphalt lips that curve into their driveway, to make Route 341 continuous and seamless as a country road. "That's so smart, Turi! I would never have thought of that." They also plant bushes up against 341 to further mask that entrance into the Torgersons' house. They dump the asphalt chunks into a ravine next to a giant boulder of mica and cover them up with leaves.

"Doña Dolores was a teenager during the Revolution, between 1910 and 1920. I think she was an older teenager by the end of it," Turi continues where they left off. He remembers how Molly was shaking last night in her sleep, how even his arms around her only calmed her body for a few seconds at a time.

"Did she still live in The Puddle? Or did they move there after she first got married?"

"When she was a younger teenager, she lived in El Ojo del Obispo. The Eye of the Bishop. Really strange names for small towns, but I've looked them up in an atlas on Mexico in the study, and they're there. Not The Puddle, but El Ojo del Obispo. Satevó, La Natividad (The Nativity), La Jabonera (The Soap Holder). South of Chihuahua City, the state capital. My mother wasn't lying to me."

"Why on Earth would she lie to you? The Soap Holder? That's great." Molly is perspiring, but she is looking at him, waiting for him to continue, the autumn light flashing on her freckled skin. In her eyes, Turi can see no trace of the fear he sometimes sees at night when they have nothing to do but wait for the morning.

"Well, she wouldn't. But it's only my memory of my grandmother's stories, I wanted to make sure I'm remembering them right," Turi says, as he squats to lower another boulder on the driveway. They continue covering the driveway after they are satisfied that, from the road, the entrance is invisible. For two days, they have not seen a single car pass on 341. Molly has dropped grass seeds on the upturned soil, although Turi doesn't think anything will grow much before winter sets in. She even plants a small tree right in the middle of what used to be the entrance. "During the Revolution, Francisco Villa controlled Chihuahua. He was from a tiny hamlet—if I remember what my father said—called La Coyotada, which I think means 'The Coyote Party.'"

"The Coyote Party? Wow, that's so cool. Sorry, but that's a lot cooler than naming your town 'Kent' or 'Cornwall.'"

"Doña Dolores also had two uncles who fought and died for Villa."

"They were fighting for the poor?"

"They were fighting for the poor. In the south, another leader was Zapata, the one Mr. Torgerson mentioned."

"Maybe these guys would be on our side now." She is spreading dried leaves around the small tree and smiling to herself, which thrills Turi. In a few weeks, the ground will be covered with layers of leaves: the color bursts above their heads will cover every inch of the landscape below.

"My mother said there was chaos everywhere. Different factions fighting each other. A guy named Carranza also had an army. One of the streets near Corralitos is named Carranza. Anyway, armed horsemen entered your town, conquered the ranches. My mother said they would take control of the stores, they would force men and older boys to join them, or they'd kill them. They would take the women."

"You mean, like, rape them?"

"Think so. My mother said Doña Dolores told her Villa would also string up local bankers and lawyers by telegraph wire, hang them."

"Holy shit. He wasn't screwin' around."

"Violence everywhere. Confusion. Panic. A society collapsing."

"You think your abuelita was raped?"

"Well, according to my mother, Doña Dolores shot and killed two men who attempted to rape her in El Ojo del Obispo."

"Shot them? That is so badass! My god!"

"Maybe that's why they had to hide later in El Charco."

"From Villa's men?"

"My mother never told me. But I wouldn't be surprised."

"Love your grandmother. Doña Dolores. She's so cool. Such a tough lady. Like Rudy."

"I wish you would've met her. I wish I would've known her better. She never gave up."

"Yeah. That would've been something. To meet someone like that."

"My mother always said I reminded her of Doña Dolores. Terco. Super stubborn."

"Muy terco."

"That's good. You've been practicing?"

"Of course." Molly smiles.

Mrs. Torgerson has a framed photo of a winter scene in the mudroom, a scene of their backyard. Two or three feet of snow have reached almost the top of the doorknob of the forest-green garage door. The elevated garden surrounded by a rock wall, waist-high, is covered—invisible—underneath gigantic mounds of snow. The photo of that winter desert is what Turi fears they will need to endure until the spring. With or without electricity. When the leaves start falling in November, covering every bit of the driveway, adding layers on top of what they created next to Route 341 to hide the entrance, Turi knows no one will find them. No one will imagine a house hides deep within this forested valley if they have not found it already. At once he feels protected against whatever is happening beyond Kent, but also entombed.

Molly has still been sleeping fitfully, and during the day Turi has again found her sobbing for no apparent reason.

Turi remembers how the leaves switched on, *all* of them, like lights in the trees—with swaths of bright yellow, streaks of greenish orange, and dots of a red so deep that Turi imagined a giant, injured pterodactyl had criss-crossed the sky. The air began to have a permanent chill at its edges. "This is what we should do next," Turi told Molly. They spent days splitting logs from the woodpile, with wedges and sledgehammers, and carting the wood and stacking it inside the garage. Stacks and stacks of wood. About double what Jorge the Brazilian landscaper originally left them. The work kept them from thinking too much about the lack of any news from anywhere. The isolation still keeps Turi up at night, but he never reveals this secret to Molly. If both of them panic, where will they be? So Turi pretends not to panic, or thinks about something else to do, or distracts them with another project, or tells her a story.

He remembers how he used to think about Connecticut: the woods and the leaves, pumpkin patches, and playing baseball. While Molly takes a nap in the late evening after chopping more wood, Turi remembers what he loved about Connecticut long ago, this sense of belonging and peace, which seems to have been lost along the way to the real Connecticut. It looks as he once envisioned it in El Paso, and he loves the woods around him, but . . . the real Connecticut has been hard. To reach the real Connecticut has been a gauntlet of pain and fear and the whimsy of luck.

It begins to snow heavily outside, for the first time this season. Already the blades of grass are only greenish tips in a ground of white. The birds frantically fly in and out of the arborvitae trees by the fishpond as it freezes. The electricity has been on for a few hours, so they have heat from the furnace. Their oil tanks are full, but they do Turi and Molly no good if the pilot light is not on. After the electricity returned, Turi figured out how to turn the pilot light on by reading the manual in a gallon-size baggie in the basement. Turi has also started a fire in the Quadra-Fire fireplace in the Stripe Room facing the backyard. Before she fell asleep, Molly brought in cut wood from the garage and stacked it on newspapers in a corner.

The snow is falling at a slant: heavy snowflakes that look more like feathers and pieces of feathers are quickly engulfing the knee-high wall of the fishpond. In a few hours, the pond will only look like a white, cold mound.

It doesn't matter what Connecticut looks like on the outside. What matters, Turi realizes, is that Molly is here with him. What matters is both of them together fighting for their new home. Connecticut the place was never the answer . . . but it was a place like Connecticut with someone he loved.

This is the land they know. They know it because they know each other.

Connecticut is the place where they begin.

Those trees and forest and hills, and their histories, even in the winter, become the beginnings of their beloved, fragile new country.

ACKNOWLEDGMENTS

I am eternally grateful to my editor Jessica L. Powers for believing in this novel and helping me to sharpen it with her incisive comments and dedication to our literary craft. She remains one of the best editors I have ever encountered, and I am lucky to also call her my good friend. I also want to thank Bobby Byrd and Lee Byrd for Cinco Puntos Press and their dedication to our border, in and around, El Paso, Texas, and beyond. They have set an example for all of us who write about the border, who take themes about the border deep into the issues that affect all of us in the United States, and who care about writers and writing.

I wrote this novel, turning in the final draft on February 29, 2020, many months before COVID-19 became major news anywhere, and so in many ways the novel predicted a pandemic that would plague our country and the world. What has always mattered to me is how people—characters—survive a difficult world, through friendships, luck, guile, and guts. Little did I imagine that the world I created about the border and beyond, about three teenagers escaping and creating their lives, and the virus Marburg-B unleashed, and their relationships under stress, and the tests they would endure to survive, that some of this would be reflected in our real world as my book awaited publication. Perhaps I have discovered a portal into the future, and that portal begins and ends with imagination and literature.

Finally I want to say thank you, again, to the three most important people in my life: my wife Laura Drachman, and my sons Aaron Troncoso and Isaac Troncoso. Our family is dedicated to each other, we help each other even during a pandemic, and we remain as close as we ever were. Laura and I have celebrated our thirtieth wedding anniversary, and my sons, in their mid-twenties, have graduated from Yale College and the University of Chicago. We are a family that works hard to improve itself and to question itself. These family values came as much from the Mexican-American family that began in El Paso, Texas as from the Jewish family with Eastern European ancestry from Concord, Massachusetts. We are, I hope, just another example of the good that can happen when you mix disparate worlds together, when you create a unique whole, a group bound by love, and a quintessentially American family.

A PECULIAR KIND OF IMMIGRANT'S SON
by Sergio Troncoso

Winner, Best Collection of Short Stories,
International Latino Book Awards

How does a Mexican American, the son of immigrants, a child of the border, la frontera, leave home and move to the heart of gringo America? How does he adapt to the worlds of wealth, elite universities, the rush and power of New York City? How does he make peace with a stern old-fashioned father who has only known hard field labor his whole life? With echoes of Dreiser's *American Tragedy* and Fitzgerald's *Gatsby*, Troncoso tells his luminous stories through the lens of an exile adrift in the twenty-first century, his characters suffering from the loss of culture and language, the loss of roots and home as they adapt to the glittering promises of new worlds that ultimately seem empty.

"An inherently fascinating and compelling read from first page to last, *A Peculiar Kind of Immigrant's Son* is an extraordinary and deftly written collection."
                                                    —Midwest Book Review

"It's his most powerful work yet, and an essential addition to the Latinx canon."
                                                    —The Texas Observer

"*A Peculiar Kind of Immigrant's Son* is Troncoso at his absolute finest . . . a masterwork bursting with immigrant intimacies, electrifying truths and hard-earned tenderness."
                                                    —Junot Díaz